Days of Wine

And

Tomatoes

Trials of Katrina Novel #3

Dale J. Moore

Days of Wine and Tomatoes / Dale J. Moore - 1st Edition Trade Paperback

ISBN 978-0-98128179-7

This book and others by Northern Amusements are available in electronic format. Visit our web site at www.northernamusements.com.

e-Pub version
ISBN 978-0-98685340-1

Cover by Ami Moore

Edited by Maureen P. Moore

Author photo by Linda Moore

Printed and bound in the United States.

Dedications

To my wife Linda, for turning research of local wineries into a truly pleasurable experience.

To my sister Maureen, for envisioning the characters at the heart of this series.

To Cecile,
I hope you enjoy Katrina's
trip to Leamington!

Dale J. Moore

0   Vacation

"Leamington? Really? I mean, who goes to Leamington for vacation?" Jake's pained expression said more than his words.

Katrina smiled sheepishly. "I know it's not glamorous like Haiti..."

"I wouldn't call Haiti glamorous."

"Okay, it's not as tropical as Haiti, how's that?"

"Better. But seriously ... Leamington?"

"Cathy's aunt has a cottage there. Right on the water. From what she says, the sunsets are gorgeous."

"From what she says."

"Yeah."

"And Stewart agreed to go?" Jake expressed disbelief, knowing how prudish Stewart Windle could be.

"It was Stewart's idea!"

"No shit?! Why?"

"Cathy says he needed to get away to someplace with a lower profile and a slower pace for a while."

"Well, David Letterman called Leamington an obscure Canadian town or something like that, didn't he?"

"Cathy told me it's quite nice. Point Pelee is great for nature walks and bird watching."

"Not interested."

"What?"

"Small town. Bird watching. Sorry, no."

"But you've been working a lot of hours. We need some time away."

"Can't argue with that. But not Leamington. Cancun, all you can drink, jet skiing, parasailing – yes. Leamington – no."

"But I promised Cathy already … "

"Sorry, but you'll have to break your promise or go without me. I only get two weeks' vacation the whole year. I'm not wasting a week in Leamington."

"It's not a whole week. It's a long weekend. We leave Wednesday morning and come back Sunday night."

"Sorry, no."

Katrina hung her head, closing her eyes as she put a hand across her forehead to cover them. "I'm at the salon all day, and you're out protecting the city all night. I barely see you anymore. I just don't know where this relationship is going."

Jake came over to her and put one hand gently on her shoulder. With his other hand he tenderly placed a finger under her baby-soft chin and slowly raised it until her red, teary eyes looked up at him.

"I know where it's not going, and that's Leamington."

1   *Busted*

The new moon offered good cover on a stakeout, but conversely could prove a detriment to seeing what exactly the bad guys were up to. Jake and his new partner were sitting in their black unmarked car, parked about ten metres down an otherwise deserted alley. The alley provided the necessary vantage point, without exposing them to people entering the after-hours club across the street. He'd waited since two A.M., and it now closed in on four-thirty. Another hour and the early summer sunrise would squash their third attempt at busting this bunch of drug peddling creeps. The moving drug store became a full time job to track. They'd established position two times before, only to have the bust called off by the operative inside. Jake hated the thought, but wondered if the operatives were helping the bad guys as much as the police. One more failed bust and surely others in the department would start thinking the same.

The late hour and lack of activity made Jake restless. Tired, but restless. His butt numbed sitting in the same place. He tried to keep his mind from doing the same. He hoped his new partner continued to be the silent type. Jake hated getting on a stakeout with a partner who thought dumping all his personal problems into the car was a good way to kill the waiting time. Jake understood the whole bonding-with-your-partner thing, but didn't think hearing a partner's marriage problems qualified. Fortunately, tonight's wait was over.

A voice came over their radio from the other stakeout vehicle: "Confirmation received. Move in."

Jake and his partner exited their vehicle, walking together from the darkness of the alley into the dimly lit street, their strides directed to the front door. Another pair of detectives was assigned to the back entrance. Uniformed officers would be arriving in a few minutes, dispatched with the same confirmation.

The after-hours club took temporary residence in a vacated store. Black tar paper blanketed the front windows, obscuring any view inside. People got into the club via an entrance in the back alley. So Jake's position at the store front was not the lead, but to grab anyone trying to escape through the 'back' front door. The more experienced team led the charge through the back, and their entry cued the operative inside to also raise his previously concealed weapon. The late hour meant only the die-hard clubbers remained – and the dealers whom the police so desperately sought to bring to justice. Most of the thirty or so occupants froze. A few bolted.

Jake and his partner stood in position at the store front. Their weapons remained undrawn, but occupied their minds. He didn't like showing his weapon in public, even on a deserted street at four-thirty in the morning. The potential paperwork alone was enough motivation to keep it holstered. Jake tried getting a glimpse through a small slit in the tar paper blinds, his partner still in position in front of the door. As Jake squinted further, he detected some movement coming toward them.

"Andy! Coming at you!" Jake pulled away from the glass as he hollered his warning.

An enormous figure flung open the twin front doors and barrelled through the opening. The size and speed of the suspect caught his partner off guard and the two of them went crashing into a car parked out front. Andy went down in a heap. The behemoth criminal bounced off the downed officer like a pinball, fleeing toward the alley where the officers' car remained. Jake looked at his unconscious partner and reached for his phone, only to see the uniforms arrive.

"Officer down!" Jake threw his arm up and pointed in the direction of Andy to signal the officers to assist, while barely slowing his pursuit. Jake re-entered the darkness of the alley that had only minutes earlier provided sanctuary from the sight of the criminals they were watching. Now the lack of light betrayed him. His pace slowed as the way in front of him faded to black. He suffered the disadvantage now, as he knew the light behind him would expose his position to the suspect. Yet Jake could see nothing, until an object appeared out of the corner of his eye. Instinctively, he ducked to dodge the incoming two-by-four, but the attacker's advantage caused a glancing blow.

"SHIT!" Jake screamed, as the two-by-four rattled off the ground, followed by the sound of the culprit running off. Jake wiped his sweating and now bleeding brow, thankful the lumber only nicked him. He transferred the blood and sweat from his hand to his jeans as he hit stride after his attacker. The alley was long, and Jake's speed, combined with the lack of it from his lumbering giant opponent, closed the gap very quickly. Jake lunged onto the back of the grizzly-like man, throwing a couple of punches toward the head as he rode the man's back. He soon discovered it was a bad idea trying to wrestle this beast down. The man tossed Jake like a rookie bronco rider. Determination was one of the young detective's strengths though. He tried the upper body tackle once more with another flurry of roundhouse punches. And again, he was thrown to the ground, first bouncing off the side of a dumpster. By the assailant's huffing and puffing, Jake knew his attempts were wearing down the monstrous man. As they say, the third time's the charm. Remembering the words of his high school football coach, Jake brought his attacker down with a leg tackle. A loud thud followed, the sound of a tree falling in the woods. A very big tree. With a knee planted firmly in the man's back, Jake grabbed his cuffs and secured his prisoner.

"Alright, get up! Don't you put up a fuss, and don't make me lift you." Jake kept one hand on the man's very thick arm as he stood up. They had almost reached the darkest end of the alley by the time the takedown occurred. Halfway back to the open street, the man turned, and as the distant street light penetrated the alley it finally revealed the bloodied face of his assailant.

"Oh, shit!' Jake exclaimed.

2   *A Mid-summer's Nightmare*

The pounding sounded muffled at first. Then it became real. Katrina woke to realize it was not a hangover pounding throughout her grey matter, but a physical assault on her apartment door. It woke her from a deep sleep that had taken forever to come. She'd tossed and turned until about four, worrying about Jake and if this was yet another relationship destined to doom. *I guess it's not just nice guys, but nice girls too that finish last.* Disappointment was her last thought before succumbing to fatigue, and it was the first thought this morning. Followed by *who the heck is pounding on my door at seven-thirty?*

Tying her granny gown as she neared the door, Katrina paused to complete the bow at the front. The comfortable, quilt-like gown was a gift from her mother. It hung in the dark recesses of the closet most of the time, only to make an appearance when she was upset or depressed and longed for the comfort only a mother could provide. Jake's attitude last night had sent her seeking the gown's solace. Leaning forward, she peered through the peephole, not knowing who to expect, having paid her rent on time. On the other side was a circus mirror view of Jake, enormous head leaning forward in front of overly elongated arms. The gigantic head shrank away from the door, turning down towards his shoes. She fluffed her hair, in contradiction to the resurfacing disdain towards her boyfriend.

She undid the chain, released the deadbolt, and pulled open the door.

"Hi," he said, as she stood with one hand firmly holding the door partly closed.

"Hi."

"Can I come in?"

"Yeah, I suppose. But I've only got a few minutes before I've got to get ready for work."

She inched back enough to allow the muscular detective to pass, and then secured the door shut. Katrina took a deep, anticipatory breath before turning to her boyfriend. Jake was again looking at his feet, which nervously shuffled beneath him. As his head rose, she spotted the gash on his temple. Katrina stepped close to him and reached forward to brush back a lock of his brown hair for a closer look. Jake clutched her hand and she felt the cool of the night transfer to her skin.

"It's nothing," he said, playing down his wound. "Been hurt worse playing hockey."

"So why are you banging on my door so early, if you're okay," she said, her tone turning sharply away from the sympathy that had filled her eyes only seconds earlier.

"I liked it better when you thought I was hurt."

"Okay. Poooor baby," and she paused briefly. "Now, what do you want?" Lack of sleep increased her irritation, and losing the last fifteen minutes of sleep always irritated her.

"Apparently you're not interested, but I got this nick in a chase after a drug bust," he said, lightly rubbing his forehead. "The guy took flight from the ensuing melee and I had to run him down. He caught me with a board as I entered an alley. It was quite a scrum before I was able to pin him down and get the cuffs on him."

"Congratulations on your arrest. So what does that have to do with coming here?"

"Well, the guy was really big. I'd say six-four and easily two-sixty or two-seventy."

"I hope you're talking pounds and not kilograms."

"Pounds. It was a guy, not a bear, although I wasn't sure for a minute."

"And?"

"And it took me a lot of effort to get this guy to go down and stay down. Boss says too much force. The kid's beat up pretty bad."

"*Kid?*" Katrina's eyes went wide with horror.

"Yeah, I guess he's only fifteen, almost sixteen."

"And you beat him up." Her look went to disgust.

"I told you. He was huge. It was dark. I couldn't tell he was a kid until after I cuffed him and got him off the ground."

"Instead of chasing him, why didn't you just shoot your gun in the air and tell him to stop?"

"That's only in the movies. I'd be in as much trouble or more if I discharged my firearm without an appropriate threat."

"So why are you here? Sympathy?"

"First, I want to apologize for last night. I was too abrupt with you. I'm sorry."

"Apology accepted, for now. And?"

"I've been ordered to take some time off and disappear. Boss figures the media's going to have a field day with this. They don't want me around to make it any worse by saying something they take out of context, or simply saying something stupid."

"Imagine that, a man saying something stupid."

"And they're making me take anger management classes when I get back, to cover their butts."

"So where are you going to disappear? Going home?"

"I figured where better than an obscure Canadian town like Leamington."

"So now you want to go."

"It's leave. I don't have to use vacation time. And it definitely sounds slower paced and away from it all." Jake put his arms around Katrina, holding her close.

"And it's not just because you have to go away?"

"Well, partly. But if I have to get away, I want it to be with you."

"The sunsets over the lake are supposed to be spectacular. I'm glad you've warmed up to the idea."

"I'm warming up, alright," Jack said, and he kissed her neck.

"See, you're already forgetting about work."

"And surely trouble can't find my Katrina way down in sleepy little Leamington."

Dale J. Moore

3   *The Ride*

"Stewart's rented a mini-van," Katrina said, as she and Jake waited on the sidewalk outside her apartment.

"I didn't know Jaguar made a mini-van," Jake responded sarcastically.

"He's not really a snob like you think," she said in Stewart's defence. "He calls it image management."

"And only a snob would come up with a term like that."

A van turned the corner, with Katrina's friend Cathy waving out of the window like she hadn't seen her in months.

"Here we go," Jake said to Katrina, "our road trip to obscurity."

Katrina pushed her forearm up against his as a sign to stop.

Cathy jumped out of the van and grabbed Katrina's bag off the ground beside her. "I'll load 'em up. Saved a couple of spaces back there."

"You loaded the van?" Katrina asked.

"What? You expect Stewart to do it? Remember, Stewart and manual labour don't mix. That's like oil and water, sex and the Pope, Ellen and men; you get the idea."

"Yeah," Jake moaned, "like Leamington and excitement."

Cathy looked at Katrina, then at Jake. "Did Mr. Crabby Pants wake up on the wrong side of the bed this morning?"

Jake gave her a quick snarl, then slid open the rear passenger door, which Katrina had fought to open for the past thirty seconds. Jake was confused upon hearing a hello coming from inside the van. He glanced inside to see a couple he'd never met.

"Hi, Jake! I've heard so much about you!" An attractive woman extended her hand. Her bright red lipstick was a stunning contrast to her baby powder-white skin and jet-black hair.

Jake reached into the van and shook her hand. "I have absolutely no idea who you are – sorry."

"Iris. And this is Tate." But her hand remained firmly enveloped in Jake's. She didn't even motion toward her companion, continuing to stare into Jake's eyes.

"Nice to meet you. You too, Tate," said Jake, as he looked at Iris before leaning slightly to see around her to acknowledge him. Tate was fast asleep.

"Two Gravols. Tate doesn't travel well," Iris smiled, still focusing on Jake.

Cathy pulled her door firmly shut and bellowed toward the back. "Iris, release your claw from Jake and let the poor guy get in. Not to mention Katrina."

Stewart chuckled, and soon pulled the gleaming glory of the Windsor mini-van plant away from the curb. Iris and Tate occupied the back row of seats, while Katrina, Jake, and a small cooler filled the middle row.

The ride out of Toronto consisted of light traffic and heavy delving into Jake's life story from Iris. By his repeated squirming, Katrina could tell Jake was wondering if he would have been better off grilled by the press over his recent incident. Frequently, yet fruitlessly, Jake tried to change the topic. Cathy subtly turned up the music a notch here or there, hoping Iris would give up trying to talk over the increasingly loud classical music that Stewart was enjoying with little regard for anyone else's musical tastes. Cathy finally gave up on this tactic, turned down the symphony, and began talking over Iris to Tate, who had momentarily emerged from his Gravol coma. Iris realized talking over Cathy was futile, and silenced her questioning of the young detective.

By now they were well out of the GTA, rambling southwest along the 401.

"So, Tate. How are you doing? Okay so far? I mean, this is a big step for you. I'm proud of you for coming on this trip!"

Jake shot Katrina a puzzled look, but felt relief that his interrogation was over.

"Tate's a recovering agoraphobic," Iris added to clear the air.

Katrina looked startled. "Should he be going to Leamington? I mean all those tomatoes, corn, and grapes?"

Jake chuckled. "Katrina, that's funny. Agoraphobic means he's afraid to leave his house, not afraid of agriculture." He turned to Tate. "Really though, how long have you had this?"

"That would be funny, what Katrina thought, since I used to do some landscaping on the side in the summer months. Nine months, give or take, to answer your question," Tate replied, his eyes fighting to stay open.

"No shit!" Jake exclaimed.

But Tate had faded back to dreamland.

Iris explained. "It started innocently enough. He told me that he became afraid to go out at night. Thought someone was hiding around every corner, behind every bush – waiting to jump out and mug him."

"That's awful," sighed Katrina.

"Then his company started letting the employees work from home. A green initiative. You know, save the environment by not driving, although most of them took the subway anyway. He didn't have to leave the house, and started making excuses not to. He started trading errands for chores. I was more than happy to run to the corner store for a bag of milk in exchange for doing the laundry. Or swing by the LCBO for a bottle instead of mopping the floors. They were good trades and I didn't realize he was hunkering down in the apartment."

Jake was fascinated by the illness. "So how did he overcome it?"

"He got some professional help as a start. A local doctor talked to him through a webcam over the Internet so Tate didn't have to leave the house. Pointed him to some websites for further information and they set up regular chats. We learned and practised relaxation techniques together – agoraphobia is really just acute anxiety, where the person fears having panic attacks if he leaves the comfortable, safe confines of home."

"Still sounds awful to me," Katrina repeated.

"And we try to avoid stressful situations," Iris said.

"Like long car rides with perfect strangers?" Jake replied.

Iris looked Jake over. "Perfect … mmm … maybe."

Jake squirmed. Then blushed.

"Hence the Gravol, Jake," came the answer from Cathy up front.

"The latest thing we've been working on is called Systematic Desensitization. Tate has to image himself in fearful situations, and then use the relaxation techniques to combat the anxiety. Once he conquers the fear in his imagination, he can apply the same process in real life situations."

"And does it work?" Katrina asked.

"We've had a few successes, and a few meltdowns. Overall he's progressing in the right direction."

Jake scratched his rugged chin. "It seems to me that this trip might not be a good idea for Tate."

"Au contraire. He'll get to practise what he's learned, but he'll have the safe haven of Aunt Verna's cottage to escape to if need be. It's a small town, so it won't be too bad."

Cathy laughed, "Even with something as huge as the Tomato Fest?"

Iris returned the laugh. "Well, if the crowds are too much for him, I can always medicate him until we get him back to the cottage. I'm sure a big, strapping guy like Jake can handle dragging a toothpick like Tate."

Katrina examined Tate. He didn't look scrawny to her. The guy wasn't built like a WWE wrestler, and didn't have the muscles of Jake, but from what she could see of his arms and chest, he looked fairly strong. Certainly not a pencil like Iris implied.

As the kilometres clicked by, the eastern outskirts of London rolled by through their windows.

"Stewart, exit up here at Wellington," Cathy directed her companion.

"We don't need gas, love," he replied.

"I'm hungry," she answered.

Katrina laughed and responded, "You're always hungry!"

"Not true," Cathy turned and smiled, "sometimes I'm thirsty."

Stewart reminded his girl, "We packed snacks to tide us over, remember?"

"I think Jake's eaten them all," Katrina joked from behind.

"Just take this exit. My folks always stopped at the McDonald's here whenever we went to Aunt Verna's for a visit. It's tradition."

"McDonald's? Really! How grease-tacular this will be for all of you."

"What, you're not going to have anything, Stewart?" Katrina asked the driver.

"I've never eaten at McDonald's in my life, and plan to keep my record intact."

"Never?" asked Cathy. "Not even an order of fries?"

"Never."

Jake whispered to Katrina, "Not a snob, eh?"

Minutes later the van settled into a parking spot at McDonald's. Tate was prodded enough times that he finally woke and joined the rest of them in exiting their urban chariot.

"I'm hitting the head first," Jake announced to the group. They neatly split into two small lines heading to opposing doors.

"Thank God they're clean!" exclaimed Stewart.

Jake responded, "McDonald's usually are very clean. It's one reason that I like using them for pit stops. Plus the fries."

The tallish Tate wobbled in front of the urinal. Jake feared for his shoes, or even his bare legs, standing so close to the leaning tower of pee. Tate responded like he was in some drug-induced dream – which he was from all the meds he'd taken. "Mmmm, fries. Munchies…"

Stewart emerged from the stall, fastening his belt as he walked to the sink to wash his hands. "Mmmm, indeed! I'll see you grease jockeys out in the vehicle."

"So to-go, then?" Jake queried as he held the door ajar.

"You don't want to keep Leamington waiting now, do you, Jake?"

"Mmmm fries ...," mumbled Tate.

"Indeed," Stewart said, strutting toward the exit.

They sped through the ordering process, and armed with bags of Mickey D's delights, munched fries on the way through the parking lot. Tate's eyes rolled up under his lids as he savoured the salty potato morsels. Jake wondered why people bothered buying street drugs if you could get that kind of contented feeling from motion sickness pills.

Stewart was devouring a granola bar when the van doors opened. From the wrappers between the seats, it looked to be his third.

The crew buckled up, successfully managing not to spill any drinks or dump any fries on the seats or carpet. Another check of the gas gauge by Stewart determined they were good to proceed without a fill-up. Silence ensued as the passengers were engrossed in their lunch. Fast food aromas soaked the air of the van. Tate finished his three large orders of fries – "nothing else, thank you." Jake finished shortly after. Katrina had eaten half of her chicken sandwich and fries and pronounced she was full. Tate finished the rest of her fries.

Cathy got to within a few bites of finishing her Big Mac and stopped for a breather. "You sure you don't want some, Stewart?"

"None for me, thank you," he said somewhat adamantly.

"I can't believe you've never had McDonald's! You know, it's not like your body's a temple or anything," Cathy smiled, observing Stewart's roundish figure.

Stewart glared slightly. Only slightly though, knowing full well she was correct.

Cathy tried again. "C'mon, just have a bite. It won't kill you to try it."

"None for me, thank you."

Cathy leaned closer to him. "You know if you try some, I'll …" and she pushed her lips up against his ear and warmly whispered something provocative, causing the hairs on his neck to stand up.

The van tires suddenly made a loud vibrating sound as the van swerved toward the shoulder, before a blushing Stewart course-corrected the pride of Windsor Plant Three back into its lane.

Cathy broke the remaining bit of Big Mac in half and slid it into the awaiting open mouth of Stewart. He chewed it for a minute before swallowing it.

"Well?" Cathy asked.

"Not totally putrid. But a long reach from filet mignon," Stewart replied.

"In price too," Jake quipped from behind.

"If the fries weren't cold, I'd give you some of those too," Cathy added.

"Oh, be still my bleating palate!" Stewart mocked.

Katrina started to doze off. Tate dropped off twenty seconds after finishing the last of Katrina's fries. He was drooling against the side window, all the while snoring with his eyes wide open.

Iris was texting at a speed somewhere between sound and light.

Jake had grabbed Katrina's iPod, only to discover that she had only three songs on it because she didn't know how to load songs. Her salon employee Kevin had tried three times to show her on the office computer how to download songs from iTunes, but only his three test downloads were present. Jake wondered, was it better to listen to Tate's snoring and Iris's texting, or a constant replay of 'Rhinestone Cowboy', 'YMCA', and 'Get Down Tonight'. He chose the snoring and texting.

4   *Welcome to Leamington*

Highway 77 beckoned the travellers south, greeted by the ubiquitous
Tim Horton's as part of a new plaza that was a stark contrast to the
quaint town of Comber. It reminded Katrina of her hometown of Pipton
as they slowly passed through. Canadiana was on display at its finest,
even in this corner of the country that many Canadians had long since
dismissed as part of the United States. Every little town had an arena, or
a community centre which housed an arena. Most of the barn-like
structures in these rural hockey hotbeds had disappeared, replaced by
aluminum-clad buildings resembling large storage facilities. Not much
character on the outside, but bursting of it within their hallowed walls.
And a church that looked a hundred years old, a grand old dame of
large cornerstones and stained glass, with a tower reminiscent of an
English castle. All it was missing was the typical steeple of many other
older county churches, a beacon to invite anyone within sight to
worship. A siding-clad Royal Canadian Legion hall completed the
picture, a haven for the elderly to reminisce over dirt-cheap draught
beer, while serving as a means to bind the community. Suffering from

dwindling numbers and struggling to attract younger crowds from trendy bars, some of the halls were simply disappearing from the landscape, a national treasure gone.

"What are those in the distance?" Katrina asked.

"Wind turbines," replied Cathy. "They're springing up all over the place down here. There's quite a divide on whether they're welcome or not."

Stewart took a quick look to the distant left horizon. "I suppose some people don't want those monstrosities in their back yard."

"They reduce our reliance on oil and nuclear energy," added Jake.

"There's a push to put some right in the lake, but after the gulf oil disaster, there's a lot of concern about something going wrong," Cathy said.

Stewart added, "Yet with these modern power generating machines in our own province, our hydro rates keep skyrocketing to pay for them. I thought half the point was to save us money as well as get 'green'. Someone's getting wealthy on this racket at our expense."

"I'm glad I don't have to decide," said Katrina.

"So you see why people are at odds over them," Cathy told her friend.

"Whoa, look at the size of that greenhouse!" exclaimed Jake, changing topic.

"That's a smallish one," Cathy explained. "There are some really big ones up ahead. I think Aunt Verna's arranged a tour one morning for us."

"Cool!" Tate had awoken from his drool fest, and used some leftover McDonald's napkins to dry his chin and smear the rest around the adjacent window.

"Look, Mersea side road," Jake said, then using his best, but not very good, British accent, "like the Beatles. You know Mersea Beat and all that rot."

Stewart rolled his eyes in the rear view mirror at Jake. "You sound like my Aunt Edna with hemorrhoids! And that's Mersey Beat – s e y , – not s e a."

"Maybe that's because we're getting near the sea," joked Katrina

"*Lake*. Lake Erie," corrected Cathy.

"Lake, sea, big diff. They're both huge bodies of water that you can't swim across and could get lost on in a boat."

They entered the town from the north. Continuing toward the lake per Cathy's guidance – Stewart had insisted that he was not getting a GPS for such a simple trip – they soon came upon the town's historic landmark, the H.J. Heinz plant and its prominent brick smokestack with Heinz emblazoned down the magnificent column.

"Okay, it's time for your first of likely many tomato facts!" Cathy sat up in her seat then swivelled as much as possible to face the back. "My father filled my head with all these facts when I was a kid, so it's my turn to share. You know, in 1907 the town of Leamington put to vote whether to give Heinz 20 years of free water, no taxes, and $10,000 to buy an existing building and land."

"A whole $10,000? That's not much." Katrina laughed.

"Considering a loaf of bread cost a few pennies, not a couple of dollars like now, that was a lot of money. It was a big gamble to a town of about twenty-five hundred people with no paved streets. So here's your fist trivia question."

"First?" moaned Jake. "God I hate trivia."

"What was first manufactured at the plant?"

In unison the van filled with "Ketchup."

"Wrong. Horseradish and pickles. Ketchup came two years later. Now they make well over a hundred different products, including baby food."

"Do they make Dijon ketchup?" Jake asked.

This brought forth a chorus of the Bare Naked Ladies song, 'If I had a Million Dollars.'

The group was surprised at how big the town was. They'd expected something the size of Comber, the town they had passed through in a matter of minutes.

"All the modern conveniences," remarked Jake. "A Tim's, a Canadian Tire, an M&M Meat Shops, and a Shoppers. What more does anyone need in life?" He laughed at his own comment.

Tate squirmed in the back. "How about a John?"

Cathy asked, "How bad? It's only ten minutes to my aunt's place."

"I can hold it. But no stops for sightseeing!"

5   *Aunt Verna*

It was mid-afternoon when the dark blue Dodge Caravan edged slowly into the mixed gravel and dirt driveway of the cottage. A grey-haired, petite lady stood from her front porch rocking chair.

"Aunt Verna!" Cathy bellowed as she stuck her head out of the front passenger window.

"What's with the sweater?" Jake asked, verbalizing what the rest of the crew was thinking.

Stewart sarcastically added, "I know this place is the anti-Toronto, but didn't realize Christmas came in July down here."

Unbuckling her seat belt as she prepared to exit the van, Cathy explained. "Aunt Verna always wears Christmas sweaters. It's her favourite time of year. She says everyone is so much happier at Christmas, and that the sweaters make people smile."

Stewart laughed. "She'd get locked up in Toronto. Or people would think she's homeless and only had one sweater."

"I think it's sweet!" Katrina gushed.

By then, Cathy had already exited the van and was embracing her aunt and her sweater, reindeer and all.

Following brief introductions, Jake and Tate grabbed the first of the suitcases. Stewart ignored the task at hand, and trekked into the cottage, trailing behind Aunt Verna.

Katrina stood out front, taking in the panorama. It wasn't so much a cottage as it was a home that happened to be located on the shore of Lake Erie. Not small and rustic, nor gaudy and over-the-top like some of the so-called cottages in Muskoka. A nicely stained cedar deck adorned the frontage. The back yard was small and, from where she stood, there looked to be a slight drop down to a narrow band of sand, likely a few steps' worth. A gazebo stood guard near the ridge, about midway between the house and the lake. It looked like a great place for a few drinks while recounting the day, telling some old stories, or taking in the sunset. Perhaps a quaint spot for a good book in the morning. Better yet, for chilling to some smooth jazz in the afternoon; Katrina had gained an appreciation for it from one of her funeral home acquaintances.

Most noticeably, a fully decorated Christmas tree stood in the front living room. Even without the lights on, it was visible from outside. Inside, the knickknacks on the walls and end tables all reflected the spirit of the December holiday. It took two trips to lug all the bags inside. After the second trip, the men returned to the front door and flipped their shoes off. As they traipsed down the hallway, bags in tow, Aunt Verna directed the couples to their rooms for the weekend.

"Stewart, I think you'll find Cathy's reindeer room cozy." Aunt Verna swung open the door to the room, revealing what she meant. The wallpaper, carpet, blankets, and every little thing in the room had reindeers playing, flying, or blinking. Katrina's eyes lit with amazement – for sure she'd have to check out the room later to see all the trimmings. Cathy waltzed across the Rudolph throw rug and flopped herself across the bed, landing on Santa and his sleigh flying across the sky.

"This room gets more charming every time I visit!" Cathy exclaimed.

Aunt Verna continued a few more steps to the next bedroom, also quaint in size. "This one can be for Iris and Tate. It's the Coke room."

"You don't know how bang-on you are with this match for Tate," Iris laughed.

"I'm glad to hear it," Aunt Verna smiled, not aware of Iris's intended meaning.

In passing, Katrina glanced into the Coke room. To her it looked even more amazing than the reindeer room! Coca-Cola stickers adorned each blade of the ceiling fan. Coke bears and baby bears covered the bookshelves. Santa Clauses drinking coke were painted on a row of decorative plates hanging on one of the walls. Coke tree decorations hung from an extra curtain rod above the window. Katrina wondered how long it had taken to collect all of the assembled artifacts.

"And last, but not least, the elf room for Katrina and Jake."

The door slid open to reveal a room full of elves. Katrina felt she'd gotten the short straw, so to speak. Elves scared her. For some reason, they reminded her of trolls in disguise, and everyone knows trolls are evil. The only good troll she'd ever seen was a little troll doll that her mother had as a child and had passed on to Katrina – and even that one scared her sometimes when the shadows in her room caught him in just the wrong way. Nightmares were a certainty on this trip. Good thing Jake had come, or she'd get no sleep all weekend. The only thing worse, she imagined, would be a nativity room. She'd hate to see baby Jesuses everywhere. At least she could have sex in a room with scary elves –she could never do it with Baby Jesus watching, not to mention Mary, Joseph, and all the wise men.

With bags stashed in their rooms, still packed, the six Torontonians joined Aunt Verna outside in the backyard. She sat on a large cardboard box.

"You boys have to earn your supper tonight." Aunt Verna stood up and patted the box on the top. "Brand spanking new BBQ. Ready to be assembled." She sized up the three young men. "Got a feelin' that Jake better take lead on putting this sucker together."

About four hours later, the erected BBQ had successfully grilled its first dinner, and the group sat around talking after a rather spirited dinner discussion. A few wispy clouds had turned into a light cloud cover, dashing Katrina's hopes for a glorious sunset, at least for their first evening. The sky darkened after a few more drinks, triggering some arm and leg slapping. The mosquitoes were out looking for their dinner.

"I forgot about lighting the mosquito repellent canister I have," Aunt Verna apologized. "Perhaps we should head inside."

With that, the group collected up the few dishes not carted in on earlier beverage runs, and traipsed indoors. They reassembled at the kitchen table for coffee and maple cookies. Short a chair, Jake located a folding one in the corner, flipped it around, and planted himself on it, next to Katrina.

Aunt Verna smiled. "You always sit bass ackwards on your chairs, Jake? Anywho, you guys picked a great weekend to come down." She refilled Stewart's coffee and continued. "Lots to do around town, with the festival going on. Motels will all be full, no bout adout it."

Cathy loved the little mannerisms in her aunt's speech.

"Please do tell," prodded Stewart.

"Well, it's only Wednesday, so there were only a few things today. The scramble's tomorrow."

"What's a scramble?" Iris asked.

Feeling smart for knowing, Katrina replied, "It's a golf tournament. Four people play as a team and they all hit from the tee, then choose which one had the best shot and they all hit from there." Beaming, Katrina looked at Jake, who'd taught her this tidbit of information one day after explaining to Katrina that it had nothing to do with eggs. "Did I get it right, Jake?"

"Close enough to understand the idea." He smiled at Katrina for paying attention to him when he spoke about sports.

Aunt Verna continued to run down the events. "Opening ceremony is Friday. Just a few thanks and singing of 'Oh Canada', followed by some local bands playing. And there'll be local vendors, you know, selling homemade crafts as well as food. And a tent with some local wines too. It's usually a lot of fun."

"Sounds charming," Stewart politely replied, reminding himself the purpose of the visit – get away from the stress and crowds of Toronto.

"Oh that's just the start of it. There's an old car show, of course there's a parade, and there's the races. And I told Cathy that I booked you some tours too."

Tate sat up, "Yeah, I heard about the tour of the growhouses!"

They laughed at his comment, then Iris clarified. "Greenhouses, Tater. Tomatoes, not weed."

"Still cool," Tate smiled and slumped back in his chair.

The conversation ended abruptly with the shattering of glass in the living room.

"What the hell was that?" Cathy yelled.

"Everyone stay here!" Jake motioned with his hand up like a crossing guard. But Aunt Verna was already out of her chair and a few steps closer to the living room than Jake. Of course Katrina was right on Jake's coat-tails.

Katrina stopped dead as she entered the room. The living room was a mess of glass and knocked-over objects. Aunt Verna, in her green and red elf slippers with curled up toes, bent down to pick up a brick from the floor. The projectile had strewn shards of glass over everything within ten feet of the cavity that used to house a pane of glass. Katrina didn't dare walk around for the risk of slicing open her unprotected bare feet. Jake was much bolder. He'd already passed through the living room, had whipped open the front door, and taken a few running barefooted strides outside in hopes of perceiving some activity amongst the darkness. The same cloud cover that had prevented their view of the advertised sunset obliterated all natural light. A faint street light about twenty metres away failed to show any signs of movement.

Distracted by watching Jake through the broken window, Katrina almost missed Aunt Verna slipping something into her pocket.

Jake walked backward into the house, still hoping to see some trace of the culprit. Closing the door, he turned to the two ladies. "Couldn't see anything. Probably kids on a dare. They were too fast and it's too dark out there tonight." He slipped on his sandals to observe the damage.

"What was that?" Katrina asked Aunt Verna.

"What was what?" asked Jake.

"Sorry, I was talking to Aunt Verna. I thought I saw her slip something into her pocket," Katrina replied.

"Oh, this," and Aunt Verna pulled a beige Kleenex out of her pocket, "it just slipped out of my sleeve." She took the tissue out and slipped it under the edge of her Christmas sweater. "Just an old trick my mother taught me."

Katrina didn't pry any further, but knew she'd seen something white slip into the pocket, not the beige Kleenex as claimed.

Stewart entered the room, coffee cup in hand. "That's a bloody shame, Verna. Come back in the kitchen and have another cookie. I'm sure the girls will clean it up."

"And Stewart can help me get a tarp over the window to keep the mosquitoes out for the night," Jake replied, triggering a grimace from Stewart. "C'mon, ol' chap. A little manual labour's good for you. I'll try to keep you from breaking a nail," and he laughed as he pounded his semi-British friend on the back.

6 *Miss Popular*

Verna sat alone at her kitchen table, having her Thursday breakfast of a slice of cracked wheat toast, gently brushed with orange marmalade, half a grapefruit, no sugar added, and a glass of cold water. She had a specific breakfast for each day of the week. The exception being Saturdays, when each week she took one more step eating her way alphabetically through the menu at the Breakfast Station.

As mornings went, summer was her fourth favourite season on the lake. Autumn led the list - the smell of settling leaves and the vibrant colours all around her modest home awoke her senses like no other time of year. Winter was a close second – when there was snow. She loved the blinding brilliance of the ground powder and the refreshing cold air in her lungs. Spring's promise and delivery of renewal brought the return of the sounds of nature's small creatures, which always gave her a smile to take to work. Summer – well, it was nice to wake up to the bright mornings that accompanied the season. But the inevitable humidity, even in this lakeshore community, put a damper on her spirits. Her sweaters were much less comfortable in the summer too, except in the confines of Tim's, where as manager she was able to regulate the thermostat.

As manager of Tim's, she knew a lot of people, some just by their face or their order, but many quite well from the personal chats that happen while having a coffee, donut, or sandwich. It was the unofficial part of her job description. She figured if people felt at home, they'd stay longer and buy other stuff. Of course it didn't matter with the seniors; they'd spend hours there nursing a single cup. She didn't mind though.

It was 5:45 A.M. as she opened the door to her compact Chrysler. Not much bothered Verna. Except liars, injustice, and yellow '68 Camaros. And the rock through the window last night. If it really was kids, it wouldn't have bothered her. But she knew it wasn't. The note was simple to the point of almost comical if you read it a certain way: 'Keep your nose out of the wine.'

Pulling into a remote spot in the parking lot, Verna was grateful to have her niece and friends come to visit. She'd looked forward to it for some time, as her family didn't get down to see her much anymore. It was different when her brother's and sister's kids were younger. They'd each come for a week 'at the beach' as the nieces and nephews called it. Verna knew that since they were all grown now, they'd most likely want to dump her to do their own thing, but having the company at the house was enough to lift her spirits. Not that her spirits usually needed lifting.

"Good morning, Verna," she was greeted in the parking lot by a young girl also getting ready to start her shift. "Looking forward to the Tomato Fest this weekend?"

"You betcha! My niece is down from Toronto, so I'm going to show her all the sights."

"That's great, Verna. You'll have to bring her by later so I can meet her."

"I'll see what I can do."

"Is that a new sweater?" her coworker asked.

"Thanks for noticing! Picked it up in Frankenmuth a few weeks back, along with a handful of others, of course."

Verna went about her morning rounds, getting the shop open for business and making sure her crew was looking lively. A few hours later, with everything running smoothly, she finally grabbed herself a coffee and muffin, and sat down at a small table where she could monitor the drive-thru service. Drive-up service was the life blood of the business, and had to work like a well-oiled machine.

"Verna!" hollered the girl on drive-thru duty. "There's a guy that wants to see you at the window."

"Thanks, be there in a sec."

"Tell him to make it quick, we're backed up a bit."

"Alright, hon," and Verna stepped up to the window. She was startled at the sight of the driver.

He spoke before she could. "Sorry to meet like this. I know we were supposed to meet tomorrow at the parade, but we need to meet sooner. Tonight, 9 P.M. at the pier."

Verna nodded, and started to speak, but the man drove off in his newer model black pickup before the words came out.

"You got a new boyfriend, Verna?" teased one of her employees. "Anybody I know?"

"It's not what you think, dear. Just someone I know."

"Well that cuts it down to three quarters of the county."

7 *Morning Glory*

Katrina awoke, cobwebs lingering from the three beers she'd had with dinner the night before. Eyes still closed, she was comforted to know Jake was lying next to her. No separation rules at Aunt Verna's cottage, thank God! She rolled over, surprised to find her boyfriend was not actually beside her. Likely having his morning coffee. She reasoned that his schedule was probably all out of whack, having just come off midnights a few days before the trip. She could tell he was still bothered by the drug bust incident. He wasn't his usual self, and grumbled about things that normally wouldn't bother him. Hopefully all the activities planned by Aunt Verna would keep them busy and his mind off of his work problems, and on her.

Katrina turned to lie on her back, but quickly jumped out of bed at the first sight of elves making toys on the ceiling. She'd found time before bed last night to neatly fill the dresser drawers with her clothes for the weekend. Katrina plucked out the outfit designated for today and began slipping it on. Minutes later, her hair was brushed enough to walk through the house – at least well enough to make it to the bathroom to brush the Molson residue from her teeth and tongue.

As Katrina tiptoed down the hallway toward the bathroom, its door flung open and Tate flew out into the narrow corridor, crashing into the green-eyed beauty. He grabbed her as she began to fall, but it was too late. She was on her way down, and with his forward momentum, all Tate could manage was to grab on and get hauled to the floor with her. Although he wasn't a huge guy, Tate's fall on her still made Katrina groan in pain. The landing was much smoother for Tate. He wasn't in a hurry to get off her soft body.

"Sorry," he said, still lying on her.

"I thought you had issues with getting too close to people."

"Different phobia," and he remained laying on top of her.

The door to Tate's room opened and Iris, half-dressed if that, stepped into the hallway. "Am I interrupting something?" she asked, rubbing her slightly bloodshot eyes. She had easily doubled Katrina's beer input the night before.

"No, I just ran into Katrina coming out of the bathroom," Tate said, still on top of her.

"Did you paralyze yourself at the same time?" Iris said with a slight snarl.

Tate finally got off the fallen blonde beauty, then outstretched his hand to help her up. Katrina took his boost up, wincing as she did so.

Iris flashed Tate a glare as she bumped him on her way by, cutting into the bathroom before Katrina could arrive at her destination. Katrina's mouth hung open over Iris's line-cutting manoeuvre, before closing into a slight scowl. She looked down at her toothbrush with despair, hoping it wouldn't be much longer to scrub that day-after beer dryness into the past.

Dale J. Moore

8   *Iris*

The steady temperature of the flowing water triggered the extended finger to realize the water was as cold as it was going to get. Iris reached for the drain and plugged the bathroom sink. As it filled, she wished they'd remembered to refill the ice cube trays before they turned in last night. The post-drinking binge, morning-after ritual was much more effective with a 50/50 split of water and ice. Determined the water had reached the requisite level, Iris shut off the tap and dunked her face. She held it there, counting to thirty seconds. Pulling out, she gently toweled her face, then repeated the task. Somewhere along the line, she had discovered this trick helped relieve the hangover and had the unforeseen benefit of closing her pores and making them less visible.

Towelling after the second dunk, she leaned forward toward the mirror, initially looking to see if the bloodshot level of her eyes warranted sunglasses all day, or if they'd be recovered in an hour or so. As the mirror approached her face, she cursed to herself. *Shit, that can't be crowsfeet already! I'm only twenty-five for crying out loud.* No wonder her mother married so early, she thought. Perhaps she'd better get on with it. Or at least get on with moving on from Tate.

When Iris met Tate, he was the perfect guy for her at that time in her life. She liked to party, and she liked to have a guy to take her to parties. Especially cool parties. She wasn't into the drugs like Tate, but didn't mind dabbling on occasion. Life was to experience new things, in her opinion, which was hard, she figured, if you were addicted to drugs. So she dabbled to experience, but never did the quantities Tate did, and she stayed clear of the really hard stuff.

Great parties, even better sex. She never imagined that such a laid-back guy could be so good in bed! The first three months were heaven on earth for Iris. Then Tate started changing. She had no idea of the phobia at first. It was winter when it began, so she didn't think much about the reduced party schedule. House parties typically were more abundant in the summer and fall (as everyone tried to cram in one last bash before winter). Tate began making excuses not to go out, from illness to falling behind on a big assignment at work. In hindsight, she realized that his supposedly broken toe was a ruse to keep him inside and from having to go to the clubs. But Iris still went to the clubs. The first month or so, dancing at the clubs worked Iris into a horny frenzy, and Tate was the lucky beneficiary when she got home. When she started coming home to a non-responsive Tate, she bitched to herself about it for a few weeks before taking her appetite elsewhere prior to returning home to her feign-sleeping boyfriend.

They were still friends, but little else. Roommates. Pals. Just as Iris had decided to dump him, she was greeted by a doctor who sat her down and explained Tate's phobia. She tried reconciling whether she had stayed with him out of sympathy, or because she didn't want to look heartless leaving him after his diagnosis. Either way, too many months of dealing with his sickness wore on her. She was happy he continued to progress in certain areas, but the sex was still not as often. Nor as toe-curling as she desired.

This weekend was their last chance. She'd made the decision prior to leaving on this mini vaca: if he didn't come around on this trip, they were done. So far he was flunking the test. Maybe she had already decided in her mind that nothing he did would be enough. Whatever, it wasn't happening.

And then there was Jake. A charming hunk – a chunk, as she liked to call them. The kind of guy Iris could bring home to Mom and Dad – a gentleman with a respectable job. She couldn't see Jake and Katrina lasting anyway, so why not go for it? She was sure Jake would get tired of blondie's awkward, dipsy ways eventually. Sure, Katrina was gorgeous. One party, when she was Tate-less, Iris had stared into those stunning green eyes and wondered if she should try a lesbian experience, if only to check it off her list. Convinced the alcohol was talking, and that Katrina was too straight-laced, Iris didn't pursue it.

And sure, Katrina was pretty, but Iris was *hot*. She might not be stunning, but she knew how to make a man squirm. And she knew how to act, having performed roles in a few legitimate plays – not those lesbian-artsy things Cathy had written with her ex-roommate - with aspirations to get into bigger productions. She'd use her body to bait

Jake, and her acting to be whatever type of woman he desired. But first, she'd have to drive a spike between the two lovebirds.

9   *Tim's*

Katrina entered the kitchen expecting to find Jake sitting at the table with a coffee. Instead, the hub of the house sat empty. Beyond the sliding door, the gazebo had occupants. Jake sat on top of the picnic table, feet resting on the attached bench. Iris had strategically taken up position between Jake and the water, resting her hands on the gazebo railing so that she faced the water. Her butt, barely covered by extremely short shorts, tantalizingly moved slowly back and forth in front of the young detective as she shifted her weight from foot to foot. At the sound of the sliding kitchen door, Jake straightened up slightly and stopped staring straight ahead.

"Where's everyone else?" Katrina asked.

"Aside from Aunt Verna, I think everyone else is still crashed," Jake replied.

"What about Tate? I ran into him earlier in the hall. Literally ran into him," Katrina added.

"Yes, I saw the embrace on the floor," Iris added.

Jake was puzzled, and Katrina felt compelled to explain. "He barrelled me over in the hall and fell on top of me. That's all it was."

"Well, Tate seemed to be enjoying it," Iris teased. "He's likely climbed back into bed. Yesterday was very tiring for him."

"But he slept most of the trip," Katrina said.

"Yeah, but emotionally it's exhausting for him to be around so many people," Iris explained.

"So Aunt Verna's gone to work?" Katrina asked.

Jake stood up and replied. "Yes, very early. Iris and I were just talking about going to grab some coffee at the Tim's where Verna works."

"Is *that* what you two were doing?" Katrina gave Jake a look like she'd caught him with his hand in the cookie jar – or at least looking at the cookie jar like he wouldn't mind taking a cookie.

Jake blushed slightly but ignored the remark as he walked over and gave her a good morning kiss. "Happy Thursday!"

Iris brushed by the embracing couple. "Let's go! I need some caffeine."

It was a short drive to the edge of town, and only a few more minutes until they pulled into the Tim's parking lot.

"Gotta love that commute!" Iris exclaimed. "Less than ten minutes to work, and no traffic. No wonder she lives out here."

"And great sunsets," added Katrina, although the cloud cover had prevented them from seeing one the night before.

As Jake pulled into the parking lot, he was almost sideswiped by a black pickup racing out of the lot. "Asshole!" Jake yelled, raising his hand to give the guy the business, but stopping as he realized the speed of the vehicle made it futile.

"Jake! You are supposed to be relaxing, remember?" Katrina barked at him.

"No, I'm supposed to be getting out of the limelight. The anger management comes later." He put the van into park and stepped out. He opened the back driver's side door to let Iris out. Katrina got out the passenger side and looked at her gentleman putting his skills to use for another woman. She wasn't happy, but figured Iris came out his side of the van, so no big deal. He'd likely do the same for Cathy, Stewart, or Tate.

"I can smell the coffee out here!" Katrina closed her eyes and smiled at the blessed aroma.

"That's because the KFC down the road isn't open yet. Otherwise all you'd smell is fried chicken!" Jake replied.

"You are so right about that," Iris added. "There's one near my work downtown, and that's all I smell all afternoon. It was great the first week, aside from me bringing it home every second day for dinner. But after that, I got sick of the smell."

"I'll have to make sure we drive by there with the windows open this afternoon!" Jake joked as he held the Tim's door open for Katrina, who was followed by Iris.

Verna came out of the back as they entered.

"Hi guys! Nice to see you. Where's Cathy, still sleeping?"

Katrina laughed, "We didn't want to wait till noon to have our morning cup of coffee!"

"Good thinking. She's a night owl, that one. Always has been. When she came to visit as a kid, she'd sneak out of bed and we'd be up playing crazy eights, or speed, or go fish half the night. I didn't have the heart to tell her I had to go to work at 6 A.M. She was cute as a button!"

An elderly man came through the door and gave Verna a half wave.

"Hi, Virgil! How's Mary doing?"

"Better, Verna. Hip's almost good enough for her to get around with a walker. She says hi, and thanks for the flowers you sent last week. I thought she was going to walk at the sight of them!"

"Tell her she's welcome, and that I miss her smiling face."

The man nodded and headed for the counter to order.

"Sounds like you have a lot of friends, Verna," Katrina stated.

"In a job like this, you meet a lot of people. If you want to, that is. And I choose to. People have a lot of stress in their lives these days, scurrying here and there, always got something to do, someplace to be. I give them a smile with their coffee – what they choose to do with it is up to them."

"I wish a few more people in Toronto smiled at me when I was getting coffee," Jake replied.

Katrina laughed. "You'd think for the six bucks you pay for that latte frappe crappe, they'd give you a smile, a hug, and a free gift."

Iris smiled. "Well, I think it's refreshing. It certainly sounds like everyone in town loves you, Verna, and your smiles!"

"Oh, that reminds me." Verna held up one finger and moved it slightly from side to side, like it was an antenna holding her thought. "Don't forget about the greenhouse tour that I arranged for you this afternoon. It's at Refreshing Farms. I left the details on the fridge."

"I think we'd better stick around and make sure your window gets fixed," said Jake, with a slight note of disappointment.

"Don't be silly. I called them this morning and they'll be out this afternoon to fix it. It's not like they need a key or anything."

"I guess they can just walk through the window to get in," smiled Katrina.

"Why bother? I never lock the doors anyway," Verna answered.

"Is that safe?" Jake asked.

"You're not in Toronto anymore, young man."

Dale J. Moore

10 *Refreshing Farms*

As Jake guided the van down Point Pelee Drive, Katrina reminisced about living in a small town where no one locked their doors. Everybody knew everybody, but then everybody knew everybody's business, too. She was a private person, in her own way, and didn't like the gossip of small towns – in Toronto most people just didn't care what other people were up to unless they were in your inner circle. Although Leamington was certainly much larger than Pipton, and growing, it still had that small town feel.

The driveway to the cottage was blocked by a glass truck, forcing Jake to pull up along the expanded front shoulder. Stewart stood in the front yard, arms crossed like he was the supervisor.

"Quite an interesting process," he informed Jake upon approach.

"How long have they been here?" Jake asked.

"Maybe twenty minutes. I was just finishing my coffee, wondering if all of you were still in bed. A gentleman doesn't crack open doors to check."

"Of course. But surely you noticed the van was gone?"

"Not really. I couldn't see the driveway because of this bloody blue tarp."

"Ah, gotcha."

Cathy made her way between the workers and out the front door to join Stewart on the lawn. She still wore her sleeping shirt and shorts. Her hair looked like she'd run a brush through it once or twice in a failed attempt to tame it. Makeup was a distant contemplation. She hung onto her coffee with both hands, like it held the fountain of youth or other mystical powers.

Katrina looked at Cathy in amazement. Not because of the way her friend looked, but the way Cathy could just wake up and be herself. No need to impress anybody, except on her terms. Katrina had to at least have her hair look good. She didn't use much makeup, a welcome timesaver. She then looked at Iris, who'd already been fully made-up when Katrina found her with Jake out at the gazebo. She wondered, *who gets dolled up first thing in the morning if you're not going to work?*

"Your aunt says hello!" Katrina greeted Cathy. "Said to remind you of the greenhouse tour this afternoon."

"Yeah, thanks. What time's it at again?" Cathy asked.

"Not sure, but she wrote it on a note on the fridge," Katrina replied.

Cathy looked at Stewart and Jake, chatting and pointing at the ongoing window repairs. "Let's leave the guys to watch their show.

I need to go paint my face and wrestle my hair into place. I'd swear a squirrel or chipmunk got in there in the night!"

Katrina laughed, "After you, Cruella DeVille!"

Tate limited himself to a half Gravol for the short drive to the greenhouse. He didn't want to miss the tour by falling into such deep sleep that he couldn't be awoken.

The early Thursday afternoon sun had already heated up the parked van. Stewart and Jake both ran in to change their shirts before leaving on the trip, as the morning humidity had drenched their shirts to the point of discomfort, to them and to anyone who passed by and inhaled through their nose. If home, no doubt Stewart would have showered again.

Katrina relaxed in the front passenger seat of the van, secure in the hands of Jake's driving. She marvelled at how easy it was to get anywhere in town and enjoyed the lack of traffic. She mellowed knowing they needn't rush to beat traffic to get someplace. Everything was within a stress-free thirty minutes.

"Rurban," Katrina stated. "That's what I call this area."

"Rurban?" asked Jake.

"Rural and Urban combined. Rurban," and she put her hand gently on Jake's leg as he drove. "All the farming and greenhouses, yet many of the comforts of the city."

Stewart overheard the comment from the middle row, where he and Cathy sat, and couldn't resist commenting. "Well, I think it sounds much better than Urbal or Farmity."

"Rurban it is," smiled Jake, guiding the van into the Refreshing Farms parking lot.

As the group unloaded, Katrina pointed out a sign indicating tour guests were to enter the door to the left and sign in. With Jake's arm around her shoulder, Katrina strolled toward the door, stopping briefly as Jake pointed the keys backwards between them to beep on the alarm.

Two other couples awaited them in the tour signup area. Katrina signed in the whole group, adding both her street and email addresses.

"Good afternoon, everyone!" A comfortably dressed man in his late thirties greeted the group. Katrina could tell he was more than just a tour guide as she responded in kind with a "good afternoon."

"My name is Edgar. I'm one of the owners here at Refreshing Farms. Some of you are Verna's guests and others are Clare's. Let's go around with introductions, and let me know whether you're with the beloved Tim Horton's manager, or with my valued production manager."

The introductions were completed and Edgar continued. "I only get to do four or five of these tours a year, so I'm not sure if that makes you special or a victim."

Katrina liked his sense of humour and felt a rush of anticipation for the tour.

"So a few facts for you first," and he turned to grab a stack of pamphlets. "These are from the Ontario Ministry of Agriculture. The handouts have a lot of numbers in them, for those in the group that like to memorize such things and impress their friends later at cocktail parties."

Handing them out, he continued. "To summarize the key points, the greenhouses in this area produce about sixty percent of all greenhouse food produced in North America. Not just Canada, but North America. There are more greenhouses in this area than anywhere else in North America. Aside from a multitude of tomatoes and varieties of tomatoes, most greenhouses in this area also grow cucumbers and peppers. Between Leamington and Kingsville, there are over fifteen hundred acres of greenhouses. That's about the size of seven hundred and fifty CFL football fields, or for you NFL fans, one thousand, three hundred, and fifty football fields."

"Including or excluding end zones?" Jake joked.

"Including for both."

Katrina was amazed. She'd never gone to a CFL or NFL game, but knew from the local schools how much space they took up.

"So follow me and we'll start at the beginning of the process." Like animals to the ark, they followed neatly in pairs outside.

"We have been a Biomass facility for a few years, meaning we supplement our oil use with natural fuels. Biomass, in simple terms, speeds up nature's process of creating fuel. The yonder pile of wood waste was our exclusive source when we started, but cost and availability has pushed us to other more efficient sources. It used to be a small mountain of wood waste about thirty feet high. Follow me and I'll show what we use now."

The five couples followed Edgar into a nearby greenhouse. Katrina's eyes bulged, startled by the enormity of the space they had entered.

Tate smiled at the site. Tall grass filled the building. "And I thought you said we weren't going to a growhouse!"

"Wrong kind of grass," Edgar laughed. "This is Miscanthus. It's a perennial grass. It's perfect for fuel use because it can grow up to three and a half metres in one season, has a low mineral content, and a high biomass yield. We shred and burn it to produce heat and steam for our turbines."

At the far end of the greenhouse, Edgar stopped them. "Greenhouse work is labour intensive. We are fortunate to be able to supplement our work force with labourers from Mexico and Jamaica. They can earn ten to twenty times what they could earn back home, and they are good workers – contrary to the stereotypes. We have onsite housing for twenty workers."

In contrast to the first greenhouse's appearance of an African field of tall grass, the next one came to life with an abundance of colour. Dominated by the bright green foliage of the plants, an array of colours burst between them as the peppers sprouted to life. Hues of yellow, orange, red, and green hung like so many ornaments on a Christmas tree. Katrina felt like she'd entered a secret garden. She stopped capturing Edgar's commentary as her visual trance continued through much of the tour. The details of how often they cut back the plants and frequency of harvesting riveted the rest of the group. The number of varieties of tomatoes grown did not hold her interest either, except to the point of knowing not all tomatoes were the same. She thought there were tomatoes and the miniature cherry tomatoes. She didn't care about beefeater, or beefstick, or whatever they were called.

The cucumber greenhouse snapped Katrina out of her fog. It was a sea of green lacking the beauty of the other crops. Edgar and the two other couples had gone ahead, greeted by a woman who was no doubt the production manager Clare.

"Wow, those are long!" Katrina exclaimed, gawking at the cukes.

"Gives one a bit of an inferiority complex, I must say," Stewart chortled.

"Don't worry, dear. I'd never replace you with a cucumber. They may be longer and naturally ribbed, but they don't bring the heat like you, big fella," Cathy giggled.

"Sounds like you have experience with cucumbers," added Iris.

"At least her cucumbers don't require batteries," Tate blurted out, likely regretting the words as they came out.

Jake took Katrina by the arm. "Let's catch up with Edgar and the others."

As Edgar looked on, Clare explained some of the safety requirements of running a greenhouse, such as employing hygiene habits, safe food handling procedures, and traceability of all produce back to the specific greenhouse with the date processed. When Clare got to explaining how they graded produce by size and shape, a number of chuckles were heard, but everyone bit their tongue.

Edgar thanked Clare for her time, and after she hugged her friends on the tour goodbye, he led them all into the packing area. Katrina thought it funny some of the packing materials were called clamshells.

"This is our stretch wrapping turntable. A pallet of produce is loaded on the turntable, then the operator guides the stretch wrap around the pallet to protect it from external threats while shipping. Most of what we ship reaches grocery shelves within twenty-four to forty-eight hours, and eighty percent of that is sent to markets in the U.S."

The machine started wrapping at the bottom. Katrina walked around to the far side of the turntable, out of view of the operator and away from the group. Something had caught her eye on the produce and she stepped closer to get a look. It spun quicker than she expected and she jumped up onto the turntable to grab what she'd seen. But the turntable kept spinning. Next she knew, she was flattened up against the pallet of peppers as the stretch wrap grabbed hold of her. The machine suddenly stopped, an alarm pierced the air, and chaos ensued.

The operator screamed at Katrina as she stood helplessly hugging the pallet of veggies, her legs coated in stretch wrap, pushing her shorts up to expose the bottom of her cheeks. After more yelling, the operator cut the plastic away from the machine and freed her from the pallet's embrace.

Jake ran forward and pulled her toward him. He held her for a second before backing off.

"What were you thinking, Katrina? You could have been seriously hurt!"

The operator still fumed. "If the wrap was near the top you could have suffocated!"

Katrina, embarrassed, held out a small leaf. "I thought it was a caterpillar. I was afraid it would die. You know, suffocate or melt."

Edgar stood shaking his head. "For one, nothing gets into these crates but the produce. It's inspected and re-inspected. Second, you're lucky it's not a shrink wrap machine that heats the plastic and shrinks it onto the product, like they use for bottled water. Stretch wrap doesn't use heat."

Jake looked at Katrina again. "You are really hard to keep safe sometimes, you know that?"

Katrina stood speechless, a small tear hanging on the corner of her eyelash. Cathy stepped between the couple to give Katrina a comforting hug. Still holding on, but creating some space, Cathy looked at her friend.

'It's alright, hon. No harm, no foul. Are you okay?"

"I'm fine, thanks. Just feel like a klutz."

"That's because you are a klutz, dear. A beautiful, sensitive klutz."

Katrina smiled through her reddened eyes, acknowledging the sentiment.

Cathy returned the smile, and followed it with a hearty laugh.

"That reminds me of a story. A guy I knew almost killed himself one Halloween - "

"And that's funny? And what's it got to do with me being a klutz?"

"He got a hold of a large roll of plastic wrap, like the stuff you got stuck in. The moron laid the stuff out on the floor of his apartment and rolled on it to enclose himself from his feet to his head. He was going to go to a costume party dressed as a penis with a condom on. Problem was, he forgot about cutting air holes, and after rolling on the plastic, his arms were trapped inside his 'condom.' His face was turning purple when his roommate found him, so he apparently looked even more like his intended disguise than planned. His buddy ran and got his camera, snapped a few pics, then freed the dick, literally, from his condom of death."

"Sounds horrible!" Katrina exclaimed.

"The dufus is okay. You should see the photos the roommate took. You'll pee your pants!"

"Well," Edgar announced as he returned to the group. "That was more excitement than we want on a tour. If you'll please follow me, we're heading back to the front to end our tour. We have a small souvenir shop and some freshly picked produce for purchase at better than roadside stand prices!"

As they arrived at the small store, Edgar thanked them for visiting and shook hands with everyone. The group mingled in the store, selecting some items to take back to Verna's. Katrina's eyes caught someone looking through the storefront window. Oddly it looked like Spare Change, the homeless guy who camped out near Katrina's hair salon in Toronto. On closer view, the man didn't look anything like him, except the standard-issue grubby homeless guy outfit.

"Are you okay, Miss?"

Katrina turned to see Edgar standing next to her, opening a paper bag.

"Oh, yes. Thanks. Sorry for causing such a commotion earlier."

Edgar stuffed some produce into the bag.

"Just don't let it happen again," he teased her. "I think my operator almost had a heart attack. He doesn't have much excitement in his job. On the bright side, it was good to see our safety measures worked so well. Nothing better than a live test, I guess." He paused as he folded over the top of the paper bag. "Have a good stay in Leamington." He nodded to her, and walked to the door outside.

Katrina watched Edgar hand the carefully selected bag of fresh vegetables and tomatoes to the homeless guy. The two men spoke for a few minutes before they shook hands and Edgar returned inside. As he came through the door, he realized Katrina had witnessed the exchange.

"That's Wally. Some call him Wally the Wino. Nice man battling some bad circumstances. He's been in town a few weeks. Not sure where he came from, or how he got here, but he lost his job and is battling a drinking problem. He comes by every few days, and if he's sober, I give him a bag of produce. On the days he doesn't show up, I assume he's fallen into the bottle."

"It's very kind of you not to judge him."

"That's the Lord's job, not mine."

Katrina paid for a bottle of water and a bottle of orange juice. She took them outside and gave them to Wally, who smiled gratefully for the refreshments. They talked for about five minutes, Katrina explaining she was visiting from Toronto. Wally informed her that he'd left Toronto about a month ago, hitchhiking and hopping trains to get down here. She wondered who would pick him up looking like he did, but reasoned that he likely started out looking a lot cleaner than he did now. Why did all the homeless guys she'd seen wear jeans? Surely they'd be hot on days like today? Then again, wardrobe was probably not high on their list of how to spend their collected change.

Iris and Tate emerged from the Refreshing Farms store, and acknowledged Katrina. They pretended not to see Wally, something homeless guys were used to, he admitted.

"There you are!" Jake exclaimed, exiting the building with Cathy and Stewart.

"We were afraid you were off rescuing caterpillars again," Cathy added with a smile.

"Jake, Cathy, Stewart, this is Wally. He's also from Toronto."

"Nice to meet you," Wally nodded, knowing most people didn't want to shake hands with his type.

"Likewise," replied Jake, reaching out to shake.

Wally smiled through his grimy exterior, and shook hands. "I hope to see you under better circumstances someday."

"I'm sure things will get better for you," Katrina grinned hopefully.

"Edgar has promised me a job if I can stay sober for two weeks."

"There you go! How many more days do you have to go?" Katrina asked.

"Thirteen."

"Well, it's a start," Katrina replied optimistically.

"Good luck, Wally," Jake said. "We should get going, Katrina."

"Okay. See you around, Wally."

As they got in the van, Iris expressed her dismay.

"How can you even talk to that piece of filth? I mean, he was so gross!"

"I concur with the filthy part," Stewart said, "but he seems harmless enough."

"Thank you, Stewart," Katrina added. "He's trying to help himself. And you try living on a few bucks a day and we'll see how pretty you look!"

Sensing a cat fight, Stewart changed the subject.

"Is everyone strapped up tightly?"

Cathy looked back from the front seat at her friend. "Not as tightly as Katrina was wrapped up with that pallet of peppers!"

Dale J. Moore

11   *Pier Pressure*

"Dinner by the water! One of my favourite things," smiled Iris, noticeably absent of Tate.

"Too bad Tate's not up to going out tonight," frowned Katrina.

"Maybe tomorrow night," Iris responded, sounding hopeful, Katrina thought. "The greenhouse tour proved too much for him."

"I hope you told him to go outside the cottage to smoke his 'medicinal' marijuana," remarked Cathy, knowing full well that Tate was going to get high to relieve his latest anxiety attack.

The van slowly passed the Seacliff Hotel, Stewart searching where to park. Not sure as he cruised past, he drove onto the pier. The ferry to forty-two-square kilometre Pelee Island left from the end of this fabled dock. This quaint island has the distinction as the southernmost populated point in Canada, and lies in the middle of the southwestern corner of Lake Erie. A few scant kilometres south is the uninhabited, inverted cap-shaped Middle Island, whose southern shores precariously lie within a few hundred metres of the American border – of course it's an imaginary line in the water patrolled by both Coast Guards. Katrina hoped they would find time to get out to the magnificent Pelee Island, but the agenda wasn't shaping up that way. Stewart followed the circle drive back around, now heading north back towards the Hotel.

"Should I use this car park, then?" he asked, the British in him emerging as he spotted some spaces on the pier.

"I think I saw a parking lot behind the place," Jake said from the passenger side front seat. Katrina and the other girls had hopped in the back, herself and Iris all the way in the back while Aunt Verna and Cathy sat in the middle row.

"Right you are!" Stewart exclaimed as he came upon the short road into the asphalt area.

They exited the van and followed Verna's lead to what appeared to be the back of the place. Stewart wasn't watching where he walked, ending trapped behind a dumpster, with a three-foot drop down to the adjoining walk. Stewart of course backtracked – he didn't jump down three foot drops.

In front of them lay an outside patio. Not huge, but not small. It had a number of tables, with a small bar in the middle. Shrubs encircled the patio, high enough to obscure the view of the water to sitting patrons, but not if you stood.

"Look who's here, Katrina," Iris noted, and she pointed at the grass in front of the foliage providing some privacy to the patio. "It's your buddy, Wally the Wino."

Sure enough, there sat the derelict from earlier in the day, on the grass with a hat between his legs. A small sign sat on top of his hat – 'In need, indeed'.

The group walked by at a safe distance, except Katrina, who diverted to toss a toonie in his hat.

Wally the Wino looked up and thanked her. "Wine is Red, wine is White, makes no difference if it gets you through the night."

Katrina smiled at the prose, but was concerned Wally was back at square one for his job with Edgar. She turned and looked up at the hotel structure. It was a rather imposing older building. Obviously a glorious hotel at one time, the restaurant/bar occupied the bottom floor, with an exit out to the patio. She followed the group inside. A nautical theme soaked the establishment. Naval ropes, anchors, and portholes surrounded them as Aunt Verna showed them the inside. Katrina thought it was very dark at first, until her eyes adjusted from the extreme sunlight outside to the artificial light of the tavern. Handsomely lacquered wood adorned the walls and room divider. The interior reminded her of an expensive stateroom on an old cruise ship, from the pictures she'd seen. She was sure those voyages were portrayed as much more glamorous than in reality. Months at sea didn't sound wonderful to her, no matter how beautiful the surroundings. And look what happened to the Titanic, she thought.

After circling the inside of the bar, the group came to consensus to sit outside in the midst of the breezes off the lake. This decision pleased Katrina.

Jake led the way out to the patio, holding the door as the rest passed through. Katrina noticed him look over her shoulder and laugh. He took out his phone and took a picture of a sign hanging neatly inside the doorway.

The group passed some small stand-up bar tables on the patio as they made their way to a larger table. The circular table had attached seats that jutted out like tentacles on an octopus. There were knocking knees, until everyone figured out the right angle to sit at.

"What'd you take a picture of, sweetie?" Katrina asked after everyone had settled.

"Oh, you've got to see this sign!" Jake laughed, then fiddled with his phone to bring up the picture to share with the group. It read:

STREET GIRLS BRINGING IN SAILORS MUST PAY FOR ROOM IN ADVANCE

Sept 26, 1926

"You've got to email me that sign, Jake," Iris demanded.

"Sure, you'll have to give me your email address later," he replied.

"No need to wait," and Iris grabbed Jake's phone out of Cathy's hand as it made its way around the table. "I'll just set myself up in your address book."

Katrina wasn't crazy about Iris commandeering Jake's phone like that. The way Iris clung to Jake, and the attention she paid him, were starting to annoy Katrina.

"Goody gumdrops!" exclaimed Verna. "Helen is our waitress tonight."

"A friend of yours?" Jake asked.

"Not really, but she makes dining an unforgettable experience," Verna added with a smile. "You'll see. Just don't be offended by anything she says."

An odd comment, Katrina thought.

The university-aged waitress came by, dropping off dinner menus, and took their drink orders. Her innocent schoolgirl smile and attire made her look much younger, perhaps too young to be serving in a bar.

"Good evening, everyone," Helen said with a delightful smile. "My name is Helen, and I'll be your waitress tonight." She looked at Stewart and smiled. "By the looks of your dry skin, you must be thirsty. What can I get you to drink?"

Caught off guard, Stewart's jaw dropped, preventing a snooty comeback from emitting from his jowls.

Verna smiled, then proposed to the group, "How's about a pitcher of draught and six glasses?"

"Make that five glasses and I'll have a Guinness stout," Stewart corrected.

"Of course you will," Helen replied to Stewart, then turned to look at Katrina. "And wouldn't you prefer a fruity, girly drink, Miss?"

Of course Katrina would have, but wasn't going to order one now. "No, but thank you for asking."

After the waitress departed to fetch their drinks, Katrina looked at Aunt Verna and asked, "So what's on the itinerary for Friday?"

"Winery tour!" Verna exclaimed. "I've got a good friend who owns one, and he's going to give you the VIP tour. Actually, he and his wife are both good friends. Nice people. You'll like them."

"Sounds great," Cathy said. "Who's driving? After all, I want to be sampling, sampling, sampling," she laughed. "I may have to be carried out of there."

"Tate will," volunteered Iris. "He doesn't like wine anyway. We just have to keep the joints out of him until we get home."

"Well, you can't smoke in any of the wineries, so unless he goes for a stroll and ducks into the vineyard, you should be okay," Aunt Verna replied.

The waitress approached to Jake's left and proceeded to unload the pitcher and five frosted glasses, followed by Stewart's brown, room-temperature beverage.

"So what do you recommend on the menu?" Jake asked the young lady, as he finished pouring himself a drink, and turned the pitcher towards Katrina's glass.

Katrina was glad Jake asked about the food choices, as she was having trouble deciding for herself.

"Anything with fish is good. I'd recommend the perch though. They do an awesome job with it – nice light batter with a few spices, and our tartar sauce is good too." The waitress smiled and looked at Katrina. "I love your blouse, by the way. I got the exact one from the thrift store for my grandmother."

In the process of drinking his draught, Jake almost spit it out at the remark. Instead, he held it in, forcing the beverage to burst into his nasal cavity, causing his eyes to tear up and nose to run.

"Can't hold your beer, honey?" Helen said to Jake. She went round the table taking orders, until at last she was at Stewart.

"I will try the perch special please, young lady," Stewart ordered elegantly.

"I'll slap an extra heap of fries on there for you. You'll likely need them to fill you up."

"Gad, no fries! Do you have coleslaw or mashed potatoes?"

"Both. I'll give you an order of coleslaw and a mountain of mashed with gravy. That should fill even a guy your size."

Cathy laughed as the waitress walked away. She'd never seen Stewart verbally bested without some type of comeback.

"If that young girl didn't look fourteen, I'd have given her some back," Stewart finally replied.

"I told you she'd be entertaining!" Verna laughed. "She honestly doesn't know she's offending people, and yes, her father the owner knows. Everyone in town just loves the girl and her ways."

Everyone had finished their dinner, except Katrina. She still picked at her perch. Very tasty – just too much of a good thing. She stared at the mountain of fries still covering much of her plate and wished Tate was there so they wouldn't go to waste.

The third pitcher of draught had already replenished some of the glasses around the table. Stewart finished his Stout and announced he would partake in one glass of the golden mixture himself, before beginning his descent to sobriety for the drive home much later.

Aunt Verna's watch alarm sounded. Everyone else looked at their own watches. Katrina's read 9:01.

"Excuse me. I have to go make a call." Aunt Verna removed the napkin off her lap, folded it neatly, and covered her almost vacant plate with it.

Jake and Stewart stood as she did. Stewart looked impressed by Jake's gentlemanly manners.

Aunt Verna grabbed her purse from under the table, and walking out of the patio area, fumbled through it a bit until she extracted her cell phone from the deepest recesses of the bag.

Another thirty or forty minutes until sunset, thought Katrina. She planned to haul Jake out to the pier herself to catch a glimpse of nature's wonder.

They had almost finished off the third pitcher when the waitress returned offering dessert or coffee. En masse they declined, and asked politely for the bill. They agreed to split it three ways, with Aunt Verna and Iris splitting one of the thirds.

Katrina looked at her watch – 9:21. "Your aunt's phone call is taking a long time."

Jake stood, pretending to stretch. He scanned the pier for Aunt Verna. No sign of the festive fiftyish female. Rather than raising alarm, and knowing Katrina wanted to venture onto the pier to watch the sunset, he suggested an after-dinner stroll in that direction.

Iris footed the bill for her and Verna, assuming she'd get the other half back later. The group left generous tips. In spite of their waitress's remarks, they thanked her for her excellent service and the scrumptious delicacies, as Stewart put it.

A wonderful thing about the summer nights in Southwestern Ontario is the retention of the warm air. Not so great sometimes when you are trying to sleep and the humidity lays on you like a wet blanket, but fabulous for an evening stroll. No need for a sweater, jacket, or even a light cover-up for the women. There was a warm breeze off the water, accompanied by the smell of the freshwater lake. A glorious sunset was imminent – they just had to wait.

Katrina knew Jake well enough to know when he had slipped into detective mode. "What's wrong?" she asked him.

Comfortable that Cathy was out of earshot, he answered, "I don't see Aunt Verna. I've scanned the pier, looked down the waterfront walk on the left, and even the long beach to the right. No one that resembles her in either direction."

Katrina looked around. Certainly a woman in a red Christmas sweater would be easy to spot on this short-sleeve night. Not so. "What do we do?" she asked her boyfriend.

"She gave you her cell phone number earlier today, didn't she? We can try calling her. She was headed to the pier to make a call, and I saw her take the cell out of her purse."

Cathy and Stewart, locked arm in arm, turned back to their straggling friends, and Cathy shouted at them, "Come on you two, keep up. There'll be plenty of time for hanky-panky later."

"Just have to make a call," Katrina yelled back.

Katrina punched in the numbers and waited. And waited. Jake looked at her, then asked, "Did you press send or enter?"

She pulled the phone away from her ear and looked at it. The number was still showing on the screen. Jake knew her too well. She was always dialing and forgetting to hit the key to actually make the call. Feeling dumb as she did every time this happened, she pushed the button. The phone rang. And rang a second time.

Iris yelled from up ahead, "Hey, someone left their cell phone on the pier!" She knelt down and observed the ringing phone, looking uncertain to touch it, like it was diseased or explosive.

Jake looked at Katrina, who shut off her phone. The cell on the ground stopped ringing.

"Cathy, don't be alarmed, but that's Aunt Verna's phone," Jake informed her cautiously.

Cathy looked around, turning in slow circles to search, as did the others. With Katrina in his arm, Jake casually took a couple of steps to the edge of the pier and looked over, trying to be nonchalant so he wouldn't panic Cathy. There was nothing to see except waves slapping the pylons of the pier.

Cathy conceded there was no sign of her aunt. Stewart turned to the off-duty detective. "What do we do now, Sherlock?"

"Well, Watson," Jake smiled at Stewart. "We can report her missing, but they likely won't do anything until tomorrow. She may have simply dropped her phone. Let's go check the fairgrounds."

Verna's had enough time to get over there and get lost in the crowd. It's only a couple of blocks away in Seacliff Park."

"That sounds like Aunt Verna – take off to the fair and forget about having company. I'm sure we'll find her at Seacliff Park," said Cathy.

"Seacliff Drive, the Seacliff Hotel, and now Seacliff Park. Are we headed to Seacliff Winery tomorrow?" Iris wondered out loud.

The group walked past the front of the Seacliff Hotel, and Stewart ducked into the patio to check if it was okay to leave the van there while they went to the Tomato Fest. The waitress informed him their crowd would be light tonight, so it would be okay. Stewart returned with a thumbs-up. Not sure where they were going, they headed back up to Seacliff Drive, as they knew there was a park entrance there. As they walked, Cathy tried to keep her spirits up. Jake laid out a search pattern for them, with Cathy and Stewart heading around the walkway to the left, Katrina and Iris around the right pathway, while he went up the middle where there was no path. They would meet at the far end in the middle, hopefully with Aunt Verna in tow by one of them. If not, they'd switch sides and reverse the sweep.

As they reached the park entrance, Katrina realized the sun had set without them. It was now dark, and the local band's rhythms carried to the front of the park. The crystal clear night provided a great backdrop for the stars over the lake. Katrina and Iris split off to cover their side. Their section was composed of a couple of vendors selling t-shirts and jewellery, as well as a few health awareness stands, and freebies from a local radio station. Some of the jewellery made Katrina pause momentarily, making a mental note to check the goods out another time. There was no sign of the Christmas sweater-clad aunt. Further down the pathway, the food concessions lined the way, as well as healthy lineups for their wares. It only took a couple of minutes to reach the rendezvous point. For all of them, the pass toward the beach proved fruitless.

"No sign on our side," Cathy replied. "It was mostly play areas for kids, so it was pretty deserted tonight. I'll bet it's a nuthouse during the day. And did you see that splash area in the middle? I wish they had that when I was visiting as a kid!"

"You can run around in it tomorrow, love," Stewart replied. "And that tomato at the top can dump water all over you. I'll bet it's better than running through the sprinklers like you did as a kid."

Jake looked at them, irritated by Stewart's light-hearted behaviour at this time of crisis. "We're going to have to do the same thing through the crowd gathered in front of the band," Jake notified them. "Take the same sides. I'll take the middle. Go to the front, and if you don't see her, switch sides on the way back. She may be walking, so keep your eyes peeled. Then we'll meet at the back of the audience and go through the bar area. Don't just look for the Christmas sweater – she may have a light jacket or something over top."

A luckless pass to the front found them standing near the stage, just as the band fired up a rendition of Trooper's 'Raise a Little Hell'. This made their return search toward the back more difficult, as everyone stood up and started dancing, or at least jumping up and down, with a few inebriated souls fist-pumping to the tune. With Aunt

Verna's diminutive stature, she'd be even harder to spot. Fortunately the band had a very limited light show, so there were no other distractions. As the tune came to a triumphant finish, Cathy's friends were still bobbing around people, trying to spot her missing aunt. They continued their search through a cover of Loverboy's 'Working for the Weekend', but their enthusiasm waned as they exhausted the search area. The crowd finally sat down as the band slowed it down with 54-40's 'I Go Blind', at which point Jake had already begun scanning the drinking area. Arriving at the back perimeter, Katrina looked across the fence to Jake, who gave the 'no luck' motion with his head. She looked over at Cathy, who saw Jake's reaction, and marched over to a local police officer on duty near the fenced-off drinking section. The rest of them went to meet her.

Katrina got there as the officer flipped open his notepad and started to write. As he wrote, he spoke. "I'll take the information, Miss, but there's really not much we can do until morning. What was your aunt's name again?"

"Verna. Verna Wilkinson," Cathy answered.

"Verna? Do you mean Verna, the Tim's manager?" he asked.

"Yes. Do you know her?"

The officer closed his pad and carefully tucked his pen inside it. "Yes, I do. Most people around town do. But I have to warn you…" and he paused for the right words, rubbing his chin in contemplation.

"Warn me about what?"

"She's … well, she's … she's kind of eccentric. She's got a reputation for disappearing, that's all."

"She *what?*"

"She tends to disappear. Takes off for a week or more at a time. Nobody knows where she goes or what she does. She just takes off and resurfaces at work a week later. No explanation."

Katrina glanced at Jake, who raised his eyebrows and gave an awkward smile. Cathy stood there speechless.

The officer sensed the surprise and broke the silence. "Look, we'll check at Tim's in the morning. When she disappears, she tells the assistant manager so her shifts are covered. Sometimes she doesn't tell them until the night before or the same day, but she's always told them before."

"Can we call the assistant manager tonight and ask?" Katrina asked.

"It's late, Miss. We don't even know for sure that she's missing. I'll have the morning shift check in at Tim's." He turned to Cathy. "And when you return to your aunt's house, if she's there you make sure you call down to the station and let us know."

"But we found her cell phone on the pier. Doesn't that mean anything?" Katrina pleaded.

"I know you're worried, but we get a lot of cell phones turning up in lost and found. Second only to sunglasses, I think. Don't worry about it tonight, okay?"

"Okay," Cathy replied, still absorbing the news about her aunt's disappearing act.

The office put a hand gently on her arm. "I'm sure she's okay. Just go home and we'll get it all straightened out tomorrow."

The group milled away from the officer, as Jake lingered around to talk to him. Shortly into the discussion, the officer withdrew his notepad from his pants pocket and jotted down something. A minute later, Jake shook his hand and turned to join the others.

Katrina reached for his hand. "What was that about?"

"Just gave him my name and number, in case they find anything."

More than halfway back through the dark to the car, Cathy broke the silence that everyone else was afraid to dent. "I've always known she was a little quirky. I mean, look at the Christmas sweaters."

Stewart added, "And that perpetually happy attitude – that's just not natural."

"And what's with the disappearing?" Iris asked.

"I just don't see her doing that with us here," Cathy stated emphatically. Katrina put a hand on her shoulder to calm her.

"I doubt she'd invite you down here, just to take off," agreed Jake. "It's not normal, that's for sure."

"Well," Stewart began to reply, pausing for effect and sticking out his chest in a somewhat smug pose, "the officer did use the term eccentric. Meaning the opposite of normal."

Dale J. Moore

12 *Morning Glory*

Jake sat alone in the kitchen. The night had been a restless one. Not because he couldn't sleep worrying about Aunt Verna's disappearance, but because Katrina couldn't sleep. And she kept asking him if he was awake, which he wasn't until she asked. All four times. By four-thirty, she stopped asking and lay sleeping soundly. Jake got up thirty minutes later, made some instant coffee, and laid several pieces of paper in front of him. Page one: a few quick facts on the front led to a slew of questions on the back. Questions for the police. Questions for the assistant manager and the employees at Tim's. Questions for Cathy about her aunt's past. Other questions that he had no idea who could answer. In spite of Katrina's intrusions, and the overall brevity of his sleep, his mind was clear and focused. Thank god for coffee, he thought.

The stove's digital clock shone 6:00 as the back of page one was filled. Jake dumped the last cold ounce of remaining coffee, folded the paper in four, and scooped the van keys from the surface of the counter. Entering the living room in his quest for the front door, he looked at the repaired front window, still barren of its coverings. He wondered if the breakage related to the disappearance, and one question on his page reflected this curiosity. He started to lock the front door, then remembered Aunt Verna never locked it anyway.

As Jake guided the van into the Tim Horton's lot, he saw the OPP cruiser already parked. That was a good sign they were taking this seriously, and he mentally crossed that concern off the list on the back of page one.

"Good morning, officer," Jake said to the uniform sitting at a table, interviewing the man he assumed was the assistant manager.

"Excuse me," the day shift officer said to him. "You must be the detective from Toronto."

"That obvious, eh?"

"No reason for anyone else to approach me at 6:15 in the morning."

"Good point. Do you mind me listening to you question the assistant manager?"

"I prefer to think of it as gathering information, not questioning. Please, have a seat."

The officer reiterated what the assistant manager had told him. There was no call from Verna Wilkinson asking him to fill in. He just lived two blocks away, so when Verna wasn't there at her 5:45 start time and there was no answer at her home or cell at 6:00, they called him to come in.

"She's always told me when she was taking off on one of her junkets," the assistant manager said, worry on his face. "It's just not like her not to tell me. Or at least tell me she needed me to fill in."

"How often does she disappear on one of her 'junkets', as you call them?" Jake asked.

"Once a year, maybe twice some years. Never in the winter, which is odd, since most of us want to get the hell to Mexico, Cuba, or some Caribbean island after the first few weeks of cold weather."

"So she's disappeared at this time of year before?"

"Yeah, I think so. Seems to me she missed the Tomato Fest a few years back."

The officer wrote some notes then asked his own question. "Anything unusual happen around here recently? Any fights you guys didn't report or any strangers lurking around?"

"Nothing that I know of. I'll ask around, as the team members arrive throughout the day. I'm sure they would have reported any fights – we've only had one that I know of in the six years I've worked here, so any fight certainly would have triggered gossip. As far as strangers, I'll ask. No one I know of, but it is Tomato Fest weekend, so there are more out-of-towners than usual."

"What about enemies?" Jake asked.

The two men at the table both laughed. The officer replied, "Verna's the sweetest, kindest lady in all of Leamington, I reckon. Don't know anybody that would want to hurt her. They wouldn't have any reason." The assistant manager nodded agreement, and was excused by the pair.

"So what, then?" asked a puzzled Jake.

"Maybe she slipped off the pier," the officer proposed. "As soon as the manager told me he hadn't heard from Verna, I radioed in. The

Coast Guard will start looking for her shortly. They know the area currents really well. They'll likely spend the day looking. I'll call you if we hear something."

"Thanks, let me give you my number." Jake straightened out of his slight slouch.

"No need. Bill, the officer you met last night, made up copies of your info and left one in each of our mail slots this morning. Said you'd be following up, and maybe you'd even be able to help if something sinister happened. Do you investigate murders in Toronto?"

"No, not really. Mostly I'm on small crimes and drug enforcement, but I've got the training for the big stuff. Just too new to earn my way up there yet."

"Yeah, know what you mean. Took me ten years to get off midnights."

Jake stood and shook hands, then headed for a cup of java from the counter. As he pulled out his wallet to pay, he noticed the officer in line behind him. "What are you having?"

"Large, double-double."

Jake put the change back in his pocket and pulled out a ten. "My treat, if that's okay with you."

Jake sat alone in the gazebo. On the picnic table in front of him laid his sheets of paper. He'd covered one page completely in doodles and connecting lines. A summation of all the information he'd collected so far about Aunt Verna and her disappearance. In the first step of his process, he performed a brain dump of everything he could think of, no matter how small and inconsequential. The second step included looking at each point to see if it related to any other point on the page. If it did, he connected the points. This often resulted in lines going every which way. The second sheet of paper only started after the first one was complete. The second page organized everything to discern any patterns. His mind struggled with figuring the best way to lay out the second page.

Still transferring items from page one to page two, Jake looked up from his seat in the gazebo at the sound of the screen door closing. Katrina was walking toward him, wearing sexy little sleep shorts, arms crossed in front for modesty, as it was already warm.

"What are you up to, sweetie?" and she gave him a peck on the cheek.

"Just collecting my thoughts on the case," and as soon he said it, he wanted the words back.

"Case? So the police think Verna's missing too? And how do you know?" she asked in quick succession.

"I met one of the officers at her work this morning," he replied.

"What? You went without me? You knew I wanted to be there!" she exclaimed.

"It was really early, before six. Thought you'd prefer sleeping in on your vacation," he explained. He knew she wanted to go, but he wanted to maintain a professional relationship with the local OPP branch, and thought by dragging his girlfriend along he would give the wrong impression. He just couldn't say that to her without hurting her feelings.

"Well I would have preferred that I was there. Did you talk to all of the staff?" she asked.

"No. I'm letting the local police handle it. I'm going to call them before shift change to hear what they found out."

"We need to go down there and question them," she objected.

Jake tried to keep Katrina from getting involved. There was no need for her to be, and she had a way of falling into predicaments. She barely knew Verna, and certainly was out of her element in this southern destination. "You are supposed to be on vacation! Let the police handle it."

"And you are supposed to be suspended. Let the police handle it!" In a rare occurrence, she let her anger show to Jake.

"I'm on leave, not suspended," he said, knowing she was basically right. He shouldn't be getting involved but it was in his blood. Until this incident, he'd been going through the motions on this so-called vacation. Sure he was having some fun, but he missed the adrenaline rush of his detective work. He wasn't sure how he'd make it through the whole weekend. "And I'm a trained detective, not a salon owner." He wanted to take that back too. It was true in his mind, but he knew it was the wrong thing to say as soon as he uttered it.

Katrina glared at him, her arms tightly crossed against her chest now, like she was containing an imminent eruption of rage. She thrust her arms down to her sides, hands making fists as she did so. Jake flinched, thinking she might actually hit him. It never crossed her mind. Instead, she stomped her right foot firmly onto the gazebo floor, loudly grunted an 'Ughhhhh', took a deep breath, turned and stormed back to the cottage.

Well, that went well, he thought to himself. Now where was he …

Dale J. Moore

13 Wine Tour

Cathy flipped over in the small bed gracing her aunt's smallest guestroom. Stewart grunted as she did so, her knee landing squarely on his slightly oversized, but still cute butt. Waking next to him made her day. Lying there, looking at him sleep, she felt lucky. It wasn't long ago that she'd wondered if all that time with a lesbian screen-writing partner and her dyke friends had rubbed off. She dismissed the notion as just plain stupid, but was relieved when Stewart took an interest in her. He was so different from anyone she'd dated before. The gentleman thing wasn't simply a first date act, like she'd seen so often before. He was sincere and respectful. She was in love.

A little snort emitted from Stewart, snapping Cathy out of her dream-like trance.

"Aunt Verna!" she blurted out. "I have to know if they found her." She gave Stewart a light peck on the back of his head, threw on a robe, and ran a few fingers through her hair as she opened the bedroom door. In the kitchen, she had just picked up the phone when she heard a noise at the back screen door. Katrina fought to get the door handle open, stomping as she did so. Cathy could tell Katrina was pissed, but couldn't help but laugh as she walked over and opened the door from the inside.

"It's not funny!" Katrina cried. Tears fell down her unmade-up cheeks.

Cathy gave her a comforting hug before pulling back slightly. Her hands went up to Katrina's face, and she used her thumbs to wipe away the tears. "What's wrong, Kat?"

"Stupid Jake. Wants to play detective without me," she replied.

"He's not playing, Kat. He is a detective," Cathy responded as she gently held Katrina's shoulders.

Katrina pulled back slightly, "Now you sound like him."

"Does he know something about my aunt?" Cathy asked.

Katrina twisted her shoulders free from Cathy's light grasp. "Maybe you should go ask the detective. I just run a salon, remember?" Katrina ran off to her room, crying.

"That's not what I meant, Katrina ... Katrina!" Cathy looked up, in mimic of her mother looking to the Lord for strength. "Damn," she said quietly, in a rare moment of verbal restraint. *Might as well go see what Jake knows*, and out the screen door she went.

Cathy eyed the clock with all the patience of a student waiting for the final bell. She was anxious to do something to find her aunt, and it was already noon. Already noon, she laughed at herself. She routinely slept late while at home, yet here she was on vacation, chomping at the bit to get going. *Go figure.* Jake had calmed her down, convincing her to let the OPP and Coast Guard do their thing. She felt better that they all had his cell phone number, and that he'd already received one call this morning from the police to confirm what Aunt Verna was wearing when she disappeared.

Everyone at the cottage had finally made their way out of their beds. They were in the kitchen of their missing hostess, all dressed and ready to go.

Cathy asked Jake to give the others a quick rundown of the search for her aunt, then stood up as he finished. She took a deep sigh, convincing herself this was the right thing to do.

"So we've decided that we are still going on the wine tour that Auntie set up. She was really close to the winery owners, and Jake thinks that we may find out some clues by talking to them." Cathy saw Katrina pouting, no doubt still feeling left on the sidelines for this mystery.

"Brill!" Stewart added, "A dose of intoxication will help lift the ol' spirits, don't you think?"

"Absolutely!" A perky Iris chimed in.

Cathy wondered why someone so perky wore so much black. Clothes and makeup. Very contradictory, she thought. Maybe Iris was a Cybil.

"Alright, then. Let's go," Stewart replied. "I'll drive there, because I'll be in no shape to drive back. I'll end up on the wrong side of the road, like back in England."

Iris laughed and answered, "Tate's cool with driving back. Although I can't guarantee he'll stay on the right side of the road even if he's sober."

Tate replied, "Sure, no problem. But I'll be chillin' as soon as we get back."

Katrina sat in the middle row with Jake as the group retraced their trip from the night before, heading into town via Seacliff Drive, and past the park of the same name. Tents and equipment stood mostly idle, a few vendors setting up for the afternoon and evening crowds. Recalling the greenhouse tour from the day before, she sat in awe at the size and number of greenhouses they drove past on this peaceful lakeside drive. As they continued away from Leamington, Katrina gazed at the beauty of the countryside in this southernmost part of Canada. Flat, but beautiful.

"You do know where you're going, eh?" Jake inquired of his driver.

"I've got the coordinates back here if you need them," Tate replied.

"Coordinates?" came multiple voices.

Cathy looked at Iris, then at Tate. "We haven't dipped into the ganja yet, have we, Tate? In case you didn't realize this isn't a spaceship."

"Unfortunately no to the ganja question, and yes I realize it's not a spaceship."

"So what's with the coordinates then?" Cathy asked.

"It's right here, on this wine route guide I picked up. It has the latitude and longitude of each winery."

Stewart snorted a laugh, "Oh yes, well I can see how that is going to be exceedingly helpful guiding our Dodge Caravan." He played around with the overhead display. "Blast it! Metric and US measurements, but no latitude and longitude. Why did I ever rent a bloody vehicle without latitude and longitude!"

Katrina laughed at Stewart's fake rant and reached over to hold Jake's hand.

Tate stared in fascination at the map that he held up in front of his face, and replied in detail to Stewart's rhetorical question.

"Well, just so you know for future reference, all of the wineries are between N 41.9 and N 42.3 degrees latitude, and, let's see … between W82 and W83 degrees longitude."

Jake laughed and squeezed Katrina's hand. "Yes, I'll be sure to file that away for future reference."

Katrina pointed out the window. "There's a winery on the left. Essex County Cellars. Is that it?"

"No, here it is now," Stewart announced as he drove past Katrina's find.

"County Estates Vineyards. Sounds good," Katrina said, apparently out of her earlier funk.

Cathy looked across the road as they turned in. "There's another one over there too," and she strained back to see the name. "Migration Route Winery."

"It's like Napa Valley around here," Katrina added. "Or at least what I imagine Napa Valley is like. Wineries everywhere you turn."

"Just a wee exaggeration, I fear," Stewart responded.

"But it is cool," Jake said to Katrina.

"It is handy," Stewart replied. "I plan to drink a lot and pretend I'm consuming the exquisite tastes of Tuscany. I figure after the first few litres, I won't notice."

Cathy smacked his arm. "You keep your wine snob comments to yourself! The owners are friends of my aunt's, so be nice. Besides, I think some of these wines will surprise you."

"Oh, I'd be surprised," Stewart added, then winced as she smacked him again. "Got it," and he rubbed his arm. "It's a splendid Friday afternoon for a wine tour and tasting."

Katrina opened the side door of the van. Before she could get a foot out the door, the humidity blasted past her and quickly displaced the artificially cooled air. She heard the moans behind her as they felt the air.

"Well, isn't that inspiration to drink?" Stewart chirped, as he plucked his floppy hat from between the front seats and settled it neatly on his head.

To Katrina, the hat looked funny on his round head. "Dr. Livingstone, I presume?"

Stewart crinkled his nose at her as he closed the van door.

Katrina flung her large carry bag over her shoulder then straightened up to look around. An old country farm house stood before them, restored to better than new. Freshly painted wooden shutters accented all the windows as they enriched the rustic feel. Vineyards lined both sides of the house, with a new red aluminum barn at the end of a gravel laneway. She turned and found Jake's arm as they ambled in the front door, held open by Tate. Only two other people milled about. She'd expected more people.

Cathy had already introduced herself and Stewart to the lady behind the serving and sampling bar. Laughing, she called the others over. Katrina took a couple of steps with Jake before jumping back a step and clenching Jake's arm, startled at a sudden noise from outside. A customer had entered via the back door, and brought with him the sounds of a small ensemble band playing on the patio. Looking outside, Katrina saw a modest group of twenty to thirty people sitting around small tables as they enjoyed their wine and presumably the music.

"Look, Jake! Let's grab some wine and head out there. It looks so relaxing," she told her companion.

Cathy overhead and halted Katrina's plan. "Everyone, this is Faith. My aunt's friend." Quick introductions followed, ending with Tate. Cathy continued, "Faith's husband Don is going to give us a personal tour in about 5 minutes."

Tate replied, "Thanks, Faith! I don't do too well in crowds."

"You are very welcome, Tate. I also hear you are the designated driver for today, so Don will serve you selections from our homemade grape juices."

"Cool," thanked Tate.

"Feel free to look around until Don gets in. Our reds are along the wall on the left, and include a selection of Merlot, Shiraz, Cabernet, and our award winning Meritage. Our whites on the right include Pinot, Chardonnay, and our well known Riesling."

As they browsed the bottles in the white section, Jake whispered to Katrina. "I don't really know anything about wine. I just like dry, so I look for the '0' under the name at the LCBO."

Katrina smiled and whispered back, "Me neither. Maybe we'll learn something on our tour."

"Maybe, but I don't drink enough of it to care too much. The process will be interesting to hear about, though." Jake smiled and looked at Katrina. "Hopefully Stewart doesn't correct our host too much."

Katrina giggled, "I'm sure Cathy will take care of Stewart if he gets out of line."

"No doubt about that," laughed Jake.

A burly middle-aged man came through the front entrance. Standing out from the shorts-wearing guests in his blue jeans, he looked every bit a farmer and not a winery owner. His thick grey hair snuck out the sides of his baseball cap. Don smiled as his eyes found Faith behind the bar. She smiled warmly back at him.

"So you folks must be Verna's lot!" and he reached his hand out to shake Stewart's. He greeted each of the men with a firm handshake. Each of the women received a gentle hug, which Katrina for once didn't mind. It was like getting a hug from her dad and actually made her momentarily homesick.

"If you ladies don't want to lug your bags around, they'll be perfectly safe behind the bar with Faith."

Not one to usually part with her purse or bag, Katrina felt she had nothing to worry about and handed her bag over the bar to Don's wife.

"Let's head out the back door. We'll cut through the vineyard and then over to the barn, where we make our delicious products. I'll give you some background about this place, some statistics for the geeks in the group, and then we'll sample a few wines. I'm sure they'll please even the picky palates in the group," and he smiled at Stewart.

Stewart flinched away from Cathy and whispered, "I didn't say anything, honest!"

"To start, Faith and I began this winery almost fifteen years ago. I'd been growing corn for years on a section of my father's farm, much like many farmers around here. I was working full time at GM in Windsor and helping my dad with his farm. My crop was more of a hobby. I was tired of working on the line, and could see the writing on the wall for the plant. I took my buyout and Faith and I chose to chase our dream. It's great. A ton of work and a few early disasters, but we couldn't be happier."

Don led them a few rows deep into a series of vines with purple-reddish grapes.

"And what type of wine do you suppose this grape makes?"

A few guesses came forth of Merlot and Cabernet.

"Both incorrect. Although light purple in colour, these grapes actually are used to make Pinot Gris, one of our tasty white wines. The grapes are believed to have mutated from the grapes used to make Pinot Noir, and have to some degree retained their dark skin. Besides, the skins are discarded while making white wine, unlike red where they are used. I'll talk more about that later."

"That is so cool!" Tate rocked back and forth as he commented.

"Southern Ontario is blessed with mild winters, at least in comparison to most of Canada, and hot summers. This allows us to grow the best French hybrid and traditional European varieties of grapes, and as a result, produce world-recognized high quality wines." He looked again at Stewart, who was now getting a complex. "The province has quality standards that we must adhere to."

Katrina raised her hand as if in class at school.

Don smiled at her gesture. "You have a question?"

"Yes, what is Meritage?"

"Good question. It's a Bordeaux style wine, like those from France. But since it doesn't come from the Bordeaux region in France, we can't call it Bordeaux. A red Meritage must be made from a blend of at least 90% of two or more of a group of wines," and Don began to count on his fingers. "Cabernet Sauvignon, Merlot, Cabernet Franc, Petit Verdot, or Carmenère. Ours use a blend of the first three. We tinkered with the blend for a few years until we were satisfied – one of those early disasters was an awful Meritage that we ended up dumping. The use of the name Meritage actually requires a licensing fee as well. Any other questions before we head inside?"

"Yes," said a previously quiet Iris, who'd focused on keeping Tate from drifting away to smoke a joint. "What is Ice Wine?"

"Another good question. I won't get into a lot of details, but we leave a small section of grapes on the vine into the winter. Usually after a few days of cold weather and a bit of snow, we'll pick the grapes and make the wine. Ice Wine is very sweet due to leaving the grapes on the vine so long. Most people who crave a dry wine don't like Ice Wine at all, finding it unbearably sweet. But if you like sweet, it makes a great sipping wine with dessert."

Stewart risked asking a question, thinking back to Katrina's comment about Napa Valley. "How much wine is bottled in Ontario every year, versus California?"

"You'll likely be surprised to find out that about five years ago Ontario produced over eleven million litres of wine in less than 150 wineries. California made about 150 times as much wine in about 1200 wineries."

"Wow!" Katrina exclaimed. "That's a lot of wine. No wonder I can never decide which wine to pick."

"That's why I stick to looking for the '0'," Jake smiled.

Their guide led them into the red barn Katrina had spotted earlier. Inside, Don introduced them to Romeo, his interim Wine Master. Don's regular Wine Master had left for Italy in March to be with his dying father, and didn't expect to be back until the fall. Romeo was a local, having trained for years in the industry in the Niagara region.

"I won't go into every detail, but will hit on a few basics, okay?" Romeo, flashing a welcoming smile to the group, took a quick glance at his watch. "Feel free to ask questions, but I do have another tour in twenty minutes. But you can ask Faith or Don later if you have more questions. So let me start with how the wines differ." Romeo looked at Don. "Did you show them the Pinot Gris grapes and talk about them?" He received a yes reply from Don. "Good. Red wine is made from the pulp of red or black grapes that ferments together with the grape skins. White wine is made by fermenting juice extracted by pressing crushed grapes - the skins are removed and tossed. As Don likely said for the Pinot Gris, occasionally white wine is made from red grapes by extracting their juice."

"How long does it ferment?" Jake asked.

"It varies, but between a week and two, keeping it warm in these special tanks," and Romeo pointed to a cluster of shiny silver tanks, dimpled on the outside.

"Can you drink it once it cools?" Katrina asked.

"I wouldn't recommend it. That's just to ferment the wine. It needs to settle and age before consuming. Our wines will age between one and three years, typically. Most wines don't get significantly smoother or better tasting by aging any longer."

Cathy smiled and added, "Besides, I'd rather drink it than watch it sit in bottles."

Romeo laughed in agreement. "I can take a hint. If you go with Don, he'll lead you back to the house for the tasting."

Don corrected his Wine Master, "Actually, I've got samples out here for you to try. Verna told me you were coming, so I selected a few of my favourites that usually aren't on the tasting and set them out. Just come around the corner and you can get into the samples you have so patiently waited for."

"Thanks, Romeo," Jake said as he passed him on the way to the tasting.

Don gave some commentary on the vintages they savoured. Jake took the opportunity to find out more about Don's relationship to Cathy's missing aunt. Katrina listened intently as she sipped her wine. Verna had attended many events here at the winery, and had become good friends with both Faith and Don. They'd hosted each other for dinner many times over the past couple of years. Don didn't know where Verna disappeared every year, and unless Faith was keeping it secret from him, she didn't know either. And that would be unlike Faith. Don wasn't completely surprised by Verna disappearing, given her history, but was intrigued by her leaving with company and having set up today's tour.

Katrina, Jake, and Don talked more about the winery, and quietly Don disclosed that Romeo was fired from his former job for letting a vintage sour. Romeo's former employer in Niagara was a large winery based in Toronto and had no tolerance for such mistakes, although truthfully such a mistake would hurt a small winery much more. Don's Wine Master knew Romeo, and recommended his friend to Don. During his interview, Romeo had detailed every step in his process, impressing Don with his knowledge. Faith and Don believed Romeo when he said it wasn't anything that he'd done, but couldn't explain what went wrong. They were in a bind with their regular Wine Master's sudden departure, and based on the recommendation and his knowledge, were willing to give Romeo a second chance.

14   *Buyout*

Katrina slumped slightly in the patio chair at the winery, enjoying the afternoon heat and feeling quite numb from the wine tasting. The music from the band had stopped, but still played in her head. She would gladly nap if not for the harassment she'd face later from her friends. She could imagine comments about needing to recharge the old batteries, not to mention the granny blouse remark from the waitress the night before. She hoped the Coke that Jake was fetching her would help revive her senses.

Jake and Cathy entered the winery from the patio, in search of more wine for Cathy, Iris, and Stewart, who had agreed that he was pleasantly surprised by the calibre of the vintages available. Jake sought Cokes for himself, Katrina, and Tate, wondering if caffeine did anything to perk up the always mellow fellow.

As Faith talked to Cathy about which wine to try next, Jake followed the co-owner's directions past the offices to the vending machine in an adjoining room. Having secured his three thirst quenching beverages, Jake walked back toward the main room.

Approaching Don's office, he heard raised voices through the slightly ajar door. Jake didn't recognize the first voice.

"You will regret not taking this deal, Don. It is almost double the first offer we made last fall. If you're holding out for more, it won't get any sweeter than this one on the table now."

"I've told you before, Evan, I have no intention of selling, no matter what the offer, or how many visits you make."

"I want you to know how we find these negotiations usually go. Most of the time, we end up getting a property for a lot less than the peak offer. Sellers hesitate and their advantage is lost. They often run into one of many problems that plaque a small business, but by then the great offer is off the table. A lot of bad things can happen to small independents."

"You're not threatening me are you?"

"Absolutely not. Canawine is an aboveboard company. We don't threaten people."

"Aboveboard – maybe. But your wine is cheap. Do you sell anything in bottles anymore, or is everything in boxes or bags now?"

"We have a defined market that works well for us," the man replied, very upset with the question.

"You don't understand my dreams."

"The amount of money we are offering will pay for a lot of dreams."

"Not this one."

Jake heard chairs move as the men stood up. He stayed put in the hallway, wanting to see the person talking to Don.

The door opened and the stranger emerged, followed immediately by Don, who saw Jake standing nearby.

"Oh, Detective Jake, how's the sampling going?"

Although Don had shown no interest in Jake's job earlier when they spoke, Jake noted the intentional use of the word 'Detective' in the other man's presence.

"Fine, but I'm on a break," and he held up the Cokes.

"This is Evan Batch, from Canawine in Toronto. He's here trying to buy the winery."

"And how's it going, Mr. Batch?"

"Not well, I'm afraid. Don hasn't seen the light yet."

"Perhaps you're looking for light where there is none," Jake replied.

Cathy approached the trio, three filled wine glasses in her hands. "Who's your friend, Don?"

"This is Evan Batch from Canawine. Evan, this is Cathy, she's Verna Wilkinson's niece. I believe you met Verna a couple of times during previous attempts to persuade me."

Evan looked instantly uncomfortable, yet outstretched a hand to shake with Cathy.

"Sorry, Evan, but I don't want to spill the fruits of Don's labour here. So excuse me skipping the handshake."

"No problem." Evan looked oddly relieved. "Well, I should be going. I've got a few other stops to make." He looked at Don and shook his hand. "I'll call you in a few days to see if you've had a change of heart. And don't say don't bother, because you know me better by now.

Talk to Faith and see what she thinks. It was nice meeting you, Detective," he said, shaking Jake's hand also. "Cathy," and he nodded to the hands-full woman, although one glass had been relieved of half its contents.

Jake hadn't noticed, but Katrina watched the gathering after she'd slipped inside to escape the heat. She wondered what had delayed her usually punctual boyfriend. As Cathy carted the wine outside, Katrina thanked Jake for the Coke and took a quick, refreshing sip.

"What was that all about? That guy looked like he'd seen a ghost when Don mentioned Cathy is Verna's niece."

"You saw that too, eh? Thought maybe it was just me."

"Who is he?"

"Buyer from Toronto. Trying to purchase the winery."

"Oh no! Don wouldn't sell this, would he?"

"You mean Don and Faith wouldn't sell. No, he flat out turned him down, for apparently the umpteenth time. Gotta give the guy marks for persistence, but he seems a little shifty to me."

"Did your detective radar go off?"

"Loud enough that I thought maybe that's why you came in."

"Well, who do we know that knows everybody that knows anyone in Toronto?"

Jake paused to rewind and replay her sentence a few times. Finally comprehending the question, he replied, "Stewart!"

A few hours later, after the band had packed up and left the patio strangely empty, Katrina and the gang agreed to head inside to purchase some wine for after dinner, as well as secure a bottle or two to take back to Toronto. They heaped thanks and praise on Faith and Don for their hospitality and their fantastic winery. Stewart even praised the vintages produced, saying they had opened his mind. Iris quipped that Stewart had flooded his mind with all the wine he'd consumed.

Cathy invited the couple back to Verna's for an early evening barbecue, and they accepted, although admitting they had some catching up to do. Tate jumped behind the wheel of the van, and shortly after exiting the winery, Cathy, Iris, and Stewart were fast asleep, done in by the sun and wine. Katrina fought sleep for most of the trip back, succumbing in the final minutes before they stopped. Jake sat wide awake in the front beside Tate, keeping the driver talking and alert. In spite of having no alcohol and not slipping away for a joint, Tate looked two blinks from a nap.

Dale J. Moore

15   *The Butcher*

Katrina's green eyes opened to the sound of the van's engine shutting off. She gently rubbed her eyes as she focused her vision. Leaning slightly to look out the window, she saw the sign for a local grocery store. The two front doors closed on the van, completely waking her but not disturbing the others from their blissful naps. Unbuckling her safety belt, she quietly slid open her door and slipped out.

"Hey, sleepyhead," Jake smiled as Katrina approached.

"You could have woken me up," she replied.

"You just fell asleep. I thought you could use the rest. All that sun, you know."

"I'm fine. What are you guys getting?"

"Dinner. We've got company coming, remember?"

"Of course I do. I'm perfectly sober now." She wasn't entirely truthful. She still felt a bit of a buzz, even hours after her last sip of wine. Her tolerance sucked; who was she kidding? She'd like to blame it on the combination of wine and sun, but knew better. "So what are you getting?"

"Steaks and chicken for starters. Tate spotted a farmer's stand just before town and we picked up some fresh corn and veggies. We picked up a fresh blueberry pie from that place Faith raved about, too."

"I didn't even notice you stop," Katrina mumbled meekly.

"None of the zombies in the back did either. At one of the stops Stewart let out a loud grunt and mumbled some incoherent British-sounding gibberish and went back to sleep. Tate tried to video it with his phone but wasn't quick enough."

Jake went back to the business of picking out steaks. Katrina watched with interest as her boyfriend examined the various cuts available from the butcher. She listened as he first exchanged pleasantries with the white aproned gentleman behind the counter. The men next discussed which cuts the local butcher recommended for the evening's barbecue. As Jake grabbed the wrapped steaks from the counter, he asked the man if he knew Verna.

"Of course I know Verna. I need my cup of coffee in the morning just like everyone else. Strange she wasn't there this morning, though. No one seemed to know where she was." He looked at Katrina. "Are you her niece visiting from Toronto?"

"Uh, no. She's sleeping in the car."

"Let me guess … wine tour?"

Jake and Katrina laughed, though her head hurt slightly when she did. *Had she already progressed to hangover?*

The butcher continued, "Just to warn you, you got to be careful of the cops. They've been cracking down lately. End of summer blitz or something like that."

"Thanks for the tip. We've got a designated driver. Anything strange about Verna lately?"

"No, not really. I thought it odd when she bought all that food the other day, but then we got to talking and she mentioned you guys coming to town, so it all made sense. I figured that was why she didn't show up to Tim's today."

Katrina asked, "Do you know anything about where she disappears to every year?"

"Nope. Not my business either. Besides, it's part of the wonderfully quirky package that makes up that darling woman."

Jake finished his order with some fresh boneless chicken breasts. Katrina also thanked the butcher and they went looking for Tate. She worried he'd slipped outside for a joint and they'd find him at the cashier with a cart full of munchies. Her worries were misplaced. They found Tate comparing labels of steak sauces.

"Just comparing sodium content and looking for artificial ingredients with more than five syllables," and he laughed at his own remark.

Jake patiently watched Tate survey the bottles. "It would be a shame to waste all this fresh food by caking it with artificial additives."

"Exactly my point!" Tate exclaimed, as he triumphantly held up a local sauce and proclaimed victory.

Katrina half expected Tate to do a victory dance or at least a lap around their shopping cart. Sauce securely tucked into the buggy, they headed to the cashier, their shopping complete. Turning the corner of their aisle, Jake almost crashed into Don.

"Hey, fancy running into you here. Well, almost running into you," Jake said.

"You're going to beat us to Verna's if we don't hustle," Katrina added.

"Not to worry," Don replied. "Faith and I are on our way to visit her mother first. She's got a nice unit in the new nursing home. Or should I say the new assisted living facility," he smiled as he used the politically correct name.

"My mom still calls them the loony bin," Katrina half smiled. "She says she'd rather be shot than made to go live in one of those places."

"Well, I assume your mother hasn't been to any of the new ones. Sure, some still have secure floors for patients with Alzheimer's or worse, but some are beautiful. If you can afford it of course. Anyway, I just need to grab some Twinkies and we'll be on our way. The dear lady still loves here Twinkies." He patted Jake on the shoulder. "See you about seven, okay?"

"Sounds good. That'll give everyone time to wake up and freshen up," Katrina said.

The cashier rang up their purchases as fast as Tate could place them on the belt. As Jake bagged them, Katrina heard raised voices from the snack aisle. She leaned to confirm that Don was one of the voices, but had to take a few steps over to be sure. Not watching where she was going as she followed the voices, she bumped into someone.

"Oh, sorry. My fault, I wasn't looking." When she did look to see the person, her face flashed startled as her eyes recognized Wally the Wino.

"No problem, miss. And thanks for the change the other day."

Katrina instinctively reached for her purse.

"It's okay, miss. You can put your money away. I've got what I need for dinner." He held up a bag with two rolls in it and a small package of macaroni and cheese meat slices. "Maybe next time."

Katrina gave him an awkward smile before turning back to listen to the escalating verbal battle. The man arguing with Don stood with his back to her, holding a shopping cart with one hand and gesturing wildly with the other as he spoke.

"But Don, you know how much I need this deal," the man pleaded.

"I know you do, but it's just not right for me," Don empathized back.

"I'm going to go under without it!" The man's voice began to rise even louder. "You need to do what's best for the community, not just you. This will bring more jobs to the area."

"And get you out of debt in the process."

The man had moved beside his cart to confront Don. Katrina could finally see his face, blazing red with anger. Obviously the man possessed a temper.

"That's not the point. You should be careful. I've heard things about Evan and his crew. Some small winery in the Niagara region held out against them and the place mysteriously burned down. Is it worth it to you, putting Faith at risk?"

Katrina could tell Don was upset with that last remark and she walked up beside him.

Don took a deep breath, then a step back, bumping into Katrina. Seeing her helped him regain additional composure.

"Look, Pierre. I understand your concerns. I do not, I repeat, DO NOT, appreciate the threats. Especially against Faith. We've been neighbours for years, and I hope it works out that we can continue to be. I will not discuss this matter with you further, especially in a public place."

At this distance, Katrina could see the man was drunk. He stumbled slightly as he moved the cart from between himself and Don. Katrina now stood at Don's side.

"No, we're going to keep talking about it!" The man raised his voice and stood toe to toe with Don.

Don backed up slightly, bumping into the shelf behind him. He added to his earlier comment, smelling the man's breath. "And I'm not going to talk to you about it until you're sober."

The man lost control of his temper. He pushed Don hard against the shelf, and boxes of cupcakes and other snacks fell to the floor.

Katrina stepped in between the two of them. "Stop it!"

She was greeted with a forceful push from Don's neighbour, and fell backwards into Don, who'd just righted himself from the first shove. More cinnamon buns and brownies spilled from the shelves.

Jake heard the commotion and started for the aisle of the tussle. He was surprised to see a police officer already with the situation under control. The officer cuffed Don's neighbour.

Don talked to the officer, while Katrina put some of the boxes back in their place.

"I don't want to press any charges, officer. Can you just let him off with a warning?"

"I can give him a warning, although we don't like public drunkenness, especially in the middle of the day."

"Thanks. It's just the booze talking, I'm afraid."

"And that's why I can't just let him go. He can't drive in his condition, so he's going to sit in a cell and sober up for the next twelve hours."

Katrina looked over the officer's shoulder and saw Wally the Wino. She flicked her wrist with a little shooing motion, hoping he'd disappear before the officer put him in a cell too. He put down his items and headed out the door.

Don stopped Katrina to apologize to her for the trouble, and asked if she was okay. He then smiled at her. "And I thought getting a box of Twinkies would be an easy errand. I'll have to send Faith in next time."

Katrina smiled back, before leaving for the exit with Jake. As they got outside, the officer was putting Don's assailant in the back of the cruiser. Closing the door, the officer turned and tipped his hat to them. He started around front to the driver's side, when he stopped and put his hands on his hips in a look of disgust. Katrina pointed a finger at herself, like she was perhaps guilty of something. The officer shook his head first, followed by a tilt upwards to tell Katrina to look behind her. She turned and saw Wally the Wino urinating on the wall.

Jake spit out a laugh. "Looks like your friend is going to spend the night in jail."

Ever the optimist, Katrina replied, "Well, he came to the store to get fed, and now he'll get a meal in jail. I guess he got what he came for."

16   *Stealth Run*

A British gentleman does not obsess, nor does he act compulsively, unless perhaps it is about one of life's finer pursuits. Namely a cracking lady, a scrummy meal, or a smashing bottle of spirits. Yet, since his drive from Toronto, Stewart had had an almost singular thought running through his mind. And finally, his opportunity had come. With everyone freshening up before their dinner, Stewart had time to fulfill his fixation. Noticing Aunt Verna's fridge low on mix for cocktails, he announced to Jake that a trip to the convenience store was in order. As expected, Jake just nodded, having just loaded up at the grocery store. Stewart was relieved, since the store was simply a cover for his true mission.

Pushing open the front screen door to leave, Stewart spotted a plain red baseball cap on Aunt Verna's coat rack. Looking back to confirm no one was watching, he grabbed the cap and slipped out the door. He wasn't big on wearing caps – he preferred berets or boonie hats (not the camouflage kind) – but it would suit today's need.

Driving into town, he stopped at the first store he spotted, and quickly got in and out with a two-litre bottle of tonic water along with the same size Diet Coke. He tucked the two bottles neatly between the front seats and drove off to his actual destination. As he drove, he contemplated whether to walk in so he could see the menu and take his time to order, or retain his anonymity. He donned the red cap and entered the drive-thru lane.

"Welcome to McDonald's. May I take your order?"

"Oh, yes. I see. Could I perhaps have a minute?"

"Certainly, sir. Just let me know when you're ready to order."

He looked over the menu. *What was it Cathy had given him a taste of?*

"Hello, miss?"

"Go ahead, sir."

"I'll have a Big Mac and an order of those fries."

"Would you like to make that a combo?"

"What's a combo?"

"You get a drink with your order."

"Is that free?"

"No, but it's cheaper than if you ordered them all separately."

"But I didn't order them all. I only ordered a sandwich and fries."

"Yes, sir, but if you were to order them separately, it would be more."

"But I didn't."

"If you were to order the drink with the combo, it would be less than if you ordered the drink by itself."

"Yes, I get that. But I didn't order the drink, and I don't want the bloody drink!"

"Yes, sir. That will be $5.65. Please drive up to the first window."

Within a minute, Stewart had driven forward to the window, paid for his meal, driven forward to the next window, and received his food. He didn't understand why he had to pay for it at one window, then drive forward to the next window to get his food. There was only one window at Tim's, and it worked just fine. He pulled the van over to a parking spot, stopped the motor, and unrolled the top of the paper bag. Tentatively, he took a bite of his Big Mac. Then another. And another, followed by a quick handful of fries. He hummed with satisfaction as he devoured the sandwich in less time than it took him to go through the drive-thru, not including the combo discussion. Half of the fries had vanished as well.

He started the van, looked over his shoulder, and backed out. Stewart steered the van around the McDonald's parking lot and pulled into the drive-thru lane again.

"Welcome to McDonald's. May I take your order?"

Stewart looked over the menu again.

"I'll have a Quarter Pounder with Cheese, please."

"Would you like to make that a combo?"

"Why would I want to make it a combo, when I only ordered a sandwich?"

"It's cheaper than if you ordered the fries and drink separately."

"But I didn't order fries or a drink. I only ordered a sandwich."

"Yes, sir, but if you were to order them separately, it would be more."

Stewart was close to losing his temper again, but remembered the girl from his first order. She was a teenage girl, likely only a few months into her first job.

"Just the sandwich, please."

"Yes, sir. That will be $3.65. Please drive up to the first window."

He greeted her with a smile as he paid her, took his change, then proceeded to the next window.

"Hello, again!" The young girl at the second window greeted him. "Forget to order your wife something?"

"Yes, that's it." He grinned as he grabbed the small bag. Stewart glanced quickly over his right shoulder before guiding the van into the same parking spot. He inhaled the burger smells as he opened the bag. He quickly consumed this second burger with delight, and polished off the remaining fries. Stewart rubbed his belly with satisfaction, but still craved more. Once more, he looped around the parking lot and entered the drive-thru. Waiting only briefly for a car in front of him to finish its business, he was all set when he approached the ordering microphone.

"I'll have the Angus Mushroom and Swiss burger, just the sandwich, no combo, and yes I know it would be cheaper to order the combo than to order separately, but all I want is the sandwich. Thank you."

"That will be $5.95. Please drive up to the first window."

The girl at the first window gave him a snarky smile as he paid. Pulling up to the second window, the girl flashed a wide smile at him.

"Did you forget to get your dog something?"

"Yes, Rover just loves his Angus burgers," he replied. "But don't tell anybody because he's not supposed to eat people food."

She laughed and handed him his order.

Staying to routine, he parked and finished off the third sandwich, although his zeal was somewhat tempered by his fading appetite. Forcing down the final bites, he crumpled up the smaller bags into the first, larger bag, and stepped out of the van to dispose of the waste into a nearby trash receptacle. As he opened the van to get back in, he discovered a new problem. If he was going to conceal the true purpose of his trip – his burger voracity – he'd have to find a way to rid the van of the smell of McDonald's food. He'd forgotten how long it lingered after their earlier stop in London, and now he was quite certain the persistent odour was the reason for his craving.

Driving back to Verna's, he pulled into the same convenience store. He purchased a small bottle of Febreeze spray, which he almost emptied covering every square inch of the interior in hopes of masking the burger chain's odour. The Febreeze smell, though, was so intense, having sprayed so much, he had to wait outside of the vehicle for five minutes for the air to clear enough that he could get behind the wheel.

By the time he pulled in the driveway of the cottage, Stewart was convinced the McDonald's smell ceased to exist. But he had inhaled so much Febreeze by then, that he really couldn't tell. Getting out of the van, he remembered to pluck the cap off his head, but had to go back in to get the pop that he'd bought as a decoy. His mission accomplished, Stewart felt quite pleased with his stealthy nature. Now he just hoped dinner wouldn't be served for a while, as he was anything but hungry. If he told Cathy that he wasn't hungry, she'd know he'd been up to something.

17 BBQ

Jake listened to Katrina's recount of Don's encounter with his neighbour Pierre, someone neither of them had met. He wondered why she continually stumbled upon these situations. She always fell into the middle of something or other. He couldn't see any possible connection between the pressure on Don to sell his winery and Verna's disappearance. Furthermore, his detective senses weren't going off like they usually did. He'd completely discard the notion if not for the trend of Katrina stumbling over clues. Surely Canawine wouldn't kidnap Verna as leverage against Don, although Evan did look guilty about something when Verna's name was dropped. Why not take Faith if that was the play? Don didn't express any fear when Verna's disappearance was mentioned. Certainly Jake would be able to read Don's face if he knew anything. And Jake didn't overhear any specific threat when Don and Evan were talking in Don's office. As the barbecue heated up, Jake unfolded his mind map and flattened the creases. He added a few points on some of the existing lines, and drew some new tangents related to Canawine and the offers to buy the wineries. Still no connection.

Folding the paper back up, he stood and shoved it in the back pocket of his shorts.

He'd left the chicken breasts soaking in his homemade balsamic vinegar and basil marinade, almost since they'd gotten back. Jake preferred a longer marinade, but it was better than just slapping them on the barbecue. Starting to grill the chicken, he realized he hadn't thought of his incident in Toronto since arriving in Leamington. He was enjoying himself. Of course anytime he could grill this much was satisfying to him. Plus he had a case to work on, so Verna's disappearance was stimulating his detective appetite. If only he could keep his gorgeous Katrina out of trouble.

Checking for the correct amount of browning, Jake lifted the cooked chicken to the warming rack as each breast was done to his liking. With all the pieces removed from the cooking surface, he brushed the remnants off the grill, turned up the heat, and closed the lid. He motioned to Katrina, who brought him the steaks from the kitchen counter, where they were marinating at room temperature for the right duration. Trading a kiss for the steaks, he paused from his cooking to watch Katrina stroll back inside. A great view indeed.

The scant few minutes consumed with Katrina's delivery and exit allowed the grill to attain the perfect temperature. While not a firm believer in applying it to steak, Tate's sauce stood at the ready. The early evening sun was still hot on his brow and a few hours from setting at this time of year. He disliked grilling in the dark unless he was camping. In which case he didn't want to see the results of his efforts, often charred in parts due to the uneven temperature of a charcoal heat.

He downed the last few ounces of his bottle of beer, licked the last drops off his lips, and set the bottle on the table behind him.

Placing the steaks on the hot grill, he soaked up the sounds of the meat searing. One of his favourite sounds, he believed. Up there with opening a can of coke or the sounds a woman made if he was doing the right things. But now was not the time to think about that. Jake glanced at the list before him. Two well done, two medium well, one medium rare, and one blue for Stewart. Why bother, he thought. He placed all the steaks over the heat, save one, and resisted the temptation of many other chefs to constantly flip his masterpieces. Looking at his watch, he raised the lid and flipped the steaks before lathering on some of Tate's sauce. He placed Stewart's steak on the grill. He closed the barbecue and hit his stop watch – he preferred to cook by instinct, but he wasn't used to cooking blue. The steaks were thick cut, so he gave it just over a minute and a half. The first side of the blue steak had nicely turned dark brown, so he flipped it and again glanced at his watch. Another minute thirty should do. He lifted Stewart's blue steak, and using tongs, made sure all the outer edges were browned before placing it on the upper rack with the chicken. Some of the other steaks were ready, and within a few minutes the rest were done. Jake transferred the steaks to a large tray Katrina had brought out. He shut off the gas and moved the chicken back down to the grill. He loved the taste of chicken grilled on the juices left behind by steak. As everyone gathered around, remarking how fabulous the food smelled, he offloaded the chicken breasts as well.

Iris brought the last dish out to the gathering at the picnic table.

"What a great Friday night!" Iris proclaimed as they sat down to dinner. "Couldn't get better."

"My aunt could be here," Cathy solemnly added.

"Sorry, of course you're right," Iris apologized.

"No, it's okay. Don't want to be Debbie Downer. Let's enjoy this feast that Jake and Tate have prepared for us," Cathy said.

"Excuse me, but before we dig in, I'd like to say grace," Don stated as hands reached for plates. Everyone stopped. Don proceeded, praying for a safe return of Verna as well as thanks for the bounty before them. 'Amens' circled the table as he concluded.

Jake grabbed the plate of steaks and stood to distribute them. "Well done first," and he placed them on their requesters' plates. "Two medium well ... one medium rare," and he paused at Stewart. "And yours, Stewart. Just took the cow, ripped the horns off, wiped its ass, and threw a match at it. Done just the way you like."

Stewart scowled at Jake, but took the steak.

Katrina looked at Jake. "Gross. Are you trying to ruin my appetite?"

Iris smirked and chuckled under her breath. *What a wuss.*

Faith looked across the lake. "Let's hope you get back that appetite and we get through dinner before the storm rolls in."

"Are we supposed to get bad weather tonight?" Iris asked. She hadn't noticed the few dark grey clouds gathering on the horizon.

"Looks like just a regular thunderstorm. Nothing nasty," Faith replied.

"A regular thunderstorm?" Stewart asked.

"Sure, we get a lot of them down here," said Faith, before proudly adding, "We're the thunderstorm capital of Canada. We get about thirty-three a year on average. That's six more than Toronto."

"And that's a good thing?" Katrina asked.

"Thunderstorms are wickedly awesome!" belted out Iris. "I love the light show and watching the tree branches dance in the wind. Should be cool out here on the water."

Tate gave Iris a look, and she remembered he was like a puppy when it came to thunderstorms. Feeling a strange urge to rub it in, she asked Faith another question. "Why do you get so many?"

Don replied instead, swallowing a taste of chicken breast first. "I've read that this area, meaning the Lake Erie basin, is where most of the hot, humid air concentrates from the Gulf of Mexico."

Stewart moaned, "I'll vouch for the humidity."

Don laughed at the sweating young man. "That air creates the conditions that thunderstorms thrive on."

"Cool," Iris replied.

"I agree, most of the time," Faith nodded. "But not too long ago we had a tornado rip through here. It was terrible. Winds up to 180 kilometres per hour. The devastation..." She shook her head. "It was sad to see trees that stood a hundred feet tall crashed across the roads, into houses, levelling barns."

"Sounds awful," Katrina sighed.

"It was. You guys went to the fair in Seacliff Park the other day, right?" Nods confirmed. "Well, they lost dozens of those amazing trees. Sixty-eight trees in total. Many were two hundred years old. Think of it. They were saplings when the war of 1812 was going on."

Don added, "Four million dollars in damage in the area."

"Well, we'd better finish up," Iris added, looking at the sky. "Looks like it's coming pretty quick."

"We've probably got an hour yet, but the winds will start making a mess of the table pretty soon," Faith cautioned.

Iris stood up, brushing up against Jake as she did. She put a hand gently on his shoulder as she apologized. Stacking a few of the empty platters, she turned to head inside, this time bumping her butt up against Jake. He stood up and grabbed a few things before following her. "Let me get the door for you," Jake volunteered as he caught up with Iris. She flashed a flirty thank you smile at him, knowing she was making inroads. Noticing Jake had put his items on the counter, she asked him to clear a spot for her to place her load. Setting them down, she thanked him, then purposely took a false step. The burly detective, hands now free, caught her before she hit the floor. Pulling her up, she took advantage of the hold to press her firm body against his.

"Oh my god!" she exclaimed. "I could have cracked my head open." She locked her eyes on his before releasing her stare to give him a long, appreciative hug. She held on tight. Jake didn't pull away until Katrina came through the door.

Katrina shot Iris a glare, before turning her eyes on Jake.

"I guess it's a good thing we're getting a storm. I'd hate to waste a beautiful sunset." She strutted away, her elbow glancing off the shorter Iris's shoulder.

18   *Fun and Games*

Everything hauled in from outside, the storm continued to approach. Most of the group poured their selected drinks and gathered in Verna's living room. Katrina and Don had kitchen duty, and Jake offered to help as a way of smoothing things over with his girlfriend. Katrina washed, leaving Don and Jake to dry and put away. No dishwasher in Verna's house – Cathy said her aunt told her that washing dishes relaxed her and allowed her time to savour the recently completed meal. Katrina took the privacy to ask Don about his confrontation at the grocery store.

"So, that Pierre fellow from the store is your neighbour?"

"I was wondering when that was going to come up. Thanks for not mentioning it in front of Faith." Don paused to finish drying a plate and stack it on the table behind them. "There are three of us that Canawine have approached with buy-out offers: Faith and I, Pierre Antonio from Migration Route Winery, and Marco Genoso from Windmill Acres."

Jake smiled. "Pierre wants to sell, and you don't. So you're his problem. I assume Marco wants to sell as well?"

"Marco thinks he can relocate to another farm in the county, so long as it has windmills. I assume to keep the winery name intact."

Katrina stated, "It sounded like Pierre was begging you at first, before he got hostile."

"I wouldn't say hostile. Agitated, maybe. He's having financial problems. Started too big too fast. Won a bit of money in the lottery, quit his science research job, and sank everything he had into Migration Route. He told me when he was starting out that he was going to use his science background to perfect the wine making process. No business sense that I can tell, but knows his wines and the science behind them."

"So he needs another lottery win," Jake replied.

"I'm sure that's what he sees it as. I've suggested to him before getting interns from St. Clair College or the University of Windsor to help him with his books, marketing, etc. The government practically pays their wages for you most of the time, and it would allow him to focus on making his wines. But he'd have none of it. Stubborn pride, I think. Said he doesn't see me getting help, so why should he need it."

"So how do you manage all of that?" Katrina asked.

"Faith does a lot to help. She's unbelievable. Loves it too. And our daughter is in your fair city taking marketing at university. She's given Faith ideas to run with, like the tours, musicians in the afternoons, art and photography shows, sponsoring soccer teams. Giving stuff back to the community to get your name out. I would have never thought of that stuff."

"Sounds like you and Faith are living the dream," Jake laughed.

"Seriously, we are. I think Pierre thought the same thing when he started, but it's turned into a nightmare for him. I'm not going to give up my dream to save his. Especially after I've tried to help him out and he won't listen."

"I apologize for this question," Jake said, holding a dried bowl in his hands, "but the detective in me has to ask. Would it help your business if Pierre went under?"

"No offence taken. I'm not sure it would make a difference. We are successful because of what we do, from the quality of the equipment we use to make our wine, to all the marketing we do. I'd say we'd possibly be worse off if he went under, because someone who knows what he, or she," he paused to look at Katrina, "is doing might buy it up and be stiffer competition."

Katrina had a nagging question she needed to ask. "What did he mean when he said you need to do what's best for the community?"

Don laughed. "Evan at Canawine fed him that line, same as he did me, and likely Marco too. Told him that merging the three wineries into one would bring more jobs to the area, as a bigger operation. I ask you, when did you ever hear of companies merging and more jobs resulting? Never. Usually they trim redundant staff. So instead of three Wine Masters, they'd have one. And knowing Canawine, their Wine Master would be some guy making minimum wage."

Jake nodded. "People believe what they want to believe sometimes."

Don took the last stack of dried plates and put them in the cupboard. "Looks like we're done here. I could use a drink."

Katrina apologized, "We didn't mean to harass you. One last question, promise."

"Shoot."

"Do you think any of this can be related to Verna's disappearance?"

"Not at all. Verna knows about the offer from Canawine, but she hasn't been involved."

Jake watched as Don poured himself a glass of Canadian Club Classic 12 over two ice cubes. Don noticed him smiling.

"Can't drink wine all the time. Besides, I need to support our other local distillers."

Jake grabbed a cold beer, and Katrina a chilled glass of Don's chardonnay.

They entered the living room precisely as the first crack of thunder let loose in the distance.

"Some entrance," Cathy laughed.

As the rain began, Stewart quipped, "I'm glad Verna got that window fixed."

Faith looked surprised. "What happened to it?"

"Someone threw a brick through it," Katrina said. "Likely kids, unless you know someone who has it out for Verna."

Don laughed. "I don't know anybody who has it out for Verna."

Faith sat up. "I bet it was those kids from Tim's a few weeks back. There were four of five of them that Verna kicked out of her store. They were loud and swearing at each other. F-this, F-that, you know, kids acting tough. Anyway, she grabbed one little shit by the collar of his t-shirt and hauled him outside. Can you picture that? Little Verna in her Christmas sweater taking on that punk? Must have embarrassed the hell out of him."

Jake laughed at the mental image. "Get kids in a group like that and they get brave … and stupid. See it all the time in Toronto, but the kids I run into are pretty tough."

Katrina put her head down, thinking of the fifteen-year-old kid Jake beat up that led them to Leamington.

"That does remind me, though," Jake said, looking at his watch. "I'm going to call the locals to see if they have any update on Verna. I'll be back in a few."

Stewart waited for Don to sit down, to talk vintages. He had his favourites, and wanted to find out Don's preferences. "So Don, aside from your own wines, what are a few of your favourites?"

"I like a few French burgundies. Grand Cru wines from the Côte d'Or region. But only the reds. Not fond of the Chardonnays."

Stewart sat back and grinned. "Excellent choice."

Katrina raised her hand again, making Don burst out laughing. "Aren't all burgundies red wines? You know, burgundy is a shade of red."

"That's a good point, and actually where the name of the colour came from. The purplish red colour of the wine inspired the name. Some people simply call the colour 'wine'."

"And what else do you like, Don?" Stewart asked.

"As for whites, there are a few wineries in the Sonoma, California area that are currently tickling my palette. I'll write them down for you. And what is your decadence, Stewart?" He looked at Cathy and added, "Wine wise, I should say."

"My favourite is Chateau Sur La Mer, the 2007. Nice oak flavour, aged to perfection."

"For over a hundred bucks a bottle, the stuff had better make you high and clean your bowels to boot," Cathy added.

"You have such a way with words at times, my dear," Stewart replied.

Don was still chuckling from Cathy's comment. "That was a good year for them, all right. But I find they've really been hit or miss the past few years. If there's one thing I can't stand in a wine, its inconsistency. I mean, how can you put out two bottles of wine that don't taste the same? Especially at a hundred bucks a pop?"

Faith put her hand on Don's knee. "As you can see, Don can get a little passionate about his wines."

Stewart added, "I'll heed your advice on the recent vintages. I'd hate to drop that kind of money for something that isn't exquisite."

Jake re-entered the room and all waited for him to speak.

"No sign of her yet. The Coast Guard came up clean, but had to stop their search due to the storm rolling in. The police have no leads either. No enemies that they can find. Meaning no motive, meaning no suspects. I asked if they were okay with me snooping around tomorrow and they have no problem with it. They just want to know as soon as I find anything that looks, sounds, or smells like a motive or a serious clue."

Jake's last word was immediately followed by a thunderous clap overhead, and a flash of lightning that illuminated the street outside. Katrina noticed Tate cowering with the flash.

So, how about a little poker?" Don asked. "I brought some chips, and the people with the two largest stashes at eleven o'clock will each win a couple of bottles of our wine."

"Deal me in," Jake replied.

"I would also enjoy a game," Stewart added, hoping his run from a trip to the Caribbean would rematerialize.

"Count me in," Cathy added.

"Me too," chimed in Iris.

Katrina looked at Tate, and empathizing with his condition, opted out. "I saw a game of Scrabble in the closet. Thought Tate and I could play in the other room. Away from the windows."

Tate sat up. "Sounds good to me."

"Perfect poker game, six players," Jake stated, not realizing he slighted Katrina as she and Tate left the room.

The poker players also got up, poured fresh drinks, and assembled around the kitchen table.

Stewart shuffled the deck and handed them to Faith on his right for a cut. He smiled at the players in front of him. "Now you're going to see some lightning, as I clean you all out in a flash."

Jake leaned back on his chair. "Just sounds like thunder to me – makes a lot of noise but does no damage."

Not to be left out, Don said, "But I will be the pouring rain, and I'm going to soak all of you for your chips."

Cathy laughed at the remarks before chiming in. "Yeah, you guys are all full of hot air. When your little storms have subsided, one of us girls will be left holding all the chips. Just deal and weep, Stewart old boy!"

19   But

Katrina clutched the Scrabble game and a deck of cards, as Tate switched her drink to rest between his arm and side, freeing his right hand to open the door to the elf room. She thought this room best, as the window faced east, and the storm, as they usually do in this area according to Don, came from the west or southwest. Verna had also installed heavier curtains, smattered with elves of course, in this room to block the early morning sunlight. This made Tate slightly less anxious, not able see the lightning turn normal trees into hideous retching octopi with limbs flailing in the green night sky. Katrina felt more comfortable knowing she wouldn't have to move around someone else's stuff, or see how messy they kept their room. Not that she was a neat freak, just organized, and the thought of having to move Stewart's underwear off a bed to sit down made her squeamish. What a pair she and Tate made, she thought. Not that she thought that.

"So Scrabble or cards?" Katrina cheerfully asked, hoping her enthusiasm would distract Tate from the storm all around them.

"It doesn't matter to me. They said they're playing cards until eleven, so we probably have time for both. Lady's choice."

"Let's start with Crazy Eights," Katrina smiled, putting the Scrabble game on top of a suitcase up against the wall. The bedroom wasn't that big, although for a weekend visit it was plenty. Not much closet space, so she'd never survive if this was her apartment. She'd have to rent a second one the same size just for her things. She sat cross-legged at the foot of the bed, while Tate did the same at the other end. It wasn't the most ladylike pose, she supposed, but it was comfy. She grabbed a pillow to hold on her lap.

"So how long have you and Iris been going steady?" The moment the words came out she realized how grade-school it sounded, but Tate didn't laugh or even smirk.

"Just over a year, last month."

"I don't think I could get through something like that without someone to lean on."

"Yeah, I suppose. She's been supportive."

"Sounds like there's a 'but' in there lurking to get out."

"I suppose so," Tate hesitated, nervously pulling on his white sport socks. Looking up at Katrina, he opened up to her. "I mean, she was fantastic before I got this sickness. We had so much fun, and she was … well we had a lot of fun," he said, blushing as he recalled.

"Do you miss the partying? I guess you don't do any of that now."

"Tonight's the closest I've come to a party since it started, yet here I am hiding in another room."

Katrina frowned at his plight. "I don't care for poker anyway. Too much testosterone for me. Even from the women playing." This got a laugh from the despondent Tate. "So you're doing me a favour by getting me away from it."

Silence joined them in the room for a minute, before Katrina shooed it away.

"You didn't reveal your but to me yet."

Tate smiled again. Katrina heard her statement over again in her head and it was her turn to blush.

"Don't worry, I know what you mean. The but is that I think the only reason Iris has stayed with me is so she wouldn't look cold. Like dumping a paraplegic after the accident."

Katrina reassured him that couldn't be the case, although she wasn't too sure herself. Iris did look to be coming on to Jake this weekend, and not in just a 'trying to make my boyfriend jealous' way. Maybe Iris was more than just flirty.

Apparently, Tate had more to get off his chest, and in a rare sign of emotion, began to turn red as he blurted out his feelings.

"And another thing she does that drives me crazy. She always talks like I'm a big stoner loser. It's not true at all. When we first met, we did a lot of parties and there were guys that I knew with connections. I liked to dabble, but I've never had a problem. She always assumed I was getting zonked. I never wanted to because I didn't want to pass out and miss a night with her."

Katrina held back a tear, believing his intentions were sweet.

"So you don't do drugs at all?"

"I didn't say that," Tate said, holding up his hand. "I'm no boy scout, but I'm not a druggie either. I haven't done anything harder than pot since my fourth date with Iris. I only did on the first four because she wanted to try some new things, and I wanted to impress her. You know, not look like a stick- in-the- mud."

"But you do a lot of pot now? For the anxiety?"

"I don't even light up most days. I'm not sure why she says that stuff."

"Maybe she thinks you're too laid-back not to be smoking up."

Tate laughed.

"But do I look like I've been smoking up?" He looked at Katrina. She looked back, focusing on his droopy, partially bloodshot eyes. Then she looked down.

He took that as a yes. "That's just the anxiety meds. I guess I have to get off them."

Fearing she was pushing him to stop taking his pills, Katrina replied, "I wouldn't stop taking them if the doctor prescribed them."

"Don't worry, Katrina. I just mean I have to work harder to wean myself off them. I just hate dependency on drugs. That's why I never got into the street stuff, at least more than a taste. I've seen some friends get really messed up."

"Maybe you need to change your friends."

"I'm sure you're right on that one. They are a lot of the guys I work with. I'm thinking of quitting and taking up carpentry full-time."

"Sure that's just not an excuse to stay at home?"

"Sounds like it, eh? No, my dad taught me a lot of stuff and I've always puttered around with it. Thought it might be less stressful than what I'm doing now."

"I'm out," Katrina said.

"What?"

"I played my last card, I'm out."

"Oh, lost track. Congratulations. What's next?"

Katrina thought about that loaded question. What was next? What was Iris up to? Katrina wasn't feeling too trusting of Tate's girlfriend. Or perhaps soon-to-be ex-girlfriend. Was Tate telling the truth? She'd heard that guys into drugs lied about it all the time. Like alcoholics or people with gambling problems. What if he was stoned this minute? Could she tell? She leaned forward to get closer to him, thinking she might smell pot on his breath. Must only work with booze. Too much to worry about for now. Shuffling the cards in her hand, she blurted out the first card game that came to mind.

"How about Speed?"

Dale J. Moore

20   *Out on Parole*

Cathy enjoyed watching Stewart play cards much more than playing them herself. He exuded confidence and a sense of control over the table. Even the few times when he lost, he lost modestly, politely, and like he didn't care. When he won, he did so with grace and style. Like Bond, James Bond. An aphrodisiac for her.

Another turn-on for Cathy was having a room at her command. Telling stories, some even tainted with hints of the truth, was her specialty. She missed the Life of the Party days. Men swarming around, regaled by her tales of humourous misfortune. Unfortunately, many of her stories were stained horribly with the truth of her younger days. But if you tell enough stories, everybody assumes they are not about yourself.

The game had progressed quite nicely, from her perspective. Stewart had a sizeable lead in chips, followed by Jake in second, and her close behind in third. At least from eyeballing the stacks on the table. Iris's preoccupation with the storm whipping around diverted her attention from the game and she had almost lost all of her chips. "I'm afraid I'm going to need a loan pretty soon," Iris said, looking at her sad little stack of chips.

"Sorry, toots," Cathy laughed back. "This ain't Monopoly."

Iris leaned up against Jake and looked up at his eyes. "So no 'get out of jail free' card either, I suppose?"

Jake looked down at her and gently nudged her away, saying, "Sorry, no."

Cathy was disappointed in Jake's reaction to this woman. Sure, he did move her away, but it didn't give any signal that he didn't care for the attention.

A good time for a story, she reckoned. The weather had cleared the area, and quiet returned to nature. Birds could once again be heard on the trees above the home. She knew Stewart didn't mind talking during a card game like some people she'd played with before.

"Jail. Now that reminds me of a story."

Jake reached for his newly dealt cards. "Why does that not surprise me? I think I could say almost any word in the English language, and maybe some in French too, and you'd have a story about it."

"I believe you are likely correct there, Jake." While he may have meant it as derogatory, she took it as a compliment and grinned ear to ear. "This one is based on the word jail, although parole is likely more appropriate." She paused to sip her wine. "Before I met my dashing Stewart …"

Don interrupted her. "Aren't stories supposed to start with 'a friend of mine', when they are really about you?"

Cathy laughed. "When I tell this to a group of strangers at a party, definitely! But with friends, I'll fess up and say this is about me, pre-Stewart. I'd been living with my lesbian playwright partner and her friends for a few months. I teetered on the brink of insanity hanging around that gang almost night and day. It wasn't the kind of crowd to attract guys that were interested in women. And if a guy was straight, he was the theatrical type who thought they were god's gift, and a plain Jane type like me was certainly below them."

"Plain Jane, my ass," Stewart objected.

"Thanks, hon." She held Stewart's hand. "Regardless, I needed to have an honest to goodness date with a guy. I decided to get on Facebook and connect with some old friends and see if I made some new ones. At the time it seemed less vulgar than an online dating site." She paused to fold in the current hand. "So wouldn't you know it, I go months without a date and on this one Saturday I get two offers. One from a friend of a friend that I don't know from Adam. Looked kinda cute, but who knows with the pictures posted on these sites."

Iris nodded, "That's for sure!"

"And the second offer came from a guy I'd gone out with a couple of times in high school. Just movie dates. It didn't go anywhere, but he was a nice guy."

"So who'd you pick," Iris asked. "Take a chance or the sure thing?"

"Well, you'd suspect I'd be the type to take a chance and see what happened, and ninety-nine percent of the time I would. But I hadn't had a date in so long, I went against the grain and went with the safe bet – the sure thing as you called it, Iris. Boy was I wrong!"

"I take it the guy had changed since high school," Faith said with a smile.

"Just a wee bit," and Cathy made a pinch sign with her thumb and index finger. "So I decide to meet him at his apartment, after all, I know the guy. His address is a swanky Harbourfront condo. I was feeling pretty good about my decision at that point. Money might not buy you love, but it's a great consolation prize."

"So good to know I've achieved my dream of being a consolation prize," Stewart smiled wryly.

Smiling, Cathy continued. "So I'm worried that I didn't get gussied up enough. I was meeting a high school friend, so I didn't go all out. Undaunted, I pressed the buzzer and waited. Nothing. I press it again, nothing."

"The guy's not home because he's in jail!" Iris exclaimed, like she'd solved a murder mystery.

"Iris, if you knew my stories, nothing is ever that simple."

Stewart let out a deep rumbling laugh. "Nor are her stories ever that short!"

The others laughed, but intently hung on Cathy's next words.

"After the third time, another tenant approaches from outside. I pretend to be fumbling through my purse for my key. Not looking totally out of place, in spite of my casual attire, the man opens the door and holds it for me to enter ahead of him. Of course I checked and the Good Samaritan had a ring. So I go up to the twenty-something floor where my friend lives and ring his doorbell. Still nothing. I ring it again. He opens it partially, chain still on. For the sake of the story, let's call him Dave. He asked me how I got into the building. I told him I assumed his buzzer was broken and explained my little trick. Dave hastily undid the chain, and grabbing my shoulder, quickly yanked me into the apartment. After almost throwing me across the room, which I tell you is no small feat, he turns and carefully closes the door so as not to make a sound. Then, equally carefully, he deadbolts and chains the door."

"He sounds a little creepy," Iris cringed.

"We're just getting started, sugar. He gives me a tour and the place is fabulous. Huge and immaculately decorated. Overlooking the water – what a gorgeous view at night. Breathtaking!" Cathy held her hand to her chest as she closed her eyes in recollection. "I was actually speechless during the tour, the place was that amazing."

Stewart couldn't resist a comment, "That is amazing. I mean that you were speechless! That'd be like me not having a cheeky comment."

"You mean like when that waitress bested you?" Jake laughed.

Cathy continued, "We finish the tour and we land on the couch in his living room. A large screen television with the lake as a background. He's got Hockey Night in Canada on, but the sound is muted. Odd, I thought, as it was muted before I came into the apartment. He excuses himself for forgetting his manners, and in a whispered tone asks me what I'd like to drink. He goes over to the wall and pulls a fully stocked bar out of nowhere. It looked like part of the wall and pulled out when needed. Super cool. As he's pouring drinks, I holler over asking if he's got a lime slice to put on the glass. He just about freaks out! He comes running over, finger up to his lips, saying I've got to be quiet. He gives me some line about his neighbour upstairs, but I'm getting an odd feeling. Like you're telling me you have this million dollar condo and you can hear through the walls?"

"Does sound fishy," Faith said.

"Exactly. Fishy is a good word. When he was whispering I thought maybe he had a sore throat, but then he pulls this neighbour B.S. Anyways, Dave settles down and returns to the couch with drinks. It's a bit awkward at first, having our drinks in silence in front of a muted hockey game. Eventually I get the conversation going; you know – catching up on what life has dealt us since high school. I caught myself in mid- bellow a couple of times and smothered my laughter with my hand. Very unnatural, I must say."

"And this is where he tells you he's been in jail?" Iris impatiently asked.

"Almost there. So we're on our second drink, and I've finally relaxed and begun to forget about the odd nuances of the evening so far. Suddenly, there's a very loud pounding on the door, accompanied by 'Toronto Police – open up'. Dave jumps from his seat, landing on top of me as he covers my aborted scream. He lays on top of me as I hear another round of pounding and identification, 'Toronto Police – Dave Smith, you need to open the door!' That blew away any chance they had the wrong apartment, although by Dave jumping me, I'd suspected they had the right place. Dave gets off me, but signals to keep quiet. I don't know what the hell is going on, or what I should do. If I yell out to the police, and he's not in serious trouble, I've just screwed over a friend. A wealthy friend. But what if he's a violent criminal and if I sit quiet I'll be found floating in the harbour the next day?"

"Only you, Cathy," Jake laughed. "I thought Katrina was a magnet for trouble. Maybe it's you instead."

"Oh, trust me, Jake. Katrina does fine without any help from me!"

"So what did you do?" Iris asked, sitting forward on her chair.

"I sat quietly. I thought I was going to pee myself. After fifteen minutes, the pounding on the door stopped and the police left. Dave grabbed my hand and led me to the windows furthest from the door. I prayed the glass was thick enough that he couldn't push me through it. But he just wanted to get as far from the door as possible before speaking. He said the police might still be lurking, waiting to hear a sound. He tells me his story in whispers. He's out on parole, and part of his agreement is that he's supposed to be at his parents' house every day from 8:00 P.M. to 5:00 A.M. He said he'd never snuck out before, and didn't think they were still keeping tabs on him after four months. Dave told me that he was so looking forward to seeing me that he took the risk. It was sweet, in a way."

"In a girl meets boy, boy is a fugitive kind of way, I suppose," Iris laughed.

"You two could have been the next Bonnie and Clyde," Jake joked.

"Yes, but Cathy and Dave doesn't quite have the same ring, does it?" Stewart added.

"I felt safer," Cathy replied, "after I found out why he was in jail in the first place. White collar crime. Fudging books and bilking investors."

Jake looked at his cards, before discarding two. "They usually are less violent, at least physically. I still find the damage done to victims is horrible. People trust their life's savings with one of these guys and they treat it like play money. Ten or twenty years of scraping loonies together and the victims have nothing left because of some greedy shyster."

"Tell us how you really feel, Jake." Don said.

"So, did you go out with him again?" Iris prodded.

"No, I didn't. He asked a few times before giving up. I don't mind going out with someone who gives the bad boy aura, but I don't actually want to date one."

"Not much future in that," Iris added. Then looking at Jake she smiled and said, "You need someone with stability these days. Too many unemployed Joe's out there with not much of a future. A good job, hard worker, honest, and trustworthy – that's what you need." Turning to look at Cathy, Iris continued, "Like Stewart."

"I'll be the first to tell you I'm not a hard worker, young lady," Stewart replied. "I'm a smart worker, thereby accomplishing much more than a hard worker. But I gratefully accept the rest of your compliments. But I, my dear, am the lucky one for having Cathy." He reached for her hand and held it firmly.

"Why don't you two get a room?" Jake teased them.

"Not so fast, Jake. We have time for a few more hands before the clock strikes eleven and I can rightfully proclaim victory," Stewart responded.

Cathy looked at Jake. "The table's down to four now that Iris and Don are both out. Since we're running out of time, why don't we double the ante and bets?"

"Agreed."

Katrina and Tate entered the kitchen, both looking very tired.

"What have you two been up to in there?" Iris asked. "I didn't hear Tate screaming at all, so I know you weren't having sex."

"I don't scream!" Tate protested, in a very un-Tate like manner.

"It was just a joke," Iris apologized. "Have a toke and relax."

Katrina could see the agitation on Tate's face. She knew Iris was pushing his buttons. He looked at Katrina in a 'see what I mean' way, but bit his tongue.

"We just thought we'd see who is winning and catch the last few hands of the game," Katrina replied to the original question. She came up from behind Jake and put a hand gently on each shoulder, rubbing them tenderly.

Cathy chuckled at the sight. "You look like Rocky's trainer before the big fight. Giving the pugilist's shoulders a rub and telling him to get in there and finish the bum."

Jake smiled. "And that's what I intend to do."

Dale J. Moore

21 *Sleuthing*

Katrina was irked by Iris tagging along on her investigation with Jake, and more upset by Jake's ready acceptance of the third wheel.

"She wants to go to the drugstore and pick up a few things. It's right across from Verna's work, so I figured it wouldn't be a problem," Jake explained.

"You're right, I'm overreacting."

Jake shot her a puzzled look, like he had no clue what she could be overreacting to. She looked back at him. *How can guys be so dumb at times? And was it dumb, naïve, or just didn't care?*

"I'm ready!" An unusually perky Iris entered the kitchen. Her dark gothic look was almost non-existent now, replaced by a wholesome, natural look.

The look sent alarms off in Katrina. "At least I know the reason for the drugstore errand. You must be out of your brooding makeup."

"No, I'm not. It's just the air out here. Makes me want to go more natural. Simplify, if you will."

Jake stepped between the women. "Okay, then. Let's hit the road."

Pulling up to Tim's, Iris announced she was going to go in with them to have a coffee before hitting the drugstore.

Jake introduced himself to the assistant manager, explaining their quest to help solve Verna's disappearance. The assistant manager told them what he knew, which was nothing, and told them he'd send the employees over one at a time to talk to the young detective.

Before the first employee came over, Wally the Wino entered the shop and ordered a small double-double. The local charity case took a seat against the window about ten feet away. Katrina smiled at the man, who raised his coffee in a mock toast to her. Jake just shook his head. Katrina thought Iris looked to be laughing at her, but perhaps it was paranoia.

A high-school-aged young man sat down and answered all of Jake and Katrina's questions. Iris sat silently sipping her coffee and listening.

Wrapping up his questioning, Jake asked, "Where do you think Verna disappears to every year?"

"Aliens," the kid quickly answered. "No doubt about it, aliens. Someone is messing with her mind to make her wear Christmas sweaters all year. I mean, she's nice enough and all, but who does that?"

Jake shook the young man's hand and thanked him for talking to them, even though it revealed no new information.

Subsequent interviews revealed nothing, except the wonderful imagination of Verna's employees when asked about her annual vacations.

"Greenpeace. She seems like the save-the-whales type. You know? I once saw her stop traffic right on the road out here, so she could scoop up a toad and carry it to safety. Do you know how busy this street gets?" replied a young woman.

Another young woman suggested Verna had left to help orphans in Mexico. "It's obvious. She has no kids of her own and so she goes and helps the less fortunate children."

A young man swore up and down that Verna was in the army reserve and that he'd seen her in boot camp with him. He even went so far as to say she was amazing in the obstacle course and that she scaled the wall faster than anyone else there. Jake doubted the entire story based on Verna's slight build, but made a note to check it out - last.

The most plausible explanation came from a middle-aged female employee.

"I think she goes to Frankenmuth, north of Flint, Michigan. It's all Christmas stuff, all year round. You know, I've been in her house. Have you seen the amount of Christmas stuff that she has? It's amazing. A little weird too, mind you, but to each their own I suppose."

The last employee on shift finally sat down. In her late twenties, she explained this was a second job to support her kids. Life as a single mother was tough. She appreciated Verna's flexibility with scheduling her shifts, and even allowing the kids to sit in the corner to do their homework on school nights. Finally getting to the investigation, the woman provided the first, and only, clue of the morning.

"Verna has a lot of people come in to talk to her, but what I remember that day was a guy pulled up to the drive-thru and asked to talk to her. Verna didn't flinch when I told her someone wanted to talk to her at the window, but after the conversation she seemed quiet. Which in itself is odd."

"Kind of like Cathy being quiet," Iris added.

"Not sure what you're talking about," the lady replied.

"Her niece has the same gift of gab," Iris explained.

"Oh, I see."

Katrina asked, "Can you describe the man, or what he was driving?"

"Sure. Black pickup truck. Big one. But there are a lot of them around here. The guy had a green John Deere hat, moustache, and sunglasses. He looked pretty tall. Maybe six two, six three."

"Well, it's something, I suppose," Jake sighed. "Anything else you can remember?"

"It didn't fit," she said.

"You mean his hat didn't fit?" Katrina asked.

"No, I mean it didn't look right. He didn't look like the farmer type. Too clean-cut – soft looking hands. The inside of the cab was too neat. No empty Tim's cups, wrappers, or other stuff you usually see in a truck. Looked brand new, you know what I mean?"

"So he's likely not from around here?" Katrina asked.

"Not likely," the employee responded. "But this time of year we get a lot of visitors. But he looked fake somehow."

"Thanks for your help," Jake said as he stood to thank her.

"So now what, Detective?" Iris asked.

"Don't you have to go to the drugstore?" Katrina snarled back.

"Sorry, I got so caught up watching Jake work."

Katrina was miffed. She'd asked as many questions as Jake did. *Watching Jake work, my ass.*

Jake sensed the tension and politely suggested Iris get her shopping out of the way while he and Katrina talked over the clues. Otherwise they'd have to leave Iris while they continued to investigate, and swing by later to pick her up. Iris took the hint and bolted across the parking lot to the store.

"So what do you suggest, Jake?" Katrina asked.

"Well, the clue isn't much to go on." Jake scribbled the last of his notes on the page. "I'm sure there are lots of black pickups out there."

"What about going to the local hotels and asking around?"

"We could try, but I'm not sure it will lead to anything. The guy could be staying in Windsor, or Kingsville, or even Chatham, for all we know. Or he could be a local wearing a disguise, but that's a little bit less likely."

"Do you have any other ideas?"

"I'll call the OPP station and give them the description. Maybe they've seen someone, or if they do, they can stop him and ask some questions."

Katrina was disappointed. Jake picked up on it and added, "Then I suppose we can look at a couple of the local hotels. It may waste an hour or two, but won't hurt, I suppose."

Iris returned from the store, a small bag of items in her grasp. Informed of the plan, she followed them out to the van. Katrina buckled up as Jake started the vehicle. Iris belted herself into the middle seat in the second row, then opened her bag from the drugstore and proceeded to put her makeup on by stretching up and looking in Jake's rear-view mirror. Not impressed by this ploy, Katrina leaned over to kiss Jake on the cheek as he drove, sending her own signal to Iris, and blocking the mirror.

Driving downtown, Jake burst out laughing.

"Look to the left!"

"Where?" Katrina asked.

"At the fountain!"

Katrina looked beyond Jake in the driver's seat and began to giggle. Iris let out a not so feminine snort. The fountain overflowed with a mass of bubbles that continued to grow. A couple of kids scooped at the puffs of the feather-light balloons, causing some to pop and others to take flight across the sidewalk.

"Makes you want to get out and join them!" Jake exclaimed.

"It does look like fun," Katrina replied. "I'd like to squish them with my toes!"

Iris unclicked her seat belt and bounced across the empty back seat, pulling out her phone to take a few quick shots. "Got it! That is so cool! Thanks for pointing that out, Jake."

At the first hotel, there was no sign of a black pickup truck, and the pleasant lady at the front desk told Jake she hadn't seen any guests driving one all week. The second hotel was much the same, although a small, beat-up black pickup partially filled a parking spot at the far end of the lot.

Finally, at the third hotel they checked – a big black pickup truck! Katrina was excited, and needed calming by Jake. He feared he'd have to keep her from jumping out of the moving van in her haste to run over and check it out. But he didn't need to. As Jake maneuvered in between the yellow parking lines, a short bald man held open the passenger door of the pickup for his wife and child to enter. Even with a hat, fake moustache, and sunglasses, it was obvious this man was not the guy described by Verna's employee. The desk clerk told Jake that was the only big black pickup she'd seen in the past few days.

"Okay," Jake said as he flopped back into the driver's seat. "One more. Then we cut our losses and hope the police come up with something on this guy. Besides, the Coast Guard is resuming their search this morning. Maybe they'll find something."

Katrina pouted, but realized Jake was right. Besides, he likely wouldn't have gone on this wild goose chase at all if not for her. He'd obviously tried to make her feel better, or at least satisfy her snoop sister craving.

Iris and Katrina sat in the van as Jake sought information from the front desk clerk of the fourth, and final, hotel. Katrina looked over at the small outdoor pool, watching a few kids play with their dad. It brought back memories of her dad playing with her and her sisters. In spite of five girls in the family, her dad always found time to play with each of them by themselves. A small tear of days gone by trickled down her cheek, which she quickly caught to avoid Iris noticing.

"Hey!" Iris yelled. A large black pickup truck quickly pulled into the hotel's lot. Fresh mud covered much of the vehicle past the front wheel well. The driver parked it over two spots, something that normally annoyed Katrina greatly. A tall burly man jumped out of the truck and hastened toward the outside stairs leading to the second floor rooms. No John Deere hat, moustache, or sunglasses, but size-wise he fit the bill. And the truck matched. Jake was still inside and Katrina assumed he hadn't seen the man.

"We should tell Jake," Iris excitedly said.

"You go tell him. I'm going to check out the truck," Katrina advised her.

"I don't think that's a good idea," Iris warned her.

"You just go tell Jake," Katrina shot back as she opened the door of the van to investigate. She looked back at Iris. "The guy could leave before we get Jake back here. I'm not taking the chance!"

Iris shook her head, but exited the van from the driver's side sliding door and sought out Jake.

Katrina snuck up behind the pickup, hunching down as she went. Brushing up against the pickup as she went around to the passenger door, she didn't notice the sleeve of her white blouse get smeared in fresh mud, though she briefly wondered why her shoulder felt cold. The man looked in a hurry, so he was likely coming back very soon. She'd just pop open the door and look in the glove box for the copy of his registration. She'd get his name and address and get out. Quick and dirty. She gingerly opened the passenger door and flipped open the glove box. What she saw stopped her in her tracks. A gun!

"What are you doing!" bellowed a loud voice behind her. The man stood there, arms crossed firmly across his chest, anger filling the veins in his neck.

Katrina meekly turned around. The man laughed hysterically as she did. She felt more like peeing her pants than laughing, but was glad her large accuser had changed his tone.

Jake and Iris came running around the front of the truck. They both burst into laughter as well.

Katrina looked down at herself. Aside from her shoulder covered in mud, two wet brown circles adorned her chest, where her breasts had pressed up against the pickup when she first looked inside. She turned red and crossed her arms over her chest. In a purely defensive reflex, she blurted out, "He has a gun in his glove compartment!"

"So what were you doing in my truck, anyway?" the man retorted.

"Excuse me." Jake stepped forward. "I'm a detective from Toronto. The lady asked you why you have a gun."

The man reached for his back pocket and pulled out a badge. London Police. Then he apologized.

"I normally keep the truck locked at all times, but I just ran back in to pick up a fresh shirt," and the man held up the shirt like it was exhibit A.

"Do you know anything about Verna Wilkinson?" Katrina asked.

"Who?"

"She's a local who's gone missing," Jake replied.

"No, sorry. I'm just in town to do some off-roading with a buddy of mine. I left the three-wheeler at his place."

"Where were you two nights ago?" Katrina persisted with her questioning.

He looked at Jake. "I thought you and I were the police here."

Jake smiled, "You don't know Katrina."

The man nodded. "I was on duty in London, Katrina. You can check with my station, if you'd like. Just got into town late yesterday." He smiled at her and couldn't resist a further comment. "Am I free to go?"

Jake laughed and shook his hand. The two men went over to the driver's side of the pickup and continued their conversation. Katrina could overhear Jake give a brief summary of Verna's disappearance as he handed the man a business card. She tried to look at the bright side – there was one more officer on the lookout for Verna.

After the man drove away, Jake returned to Iris and Katrina. His smile vanished as he addressed his girlfriend.

"What were you thinking? You can't go running off breaking into someone's truck to satisfy your need to play private eye! The man had a gun for Christ's sake!"

"I didn't break in. The door was unlocked."

"You still can't go into someone else's vehicle without cause."

"But I'm not a police officer."

"It still isn't right. How would you like to find someone rummaging through our van?"

Katrina bowed her head in shame. "I'm sorry..."

"Sorry? You're sorry? You need to use your head. See what Iris did? She came and told me."

"But I didn't want him to get away. And Iris was going to tell you, we didn't both need to go."

"I don't care. You could have been hurt. Maybe killed. You need to let me handle these things."

"Why, because you're a big strong man and I'm just a girl?"

Jake pulled at his hair. "No, because I'm a trained police officer and you are a salon owner. I'm trained on how to handle these situations. You are not!" Jake let out a large gasp and headed back to the truck.

Iris looked at Katrina and wryly smiled at her before jogging after Jake. Katrina moped, knowing Jake was right about his training in such matters. But what if the man was their guy and he'd left the lot before Jake got back? At least they'd eliminated the driver of one black pickup in town from their suspect list. She held her head high and walked back to the waiting van.

Dale J. Moore

22 *Evan's Folly*

From Stewart's perspective, this mini vacation to Leamington was just what the doctor ordered. He'd started to unwind and enjoy spending time with Cathy. The quality of the local wines was a pleasantly palatable surprise, and the opportunity to discuss vintages with another connoisseur always made for a day to remember. Staring contently at the ceiling as Cathy snuggled up against his bare chest, he thought he could stay in bed all day. He got a kick out of Cathy's occasional talking in her sleep. Mostly it made no sense at all, but still entertained him. This morning's treat was 'This drink needs mango juice,' which he assumed meant Cathy was enjoying some tropical cocktail in her dream. His all-time favourite was 'put the puppies in the living room', for which neither Stewart nor Cathy could ever develop a logical interpretation. Best guess was Cathy had fallen into a slumber re-enactment of 101 Dalmatians. He hoped she was playing the role of Anita, the dog's owner, and not Cruella De Vil.

Cathy mumbled something incoherent in her sleep as she rolled away from Stewart, dragging the blankets with her. Stewart sighed, a beautiful moment ended. Rolling out of bed, he adjusted his boxers as he stood. Gently he tugged at the ball of sheets Cathy had made, first extending them out before neatly tucking them in behind her backside. Kneeling on the bed, he pecked her cheek and jiggled her butt; a daily routine performed by whichever one of them left bed first. Pulling on a collared golf shirt and shorts, he gingerly opened the door and backed into the hallway. After a quick trip to the washroom, Stewart thought of Verna's homemade marmalade jam and set out to make some toast to plaster it with. He made a cup of instant coffee, which he'd finally grown used to. He took a sip. Maybe grown used to wasn't correct – grown used to, not complaining about – that was more like it.

As the marmalade and coffee awoke his remaining senses, he recalled some phone calls he needed to make. It wasn't work. He had a strict policy of no work calls when on vacation. Talking to Don and Jake last night about Canawine's interest in purchasing County Estate Vineyards, Stewart had gone on, likely far too long, about what an abomination that would be to palates near and far. A friend, and Stewart used that term loosely for this person, once re-corked a bottle of his beloved Chateau Sur La Mer after filling it with Canawine box wine. Stewart's nose thought something was afoot, but figured the barbecued garlic shrimp had led it astray. The customary sip and swirl was followed by a dip and hurl, as he disgorged box wine clear across the table.

This morning Stewart would utilize his contacts to create a profile of the interloper known as Evan Batch, as well as his company Canawine. It might take a bit longer on a Saturday morning, but he knew a few early birds that could get on it.

On his second plate of marmalade hiding toast, Cathy emerged, planted a kiss on his cheek, and left for the serenity of the shower. Evan Batch's life was rounding out nicely from the call-backs Stewart had received. The Canawine picture was slower to develop, as most corporate ones are. Sure you can go online and find out what they are telling the press, but finding out what they aren't telling holds the key. One of his first contacts knew Canawine was under investigation, but would need time to find out why.

An hour later, Cathy emerged ready for whatever the day could throw at her. On the other hand, Stewart thought Tate looked like he'd dragged a comb over his head and taken a cologne shower. The crunching of gravel directed Stewart's attention to the driveway and the return of Jake, Katrina, and Iris. Jake carried two bags of subs for lunch. Iris walked by Tate, no sign of affection displayed. Jake and Katrina also looked at odds with each other.

Grabbing drinks, they all headed outside to eat. Stewart swallowed his first bite before informing Jake what he'd found out. The rest of the table listened in.

"As I told you, I'd heard this Evan Batch fellow's name, but the reference escaped my grasp. Fortunately, I'm well connected."

"Yes, we heard about your cucumber the other day," Iris interrupted.

Ignoring the remark, Stewart continued. "This Evan fellow has a fine pedigree, at least when it comes to ruffians."

"Ruffians?" Katrina asked.

"Hooligans, louts," Stewart replied.

"Bad guys," Jake clarified.

"As I was saying," Stewart said, "his great-grandfather was a gangster in Chicago. His grandfather moved to Montreal and was in the mob there. His father changed the family name from Bartolino to Batch, and was the first one to supposedly go legit, although that could be disputed."

"What did his father do?" Tate asked.

"He ran a private security company with his brother. Batch Brothers Security."

"You mean like private eyes?" Iris questioned.

"No, more like bodyguards. They provided protection, if you know what I mean. They were linked by police to many beatings and a couple of deaths, but there was never enough evidence to convict Evan's father of any wrongdoing."

"So they weren't the Mob. They were like the Mob-for-hire," Jake said. "I've heard of them. They folded up shop around 2005 or something. Everyone on the force referred to them as the Bash Brothers."

Stewart ingested another bite of his sub before continuing. "Apparently, Evan's father didn't want him to carry on the business. Evan was the first one in the family to get a university degree."

"I didn't know U of T had a program in how to be a gangster," Katrina added.

"MBA, actually," Stewart stated. "But daddy got him his job at Canawine. And coincidentally, Canawine's under investigation. I'm just waiting to hear the details. I'm guessing extortion and that we'll find out that Evan's dad is involved."

"So anything about Evan resorting to his father's tactics?" Jake asked.

"I'm sure the apple doesn't fall far from the tree," Stewart replied.

"Or the grape far from the vine," Katrina said.

"Something else you might be interested in, Jake. Evan Batch was best man at the wedding of Mr. Nathaniel South, owner of Essex County Cellars, and neighbour to Don and Faith."

Dale J. Moore

23   Back to the Winery

Jake still gave Katrina the cold shoulder, a substantial feat on a sultry day when the heat produced mirage-like vapours from the asphalt roads. Just another summer day in Southwestern Ontario. Stewart's investigative work provided them with a lot of information to digest, and aside from a gut feeling, she had no idea how any of it played into Verna's disappearance. Katrina envied Stewart's ability to dig up information, and so fast! She could spend hours on the internet and not find what she was looking for. Good old-fashioned detective work won out every time. There are no short cuts to solving crimes, she was learning. Although blind luck sometimes helped.

The group set their sights on visiting the festival in the late afternoon to watch the parade and take in some of the local festivities. They had a few hours, so Katrina and Jake planned a trip back to the wineries. Jake wanted to update Don about Evan, and also hoped they'd save another trip by having time to visit Evan's friend Nathaniel South at Essex County Cellars. And if really lucky, they'd swing by Marco Genoso's stake at Windmill Farms.

Cathy and Stewart opted out of the winery do-over, in favour of a stroll down the road toward Point Pelee. Tate felt anxious and thought it best to hang around the house. Iris wanted to trek to the wineries, but feared another stint as the third wheel might alienate Jake.

"Katrina! Jake! I'm surprised to see you two so soon. Thanks for last night, it was a blast." Faith came from behind the tasting counter to greet her new friends. "What brings you back?"

"We want to talk to you guys about Evan from Canawine," Katrina replied.

"Don's going to be down at the barn for a while. Why don't you go out there and tell him? I have to tend the counter anyway. He can fill me in later."

Approaching the barn that housed the fermenting tanks, they could hear Don arguing with Romeo. Katrina found Don to be a very kind man, yet here he was in his second argument in as many days. This time however, Don looked to be leading the verbal assault, not fighting it off. Katrina and Jake entered through the open door, but weren't noticed.

"So if you had nothing to do with it, how do you suppose it happened?" Don spoke loudly, but not out of control.

"I don't know how, Mr. Don. I followed all my steps."

"Are you sure you didn't miss something? Think carefully."

"I'm certain," and Romeo turned to the desk behind him. Behind the desk was a pegboard with five or six clipboards hanging on it. He grabbed one and held it out to Don. "See, I keep a log of each batch. All the details. Step by step by step. I initial and date each step myself. Look, no steps are missing. This is the log I keep on hand in case we get inspected by the VQA or Ministry of Agriculture."

Don scanned the board, a look of relief filling his face as he looked at the details. "So what do you think went wrong?"

"I don't know."

"Let's think of the variables then, if we assume the process is correct, which it appears to be."

"Yes, Mr. Don."

"Let's start with the grapes. We both sampled them and no problems."

"Yes. Second check mark, right after confirming tank cleaned and ready for new batch."

"If it was any of the additives, all the batches would be bad, not just this one, right?"

"Right. They'd all be skunky."

"Yes, like Canawine," Don tried to lighten the moment a bit. "Perhaps the tank is not working correctly. I can have someone check it on Monday." Don glanced at his watch before letting a whispered curse escape. "Do me a favour, Romeo. Run up to the house and help Faith restock the tasting bar. I was supposed to do it ten minutes ago, but I need to stay out here to think things through."

Jake cleared his throat to make their presence known as Romeo secured a hat on his dark curly hair.

"Oh, hi, Jake, Katrina. I didn't see you there. How long have you been standing there?" Don asked.

"Just a few minutes. Long enough to hear you've got some bad wine."

"Yes, unfortunately. A batch of Meritage. We'll have to flush it."

"May I ask a few questions and make a suggestion?" Jake asked.

"Certainly," Don replied, leaning forward.

"First, what's the VQA?"

"Vintners Quality Alliance. They enforce winemaking and labelling standards, and ensure integrity of our products. You know, things like making sure that we use locally grown grapes."

"Interesting. Did you experience any power outage with the storm last night? Could that have caused the sour wine?"

"Good thought, but not a chance. We're used to this weather so we have a few backup generators standing at the ready. Next question?"

"Could someone have gotten in here and spoiled the wine intentionally?"

"I didn't think of that. But the only ones with keys are Romeo, me, and Faith. I locked it yesterday when I left, and unlocked it this morning. Who do you think would want to wreck my wine?"

Katrina piped in, "Well, Pierre for one. Maybe he wants to take you down with him. You know, misery loves company."

Jake nodded. "He certainly has motive. If he can get you to give up and sell, he'll get out of his financial hole."

"Maybe," Don replied, "but I doubt it. He's all words. He's a decent guy, just no business sense."

"And what about Evan?" Katrina asked.

"That may be more his style, but the locks weren't touched. I don't think anyone could have come in here and affected the batch …" Don stopped dead in his verbal tracks. Paleness set over his face, like he'd seen a ghost. Sitting down, he spoke. "I never thought of this before, but it makes sense."

"What makes sense?" Jake asked.

"Do you remember before when we were talking about Romeo, and how I'd given him a second chance? Do you know who fired him?" he asked rhetorically. "Canawine."

Jake looked at Katrina. "Well, that's a development." Turning back to face Don, Jake inquired, "Do you think Evan put Romeo up to spoiling the wine, or perhaps Romeo is still working for Canawine?"

"It's possible, but Romeo seems legitimately upset about the whole thing," Don answered. "I just can't imagine him doing it."

"When did Evan start coming around?" Jake asked.

"June."

"And Romeo started in March? And was recommended by your Wine Master. And do you trust your Wine Master?"

"Yes, completely," Don answered quickly.

"Don't worry, it's likely just a coincidence," Jake added offhandedly, not wanting to worry the winery owner. He noticed Katrina's expression, a reminder of what he'd told her before about detectives not believing in coincidences.

Returning to the previous line of thought, Don asked, "Now, what's your suggestion?"

"Can you put some of that wine in a bottle for me?"

"Trust me. You don't want to drink it!"

"No, I thought maybe we could get a lab to run some tests on it next week."

"I guess it couldn't hurt."

"Thanks. In the meantime, I suggest you check your other batches regularly. And keep your doors locked."

Don ran some of the foul wine into a bottle, slapped a sticker on the front, and scribbled down 'bad Meritage' and the date.

"By the way," Jake asked as Don handed him the skanky brew, "how well do you know Nathaniel South, your neighbour?"

"Fairly well, I suppose. As far as neighbours and competition go."

"And what do you think of him?"

"I like him. He's always been straight up with me. We've partnered on a few events and they've been pleasant experiences. Why do you ask?"

"Did you know that Evan Batch was best man at his wedding?"

Don's expression said it all – he had no idea. He turned away to collect his thoughts.

Jake had expected this reaction, or at least hoped for it. The response vanquished any suspicion of Don's involvement that might have lurked in the dark recesses of Jake's mind.

"You know, Nate and I have never discussed Canawine. It's just never come up. I guess I assumed Evan hadn't approached him. But it makes sense, our properties being adjacent."

"I wouldn't read too much into it," Jake attempted to ease the pressure on Don's distraught mind.

"But I'm sure you are, right, Detective."

Katrina stepped in, quoting a line she remembered Jake telling her. "A detective's job is to uncover the facts, and in the process the truth will be revealed."

Jake smiled. "Just the facts, ma'am."

Dale J. Moore

24   South

The main house of Essex County Cellars sat merely two hundred metres from where Jake and Katrina had conversed with Don. They were tempted to hop the fence and cut through the neighbouring vineyard, but thinking it wasn't the right thing to do, they retreated to the van and made the short trip to meet Nate South.

The tension between Jake and Katrina had subsided, at least temporarily, and he carefully extended his hand for her to hold as they approached the door adorned with the Essex County Cellars' ECC crest. She accepted his hand without hesitation, a relief for him.

This winery resembled Don's in many ways, almost a mirror image in layout. The two barns lay about fifty metres apart, each about 150 metres from the respective houses that held the retail outlet, tasting bar, and offices. Neither winery was large, but both were doing quite nicely on the ledger.

Nate South was much younger than Don, as Jake expected having met Evan Batch. The owner of Essex County Cellars could easily play Santa in a mall, only having to grey his thick brown beard.

Jake thought a growth like that must be awfully uncomfortable in heat and humidity like Southwestern Ontario endured during its long (at least by Canadian standards) summer. His wife Deb was a petite brunette who'd fit twice in her hubby's shadow. Another curiosity for the detective - large men marrying tiny women. Someday he'd have to get the stones to ask one of these couples about the attraction. After a warm greeting by the owner couple, Nate asked if they minded continuing the conversation outside as he had to set up the patio for the day. Jake offered a hand, and the two men carted and placed chairs as they talked. Speaking frankly, Jake explained how he and Katrina knew Don through their friend's Aunt Verna who'd gone missing. Nate replied he'd heard of the disappearance, but he wasn't alarmed based on Verna's history. Although he didn't know the lady that well, rumours still spread quickly even though the town had grown.

"So what does her disappearance have to do with me?" Nate rightfully asked.

"Nothing, most likely. I find myself dragged into this winery buyout, somehow wondering if there is a connection."

"Evan. Get it. I know Evan, and you're wondering what I know about his plans. Not sure either how it fits to a missing woman, but I'll let you figure that out, you're the detective!" Smiling and pulling a cloth to wipe his brow clean of sweat, Nate stopped for a breather.

Jake paused as well, realizing the humidity must be even harder on an overweight guy. "So tell me about Evan. All I know is he was your best man."

"We went to business school together in T.O. Sort of an opposites attract thing, Deb always said. Me jovial, him solemn and serious. He said his dad was very strict, and living at home during university, was still under his thumb. We became good friends, acting as wing men for each other. You know, guy stuff. Both of us are big Leaf fans."

"Misery loves company," Jake replied.

Nate let out a grand belly laugh. Obviously he was a guy that could receive a good joke as well as he could dish one out. Resuming the task at hand, he scooped up four chairs and lugged them to start a new row. "Anyway, we'd kept in touch over the past ten years and found it neat that we both ended up in the wine business. Deb and I started this place right after we got married. Her old man gave us the seed money and still owns forty-two percent of the place. Started out at forty-nine, but we buy out a percent a year as part of the deal we made. Provided we make a profit that year. So far we have every year except the first few."

"So you married up," Jake added. He knew Katrina didn't like that expression, but if the shoe fits, as his grandma used to say.

"In more ways than one, that's for sure. Some guys say they'd never work with their spouse because of the strain it would put on their relationship, but it's been great," Nate replied.

Jake and Katrina exchanged an awkward glance before he replied, "Well I suppose making money every year makes it easier." Not pulling any punches, Jake threw out the imminent question. "So are you selling to Evan?"

Nate's expression didn't change as he immediately answered, "We've tentatively accepted his offer. He has big plans and we've taken advantage of his thirst for this deal."

"Taking advantage? Is that what you do to friends?" Katrina asked.

"It's all business, and he knows that. He thinks he's getting a good deal too, so that's all that matters."

"So, what did you get him to throw in?" Jake wondered.

"For starters, we get a lot of money. Deb and I already have a couple of other spots picked out if this goes through. Similar soil and size. We also get to keep harvesting grapes in the northern quadrant of this vineyard for two years to keep our brands active while we move."

"Smart," Jake added. "Sounds like you and Deb have thought this through."

"And," Nate said, "we get to take up to twenty-five percent of the vines from the northern quadrant with us to help establish the new vineyard."

"So why haven't you told your neighbours?" Jake said confrontationally.

Nate looked at him, surprised by the tone. "Pierre knows, and is very happy about it. But I only told him because he came over asking me about it. Thought he was going to hug me, he seemed so happy."

"No doubt," said Jake. "We hear he needs to sell to save from losing his vineyard."

"Heard he was in trouble, but didn't know how badly. As far as Don and Marco, we just haven't talked about it. I'm sure they both have offers too. My guess is Don is holding out."

"Good guess. It's got Pierre plenty pissed too," Jake confirmed.

"I'm surprised Evan's not keeping you up-to-date," Katrina said.

"We're buddies, but this is business. He has my signed offer, so I'm no longer his concern. As for Marco, I couldn't guess if he cares one way or the other. He's a tough one to read at times. Seems mostly sincere, but sometimes I just don't know. Maybe I'm just waxing on Deb's gut feeling. She doesn't trust him."

"Well, he's our next stop, so I guess I'll get to take my own read. Thanks for your help."

"No – thank you. You saved me about twenty minutes of labour in this sticky heat. Of course I could use to sweat off a few pounds!" and Nate laughed at his own appearance, shaking his belly like a bowl full of jelly.

Dale J. Moore

25   Marco

Katrina looked at her watch as they belted up in the van. She suggested they call Cathy and tell her they'd be a half hour late. It would save them a bunch of time later if they could talk to Marco now while they were out this way. Jake agreed and she made the call as he drove the short distance over to Windmill Farms.

Stepping out of the van, Katrina was taken aback by the size of the wind turbines looming on the immediate horizon. They stood like giant metallic aliens from a science fiction novel, standing in line in defence of their newly conquered civilization. A chill ran down her spine, right where the humidity had caused her thin cotton top to cling to her body.

"Are you coming?" Jake asked her, hand outstretched as she came back to reality from her War of the Worlds imagery. Perhaps she was getting carried away.

"Yes, sorry. This winery is so different from Don's or Nate's, isn't it?" she stated more than asked. While the first two wineries had taken over farmhouses and renovated them to suit their needs, the building for Windmill Farms looked more like an office building than a home. About a hundred metres further away from the road stood a large modern home, close to four thousand square feet at Katrina's best guess. A grand two- storey all-brick with French corners and steep dormers, it looked out of place where it stood, although it would have fit nicely into a couple of the waterfront communities they'd passed on their way out of town.

Entering the winery, the stark contrasts to the others continued. Young girls in a standard uniform dress code swarmed the place. Each wore a nylon burgundy sport shirt with the Windmill Farms logo as a pocket crest on the shape-hugging top. Skintight, petite black shorts completed the outfit. It looked more like a bar than a winery.

Jake politely asked one of the girls if Marco was available. She picked up a two-way radio and inquired on his whereabouts. He said for them to meet him in the outshed, which Jake assumed meant barn. The young lady put down the radio and summoned another one of her clones to escort Katrina and Jake to see the owner.

"First time visiting us?" the perky university aged girl asked.

"Yes, it is," Katrina replied.

"Well, you just have to taste our Riesling! Best in the county, if not the province. Perhaps the country!"

Katrina sized up the girl, wondering if she was indeed nineteen and old enough to enjoy this wine she hyped. Politely Katrina replied, "I'm sure we'll have time for a glass before we leave."

Entering the barn, Marco sat on a stool, tasting grapes from a nearby bin. He wore jeans and a black t-shirt. He remained seated as they exchanged greetings and handshakes – it seemed odd to Katrina, but maybe she was spoiled by Jake's gentlemanly ways.

"Aren't you hot in those jeans?" she asked.

"No, I'm used to it. Besides, there's this." Marco rolled up his pant leg to expose an artificial leg.

"I'm so sorry, I didn't know," Katrina blubbered in embarrassment.

"I don't believe it was your fault," Marco responded. "Besides, I wouldn't have this place without it." He tested another grape. "Do you want to taste one?"

Katrina grabbed one, hoping the grape might prevent her from putting her foot in her mouth again. Now too shy to speak, she was relieved when Jake asked the obvious follow-up question.

"Workplace accident and lawsuit?"

"Yep. Although I have to admit it took me a while to see the silver lining. Or the money for that matter. I became a miserable drunk after the accident. I didn't know how to cope. I used to play junior hockey and was getting better every year. I even heard talk of getting drafted – NHL, not army, in case you're wondering, doll," and he chuckled at his joke. Judging by the way he ordered his staff to dress, he likely didn't have a lot of respect for women and probably thought them all dumb. "Anyway, I was working a summer job that I'd taken because it had a lot of lifting. Figured it was as good as working out, but I was getting paid for it. One day, me and another guy are escorting a forklift with loaded drums when one comes free and crushes my leg. The company argued that I was responsible because we didn't guide the drum onto the forklift correctly and make sure it was stable before moving it. Fortunately the forklift driver testified the lifting chain snapped, resulting in the load to fall. At the time it was the worst day of my life."

"So you're an alcoholic running a winery?" Katrina asked, puzzled.

"I'm no alkie. I was a drunk. I was drinking out of self-pity, not compulsion. There's a big difference. Once the lawsuit settled, I made the choice to rejoice, as I like to call it, at what the Lord had given me."

"So you found God too while drinking?" Katrina doubted his sincerity, something Nate's wife Deb had expressed concern about.

"Actually, he found me and told me to quit drinking and make something of the life he gave me. That's when I started this winery."

"Seems odd to start a winery after having been a drunk."

"I'm not much of a wine drinker, so I felt safe. Besides, you ever hear of the expression, keep your friends close and your enemies closer?"

Katrina politely nodded as she tried to think of the phrase's relevance.

"I looked for different things I could do with the money and this was the winner."

"Better than blowing it on booze," Jake added.

"Precisely. Haven't seen many one-legged guys make the NHL. Better chance if I was Jamaican."

Jake laughed and replied, "Well, they did have a mighty good bobsled team."

"The lawsuit was like winning the lottery, and I'd heard too many stories of people that'd won the lottery and were bust within five years. I was determined it wasn't going to happen to me. The winery is perfect. It's not tough physically for me and it makes me look important. Plus, did you see all the hot girls I get to hire?" Then leaning over to Jake in a pretence of confidentiality, he spoke loud enough for Katrina to hear. "You know I've nailed over half of them already. Hoping to have the rest by the end of the season. And every year I get to hire a new batch."

Katrina pretended not to hear, but wanted to kick him in his good leg. Or perhaps between the legs. As they continued to talk, they found out Marco relied on his NHL dream when he was young, forgoing scholastic concerns while he played junior hockey. Indeed, he'd never finished high school after his accident. But it was difficult to blame the guy, she supposed. Trying not to feel sorry for the man due to his life-altering accident, and reminding herself that he was a creep, she cut straight to the chase (although she'd never understood that expression).

"So is Canawine offering you another chance to win the lottery?"

"I suppose you could look at it that way." Marco smiled, not at all the reaction Katrina hoped for. "Their offer is quite lucrative. God is smiling on me, that's for sure."

Jake had wandered a few metres away, glancing at some boxes along the side wall. "Why do you suppose Canawine wants these wineries so bad? I mean, aren't there other wineries around they could go after, or simply buy a large tract of farmland and start a new mega winery?"

"Good questions. First, the second answer. It takes a few years to start a winery and can take more to find out what grapes work best in the soil and moisture you've got to work with. So I think they want our wineries because we're all clustered together and all established. I think he's going to build some type of resort, myself. I mean, there's nothing around here. Nobody in Windsor thinks big like guys from Toronto. I don't know if they're all chicken shit, have no imagination, or are just plain stupid."

Katrina did not like this guy. Too rough around the edges for her. "So have you accepted Evan's offer?"

"You bet your bony little arms I did! Too good to pass up. Besides, the secret to the unique taste of my wines is the windmills."

Katrina wondered if this guy was for real. *He must be hanging around Don Quixote, or something.* "Windmills?" she asked.

"Yes, the vibrations of the windmills enhance the grapes as they are growing. Add vitality and other life forces that are otherwise trapped in stationary soil. I feel the same surging through my body every day."

Katrina looked at Jake who smirked back, trying to keep himself from laughing.

"So will you just relocate, or is there some other destiny awaiting you?"

"I'll probably just pack up and find another place with the same aura. We'll see what the Lord tells me when the time comes."

Jake shook Marco's hand, and this time the winery owner stood as he did so. Marco nodded goodbye to Katrina, who was relieved he didn't try to hug her.

Walking back to the shop in the front building, Katrina insisted they buy a bottle of the previously hyped Riesling. She felt compelled to do so, as they had no time to enjoy a glass as she'd told the girl they would. Tucking the bottle in between some things in the back of the van, Jake closed the door.

"Did you notice …" He stopped speaking as he looked around. "I'll tell you on the road."

Katrina couldn't wait to let loose. "That guy's an ass! He thinks he's God's gift or something."

"Interesting you mention God. Notice how in one sentence he's praising God for the wonderful things he's received, and in the next he's talking about having sex with all his staff? Nate said the guy was hard to read and didn't seem sincere. Looks like he called that one right."

Jake circled the van around the lot and stopped at the entrance to the road. Completing his turn, he restarted his thought from before Katrina's outburst.

"Did you notice what was in those boxes along the wall?"

"I'm assuming wine?" Katrina replied with uncertainty.

"Yes, wine. But do you know what type of wine?"

"Their world famous Riesling?" Katrina replied, mocking the enthusiasm of the girl at the winery.

"No, but you'd think so. It was Chateaux Sur La Mer. At least ten cases of it."

"That's odd."

"Especially when Marco says he's not much of a wine drinker. Why would he have that many cases of expensive wine, if he doesn't drink the stuff?"

26   *Festival*

Pulling onto the highway, to head back to their home for the weekend, Jake noticed something out of place. A shopping cart teetered on the gravel shoulder slanting toward the deep ditches that accompanied all the roads in this part of the province. Still moving slowly, he could see an odd assortment of bottles and cans halfway up the wire walls of the cart. Katrina had also spotted the buggy.

"Look, it's Wally the Wino! I mean its Wally," Katrina told Jake, who didn't have as clear a view from the driver's side.

"Collecting bottles for their deposit, I suppose. At least he's out working, so to speak." Jake had slowed to a crawl, having checked his rear view and detecting no traffic.

Katrina watched her new acquaintance go about his business.

"That's odd ... he just filled a beer bottle with water, dumped it, and is filling it again."

"Maybe he wants a drink of water and is cleaning the bottle first."

"That's just gross!"

"I'm assuming the guy can't afford Perrier."

"It's still gross." With excitement in her voice, she added, "Let's go, he's coming up to his cart!"

"What, do you think he's going to accuse us of spying on his bottle collecting? Is he going to attack us thinking we're stealing his empties?"

"I just don't want him to think we're spying on him, that's all."

Jake sped up and left Wally in the rear view, clambering up to his day's catch. Taking his eyes briefly off the road in front of him, Jake looked at Katrina. "You certainly have a big heart, Katrina. I wish I could see the good in people the way you do."

She smiled without replying. That was the nicest thing he'd said to her the whole trip. Hopefully a sign of better things to come.

Nearing town, Jake had to detour from their normal route as parade preparations were well underway.

"I've got to pull into Zellers for a few minutes. The police officer I met with the other day suggested white t-shirts for this afternoon's events at the festival."

"Why?"

"So we don't wreck our good clothes in case of tomato splatter. And he says the tomatoes show up best on white."

Katrina wasn't sure what that meant, but nodded okay. "I'll just stay in the car and listen to the radio, if that's okay."

"Sure, but give me sizes for you, Iris, and Cathy. I can guess at the guys."

Obliging his request, she watched him jog across the parking lot into the store. A few songs later he emerged, bag in hand, chewing on a pepperoni stick. Opening the door, he tucked the bag between the seats. Katrina looked at him chewing on his treat, a slight pout forming on her lips.

"Relax. I wouldn't forget you," and Jake tossed her a Kit Kat single.

"Are you calling me fat?"

"What?"

"You got me the Weight Watcher's version of a chocolate bar."

"You usually only eat one stick at a time anyway."

"But I eat the other pieces later."

"They'd melt in this heat before we got back to Verna's."

"That's not the point," she protested.

"It's exactly the point. I don't want to find a gooey mess stuck to the carpet of the van. It is a rental after all, and I don't think Stewart would be pleased."

Katrina ate her little chocolate bar, but it didn't taste the same accompanied by a fresh pout.

Back at Verna's they received the recap of everyone else's early afternoon. Iris and Tate had whipped up a batch of spaghetti for a very early dinner, thinking it would be good to get some substance before heading out. Besides, they were likely only going to see fair food, in more ways than one, at the festival. Katrina lost control of a forkful of noodles and they catapulted themselves onto her little cotton top.

Jake glanced at the mess on her chest. "I should have given the t-shirts out before dinner, seeing how they'll likely end up with tomato on them later."

Dishes scraped, rinsed, and stacked in the sink, the lineup for the bathroom formed. Jake distributed the white t-shirts. The girls went to their rooms and slipped them on over bathing suits. The guys just tossed their current shirts on chairs and pulled on their new white attire.

Jake and Stewart remained alone in the living room. Stewart held up a pamphlet.

"I was looking at the schedule of events that Katrina picked up. We missed the parade – it was this morning at ten A.M., not four P.M."

"Where'd we get four from?" Jake asked.

"I suppose I mixed up the time with the Tomato Stomp. It has a little red star beside it saying 'new time this year'. Sorry about that."

"Can't say I'm disappointed, but Katrina likely will be."

"Yes, but at least I don't have to worry about an arrest for knocking kids over trying to get to the tossed candy first."

"Too bad, that would have been a sight to see!"

"What would have been a sight to see?" Katrina asked, entering the room wearing her fresh white t-shirt, packaging creases still intact.

"Nothing," Jake replied. "Bad news, though. We missed the parade."

Katrina's smile drooped. "But we detoured around them setting up."

"Must have still been closed, or closed for this afternoon's activities."

The others gathered one by one in the front room as they finished prepping.

"All right. Are we ready? Did everyone use the potty?" Jake said, like a kindergarten teacher before going outside for recess.

They looked like a Hanes commercial waiting to happen, all decked out in their bright whites.

"All set," Iris responded, doing a little pirouette in her new outfit. Katrina had told Jake a larger size for Iris, hoping to make her look frumpy. Instead, Iris had taken the shirt and knotted it at each side, pulling it tight to her chest. The larger shirt was longer too, making it look like a very short skirt. She'd abandoned her jean shorts for just a bikini bottom, giving the appearance of wearing nothing under the white cover-up. Looking at the guys' faces, Katrina could tell she'd produced the opposite of the intended effect.

Having parked a few blocks from the festival, they had only a short walk to the park. A few wisps of clouds inhabited the brilliant blue sky. A light breeze trickled off the lake, giving occasional relief to the heat and humidity. Katrina sipped from a bottle of water as she walked. She glanced at Stewart and Cathy, who looked the part of a couple in love. A DSLR camera hung around Stewart's neck as he walked hand in hand with Cathy.

"Aunt Verna registered us for the Tomato Stomp. Our team name is T.O. Stomp," Cathy informed the group. "It's teams of five," she said, walking backwards to face the trailing Iris and Tate, "but Stewart's volunteered to sit it out."

"Mighty big of you, sport," Jake mocked him in an awful British accent.

Cathy added, "Stewart's going to film us. Aunt Verna was going to …" and her voice tailed off.

"Should be a hoot to watch later," Katrina said cheerfully.

Entering the park, they took the shortest path on the winding walkways toward the Tomato Stomp area back near the parking lot holding the soundstage. A massive tarp lay stretched out across the nearby grassy area. A straight line had been formed with the colourful plastic kiddie pools used for the Stomp. Each pool contained a different design and would soon be filled with two bushels of exceedingly ripe tomatoes. The object was to squish as thoroughly as possible every tomato in your pool. A dump truck full of tomatoes stood nearby, as did the twenty bushels for the pools.

A man approached the area, raising a megaphone to his mouth. Only those really close to him could hear him utter, "Can I have..." He fiddled with the voice-projecting device for a few seconds before another futile attempt to be heard. He put down the megaphone and turned to a woman a few metres away.

"Sheila. Do you know how to work this cursed thing?"

The summoned lady walked over, shaking her head. She flicked a switch on the side.

"TEST, TEST," she boomed out of the device.

"Thanks, Sheila. Can I have all the team captains, please?" The older man in an official TomatoFest golf shirt was finally heard above the chuckling crowd.

"Go ahead, Jake," Katrina encouraged her boyfriend. The others agreed. While the captains gathered for their instructions, a volunteer lifted the first bushel of tomatoes and dumped it over Dora the Explorer and her friends in a nearby pool. Other volunteers followed suit, covering the cute pictures of the Sesame Street gang and Disney movies, such as Cars, The Little Mermaid, and Wall-E. All pools oozed with the red fruit by the time Jake returned and gathered his team and their photographer.

"So the rules are pretty simple. You have to stomp the tomatoes more than the other teams to win. You can't intentionally fall and roll around on the tomatoes, but falling doesn't disqualify the team. Falling out of the pool is okay, but you can't step out to make more room for other team members or the team is eliminated. I think that's it." Jake paused, running it through his head. "Oh, one more thing. No using hands to squeeze tomatoes, unless you are bracing yourself when falling."

"Sounds like a lot of falling," Katrina said.

"Well, one good thing," Jake added, "there are two flights."

This meant nothing to Katrina, and her eyes let Jake know.

"There are five pools and ten teams. Five teams go first, then the pools are emptied and refilled, then the last five teams go. We're in the second group, so we can pick up some pointers by watching the other teams."

Katrina wasn't overly competitive in these situations. Iris made it clear she didn't like losing with the words that followed.

"Great!" Iris exclaimed. "So there are five of us and five pools. We can each watch a pool to get tips. Watch for what they do that works, and what they do that causes the team problems. We should have a few minutes to compare notes while they empty and refill the pools."

"I like the way you think," Jake replied.

"And what am I, chopped liver?" Stewart replied.

"I just thought you'd be filming the other teams, that's all," Iris said. "Sorry, didn't mean to exclude you. If you see something while filming, you can tell us too."

They spread around the area, each positioned to watch a team down the line. The first group of teams assembled by their pools. Some teams just stood in their pool waiting for the 'Go' command, but Katrina noticed the team in front of her formed a tight circle in the pool.

"Everyone get in your pool," the starter announced. "So there are three of us acting as judges today." The man pointed at the lady who had fixed his megaphone, and a young portly man with wild curly hair and a beaming, welcoming smile. "We're going to score each team, based on a system that's a secret, mostly because we're going to make it up as we go." He paused to a smattering of laughter. "Is everybody ready to go?"

A few scattered yeses came from the contestants.

"You don't sound very enthusiastic, people!" He raised his voice as he solicited a more vocal response. "I SAID, IS EVERYBODY READY?"

A roar of "YES!" came from the pool people.

"That's better! Okay, Sheila and Tom, spread out a bit and let's get this show on the road." He waited a few seconds as his fellow judges moved down the line of pools. "Okay. Ready. On you marks … GO!"

Pandemonium followed. The team Katrina watched had a reluctant young lady who appeared too shy to hurt a tomato. Katrina knew the feeling. They jumped around chaotically, bumping into each other frequently. The shy young lady had her feet cut from under her and she fell backwards hard onto the awaiting red mush. Katrina saw her future. Looking at the pool beside her, she felt more encouraged. This team had formed a neat circle inside the pool, locking arms around each other's shoulders as they feverously pounded the tomatoes below them into oblivion. The judges strolled up and down the line of pools, joking with the contestants while encouraging them. A contestant in the pool near Jake went ass-over-tea-kettle and made a red splash, much to the delight of onlookers.

"STOP!" The emcee's amplified voice carried across the Tomato Stomp area, emitting right behind Katrina and causing her to jump in the air and break out in goose bumps.

The organizer spoke again.

"Tom, are you going to measure each pool?"

The young man pulled a tape measure out of his substantial cargo pants, then proceeded to the first pool to measure the depth of the goo produced. The teams stood barefoot in the slop while the measurements occurred. He wrote a number down for each team and convened with the other two judges. The emcee wrote more numbers on his small notepad, flipped over the cover, and stuffed it into his back pocket.

"Alright. Great job, everyone! We have a winner of the first flight, ladies and gentleman! Is that you, Ronnie? Good job to you and your team! Okay, all of the teams out of the pool while they dump and refill them. You might want to step a ways back, as they are just dumping them on the tarp – remember, the tomato fight is next. Be sure to stick around for that. And even if you don't win your flight, stick around as we have a couple of door prizes donated by local businesses."

Jake gathered his team. "So what did we learn?"

Katrina tried to speak, but Iris cut her off.

"I had the winning team in front of me. They formed a circle inside the pool before the start and got comfortable about standing in it. Teams that stepped in just before the start still seemed tentative about standing in it when he said go."

"Agreed. Acclimate to the gunk," said Jake. Katrina nodded as well.

"And wrap arms around each other's shoulders. I saw one team try around the waist and it threw off their balance."

"Sounds like a plan," Jake replied. "I saw a lot of teams do what you said, and they all fared better than the others that worked as individuals. Maybe it was a rule last year, or something."

"Can I make a suggestion?" Katrina asked.

"Sure," smiled Jake.

"Well, this may be dumb," she shyly added.

"C'mon, spit it out, Katrina. We don't have much time." Iris made a rolling motion with her hand for Katrina to get on with it.

"Jake, what if only four of us made a circle and you got in the middle? Five is crowded around the outside, and there's a lot of bumping and stepping on each other. That's what causes most of the people to fall. You're the most athletic of all of us, so it makes sense that you go in the centre."

"I like it!" Jake exclaimed. "I stand in the middle and get all the tomatoes in the centre and those that squirt away from you guys on the outside. I can balance myself on two of you on the outside, so I don't become a casualty. Anybody disagree?"

Katrina beamed over Jake's approval of her idea, and the satisfaction of seeing Iris's scowl.

"Okay, flight two, take your places!"

Jake led their team to the Sesame Street pool assigned to them, and they formed their circle. "So, I go in first and you guys quickly form a circle around me. Cathy and Iris face each other and I'll balance myself on you two, as you're about the same height."

Katrina closed her eyes and gingerly dipped her bare toe into the pool, turning her head and wincing as she did, like she'd stepped into a pool of cacti. Jake grabbed her hand and helped her step the rest of the way in.

"On your marks…GO!"

They quickly got into formation and began stomping for all they had. Katrina had lost her shyness about stepping on tomatoes, imagining Iris's scowl on each one she flattened it. Katrina thought they were doing awesome, as the availability of tomatoes underfoot became harder to spot. They were down to their last few tomatoes and began excitedly pointing out wayward tomatoes to each other.

"STOP!" hollered the voice over the megaphone.

"Woo hoo!" hollered Cathy, pumping her fists in the air.

Katrina reached for Jake to hug him, but suddenly her feet went from under her and she landed butt-first into the stew-like mess. She looked up to see Iris giving Jake a hug – not Tate, who reached down to pull up Katrina.

The organizer spotted the fall and bellowed out a laugh. "No sitting in the pool while Tom takes his measurements! We'd hate to have to deduct points for squatting."

Katrina was self-conscious of the large wet spot on her butt as Tate lifted her up. Tom grinned at Katrina as he knelt next to her to measure their production of stewed tomatoes. As he got up, the heavyset man leaned toward her and whispered, "It's not that noticeable," and nodded his head.

As Tom left, Jake nudged Tate aside and pulled Katrina towards him.

"Great plan, Katrina! You were awesome!" Changing tone, he asked, "Are you okay? You took a pretty hard fall."

Hard fall, my ass, Katrina thought, rubbing her tush. She knew Iris had slew-footed her – at least that's what she remembered Jake calling it in hockey when one player takes the feet out from under another one. "Yeah, I'm fine."

After Tom had measured the final pool, he returned to consult with the other judges. The results of the second heat came shortly after. "First, we'll announce the winners of the second group, and then we'll announce the overall winner. Second group winners, with an acrobatic landing at the end, T.O. Stomp! Let's hear it for our second group winners!"

Excited, Katrina leapt into the air, but unfortunately for her, didn't nail the landing. Splat! On her butt again. The crowd erupted in laughter.

"You already won, young lady. No need for more gymnastics!"

Katrina sheepishly stood up, helped by Jake.

"If the winners of each group could come up, we'll announce the overall winner."

The two teams collected in front of the man with the microphone.

"First place, by only two points, goes to Ronnie! Congratulations and step up here and get your trophies!"

Katrina was bummed as the winners got their miniature spoils. She knew it was hokey, but she liked trophies. Not that she had many.

"And to our runners-up! Verna Wilkinson's group. Come up and get your medals!"

Katrina smiled again. Medals were good too. She liked hanging them up as reminders. The team drifted back into the pack as the other teams moved in closer.

"And as I mentioned we have a couple of door prizes!" Each contestant had filled out a card before the event and the man proceeded to pull two names out of a drum. "Okay, first name is Katrina … I'm sorry I can't read the last name." He handed the card to a volunteer beside him, who shook her head. "Well, it's Katrina and the address is in Toronto. Is that you, young lady?"

Katrina blushed. *Was she more embarrassed at winning or because he couldn't read her name?* Either way, she ran up to the front where two items lay in front of her. One choice was two bottles of wine from Windmill Estates: a Merlot and the previously hyped Riesling. The second choice was a table lamp with a tomato for a lamp shade. Katrina didn't hesitate and plucked the lamp from its spot, hoisting it high in the air like a trophy. Her group all cheered wildly at her prize.

"Wait a minute, Katrina," and the man called her back.

Thinking she'd done something wrong, Katrina automatically gushed out a 'sorry.'

"You didn't do anything wrong. It's a set of two lamps. We just didn't have room on the table when we started." One of the volunteers handed her two boxes, one empty, the other holding the second lamp.

"Thank you," Katrina said, awkwardly trying to carry the set back and dropping the empty box twice before Jake finally got a clue and came up to help her.

The man called the second name, and the door prize winner thanked Katrina on the way by, not as enamoured by the lamps as her, and grateful for the wine prize.

"Thanks to everyone for our best turnout ever. A lot of laughs, that's for sure! And don't forget, the event many of you've anticipated will be starting in about an hour – the first Tomato Fight! If you didn't purchase a ticket in advance, be sure to get one now before they are all gone. Remember, all proceeds from the Tomato Fight go to a great cause, the Canadian Cancer Society. Instead of wearing pink today, I want to see everyone covered in red!"

"Well, that worked up a thirst!" exclaimed Stewart.

"All you did was film us!" replied Iris.

"It's still hot out here, even just filming, as you say," he replied. "Besides, if we grab a beer and a seat, you can gather round and watch your victory."

"Second place," Tate reminded him.

"But you got medals, and Katrina got those wonderfully atrocious lamps. I call that a victory," Stewart said.

"Right you are, old chap," Jake responded, putting an arm around Stewart. "I think a victory drink is in order. But I seriously doubt they'll have stout on tap, old man."

"I shall be glad to drink whatever they have on tap to quench this vile thirst. If I were less a gentleman, I would show you how dry my poor tongue has become."

"Dry as it is, it hasn't slowed down any," Cathy teased him.

Katrina and Cathy planted themselves at the first open picnic table they came across, and the guys went up to get drinks. Iris trotted off to the restroom. The guys had beaten the rush to the bar and, each carrying two drinks, returned in a few minutes. Iris had already returned. Stewart had drunk half of his beer before reaching the table. The girls were laughing loudly as they huddled together, watching the images on Stewart's camera.

"This is hilarious, Stewart," Katrina told him with an awkward snort at the end.

"I thought we were going to watch it together," Tate said.

"We haven't gotten to you guys yet," Cathy placated him. "We're just watching the first flight. There's a bit in here where two big macho guys are trying to show off to the three girls on their team. They end up cracking their heads together and going down in a heap. The look on that one girl's face is priceless! Let me rewind it for you – we've watched it three times already."

The guys stood up and moved around to stand behind the girls. The sunlight and angle of viewing caused them to all lean over. Focused on the camera, none of them noticed the approaching police officers.

"Excuse me, Jake. May we have a word?"

Katrina cleared her throat.

Taking the hint, Jake replied to the officer. "Everyone here is aware of your search, officer." Placing a hand on her shoulder, Jake added, "This is Verna's niece, Cathy. She's anxious to hear any news, good or bad."

"Nice to meet you, miss," and the officer tipped his hat, then held his hand out to the second officer who handed over a sealed plastic bag. "This morning, the Coast Guard found this floating over by the Point. They searched the area extensively, but didn't find anything else." Looking at Cathy, he placed the bag on the table in front of her. "I'm pretty certain this is your aunt's, but need positive ID."

Tears welled up in Cathy's eyes. She immediately recognized the Christmas vest as the one Verna had worn to dinner. She wiped back the tears as they escaped her eyes. "Yes, it's Aunt Verna's."

"It doesn't mean anything, Cathy," Jake consoled her.

"That's right, miss. She may have fallen in the water and taken the vest off to swim more easily. She could be just trying to get home."

"Or if she was kidnapped, they might have thrown it in the water so Aunt Verna wouldn't be so easily recognized," Katrina added, trying to think of scenarios that didn't end in death.

Jake didn't like Katrina reinforcing the idea of kidnappers, even if it was a possibility. "There are lots of possible explanations, Cathy. The main thing is the police are still investigating, and they are turning up clues."

"Can't they check the sweater for fingerprints, hair fibres, or something like that? Like they do on CSI," Katrina offered.

"Looks great on T.V., miss," one of the officers replied. "I'm sure your detective friend here will agree that there simply aren't resources of that type available to us. Same goes for pretty well anywhere in Ontario for that matter."

"Only the highest profile cases get any funding approved for that type of analysis, and even then it takes a long time to get results back," Jake concurred.

The officer lifted the evidence bag from the table. Jake came around to thank both officers and shake their hands. He walked with them for a few paces, before stopping and talking briefly.

"So, shall we head over to the Tomato Fight?" Jake asked upon his return to the group.

Iris glanced at her watch. "You're right. We'd better get moving." She stood up, and downed her drink. "Let's go!"

The others followed suit, except Cathy. "I think I'm going to stay here, if you don't mind."

"C'mon, Cathy! It will take your mind off things," Jake encouraged her.

"Yeah, it will be a chance to release some of that tension," Katrina added.

Stewart nodded, and held his hand up to her.

"Okay. Let's go smoosh some Tomatoes." Cathy said through a somewhat forced smile.

Katrina looked around the crowd already gathered around the large tarp – it looked like over a hundred people. Many of them had taken to wearing white as well. The dump truck stood about five metres from one end, tires on the tarp and tilted high in the air to show the partakers the mass of tomatoes about to be dumped. Katrina marvelled at the sight of so many tomatoes. Even in the greenhouse, she'd never seen them assembled in such a quantity – they were all neatly packed in smaller containers on the tour. The tarp already contained a mess, with the soup from the Tomato Stomp spilled in the middle as a base.

Iris came up beside Katrina and squealed, "This is going to be awesome!"

Katrina looked at her. Something was different. Katrina hadn't noticed, but Iris had changed when she'd gone to the restroom. The frayed edges of her tiny jean shorts peeked out from under her white shirt. "Oh, you changed."

"Yeah. I didn't want to wreck my new bikini."

Katrina looked at Iris's top. Sure enough, no bikini. She was free as a bird under the white t-shirt.

The crowd around the tarp tightened up, as more people jockeyed for position. People now stood a few deep around most of the perimeter.

A large lady in an official TomatoFest t-shirt tapped on a microphone, as she stood to the side of the dump truck's tailgate. "Test. Test." Tap, tap.

"Dump trucks," Jake whispered to Katrina, "another wonderful Canadian invention. New Brunswick, I believe."

"IS EVERYONE READY!" the lady boomed over the microphone. The amplification was quite unnecessary with her pipes.

The crowd clapped and hollered in anticipation. "I want to thank the Mayor here, for placing the tiebreaking vote to allow us to have this event. Try not to think of this as wasted food, but as a very healthy donation to battle cancer! The Mayor has the honour of pushing the button to release over twenty tons of our red fruit. Mayor, if you will," and she handed over the microphone.

"Welcome everyone to Leamington! Are you ready to get red?" Another roar came from the crowd. "Everybody stand back until I say go. The dump truck will begin releasing tomatoes as it drives off the tarp. Then I'll give the command to start." He held up the controls and pressed the button. A river of tomatoes began to flow out of the truck. The Mayor scrambled out of the way, barely avoiding the flow. The truck completed unloading as it reached the end of the tarp.

"LET THE FIGHT BEGIN!"

Festival goers descended on the red pile from all directions. The crowd surge dragged Katrina toward the centre. Chunks of tomato flew everywhere. Jake took a tomato and squished it on her head, oozing juice down her face. In turn, an unknown assailant from behind Jake pelted him in the back of the head, sending more debris into the air. Cathy lay on the ground, laughing in the goo. She began to roll around, knocking others down as she went. Katrina tossed a tomato lightly at Jake's chest, and seeing the result, bent down to scoop up more tomatoes and chunks of tomatoes.

Katrina watched Iris cover Tate with tomatoes in an onslaught that would have made a good YouTube clip. Tate was covered head to toe in a slimy coating, his red face not the result of the fight but of a brewing hostility. Finally at his breaking point, with Iris bending down to pick up more assault material, he placed both hands on Iris's back and pushed her face first into the slop. Iris stood, tomato skin hanging from her face. Her white shirt had turned completely red on the front, and had two tomato-induced hand prints on the back. Tate had never stood up to her before and she was shocked at the timing. She didn't have long to think though, as Cathy rolled under her, causing Iris to land splat on her back. A second later, Jake was Cathy's victim and he landed on top of Iris. He lay there for a few seconds before helping her up. Her tomato-soaked top left nothing to the imagination as she stood up. Katrina was angry at Jake for leering so long at Iris like someone in a wet t-shirt contest. Any look over two seconds was leering in her book. She took two handfuls of red mush and smashed it into his face.

"Truce?" offered Jake to Katrina, extending his hand to shake.

"Truce," and Katrina shook his hand. He latched on and whipped her around him, and letting go at the right time, sent her sliding through an open area toward the outside of the swill. Standing up, pieces of tomato fell from her body. Upset with Jake and feeling dirty with tomatoes, she turned to face away from the mayhem. There stood Stewart, filming her. What came next made it worse. Volunteers had surrounded the tarp, armed with hoses. One stood directly in front of her and began hosing her down. She let out a very girlish scream as the cold water hit her body.

"This is great!" yelled Stewart.

Katrina felt as though she stood naked in front of the world. She covered herself and turned to run away, only to slip and land again in the sticky mess. She covered her face with her hands and sat there crying into them. Stewart shut off his camera and instructed the volunteer to point the volley of water somewhere else. Stewart tiptoed onto the tarp to help Katrina up and off. "You do need to hose off, you know," he said to her.

"Yes, I know. This feels so … so …"

"Yucky?" Stewart suggested.

"Yes, yucky."

Katrina had finished hosing herself down before the Tomato Fight ended for everyone else. In fact, she'd bought a souvenir towel and t-shirt, so she almost felt clean again. She stood beside Stewart as the other four in the party slid their way off the tarp. They were all laughing as they picked bits out of their hair and off their clothes. Even Tate settled down and got into it.

"Katrina, how about a hug?" Jake joked.

Stewart stepped in front of Katrina. "I wouldn't go there if I were you."

"Right," said Jake. "We should go get in line to hose off anyway. Say, where did you get the shirt from? I think this white one's had the biscuit."

She pointed in the direction of a nearby booth, its operator smiling from ear to ear with the rash of sales.

As Jake headed off to the shower area, Katrina turned to look at the remains of the twenty tons of tomatoes. It looked like a vat of stewed tomatoes, with a few stray shoes and hats stirred in. The appearance wasn't as disgusting from this distance as it was up close. Volunteers with orange vests spread open barricades and the dump truck pulled onto the road. Watching the truck make the tight turn, Katrina's heart jumped and she instinctively yelled, "Jake!"

Jake had only gotten about ten metres away and turned as he heard Katrina's excited call. He turned and ran to her. As he approached, she started pointing in the direction of the dump truck.

"Black pickup truck, Jake! Look at the driver!" Katrina exclaimed.

Sure enough, a man in a John Deere hat and sporting a thick moustache sat behind the wheel as the pickup began to back up to leave.

Katrina cried out again, "Oh no, he's leaving! What do we do?"

"We'll never catch him from here … Stewart, give me your camera. Quick!"

Stewart, moving as quickly as he ever had, came right over. Jake ripped the camera from around Stewart's neck, soliciting a curse from the strap burn. Jake zoomed in with the camera and took a handful of shots as the driver pulled away.

"Shit!" Jake complained as he looked at the images on the small screen. "Mostly got the side of the truck. Only one partial plate in the entire lot. Ontario plate starting with a B – not much to go on, I'm afraid."

"You can probably zoom in on the driver," offered Stewart as encouragement.

"Show me," said Jake.

Stewart looked through the images and found the one with the best view of the driver. He zoomed in and handed it to Jake, with Katrina looking over his shoulder.

"Sure looks like the guy that the girl at Verna's work described," Katrina said.

"Thanks, Stewart. We'll take this by the police station before we head home." He handed the camera back to Stewart, who looked repulsed. "What?" asked Jake.

Stewart turned the camera to show tomato ooze on the handles of the camera.

"Sorry, mate. But it could have been worse."

"How's that?"

"I could have done this," and Jake took a clump of tomato off his shirt and slapped it on Stewart's face.

27 Mugging

Cathy had had a rollercoaster day so far. The morning started with Stewart and her enjoying a peaceful stroll, hand-in-hand, laughing, not a care in the world. Then the news of them finding Aunt Verna's sweater, and the dreadful possibilities brought with its discovery. That was followed by unwinding in the tomato mosh pit. Changing for a night out at the bar just down the street, she hoped to end things on a high note. Perhaps drinking herself into a coma would help.

It was past ten P.M. as they walked to the bar, and Cathy had to endure listening to Katrina moan about missing another sunset because they'd been changing. The bar could be described as more restaurant than bar. The outside had an enormous deck that wrapped around two sides of the exterior. Large umbrella-shaded tables covered the deck, without overcrowding patrons like too many of these beach-style joints did. Cathy hated places where you couldn't get up without colliding with an adjoining table's occupants, or where the closeness precluded any privacy at all. Booths filled a good portion of the inside of the establishment, with room for a few moveable tables that at this hour had made way to house the band and a small dance floor. The place had a remarkable island flavour to it. A Corona kind of place. Or perhaps Dos Equis – maybe she'd meet the most interesting man in the world tonight! The warm tropical night enhanced the mood and her spirits, as she plopped herself down on a sturdy resin patio chair.

A few draughts and many appetizers later, Cathy had fully relaxed. They'd ordered almost every appetizer on the menu and shared around the table. Now they began working their way through the bar menu. All of them were partaking, as Aunt Verna's place was a short few-hundred-metre walk down the narrow two-lane asphalt road. At least it was short on the way there, who knows how long it would feel after all the alcohol she'd consumed. Hopefully they'd head in the right direction and not end up at Point Pelee.

"Excuse me, miss," Stewart asked their waitress. "When you have a minute, could you bring us a round of Orgasms here please?"

"Cocktail or shot?"

"Shot, please."

"Certainly. Would that be Norwegian, Chocolate, Squirting, or Screaming?"

"Wow, you know your Orgasms," Stewart replied. "I want the kind that is half Bailey's and half peppermint schnapps, whatever that one's called."

"Got it. Anything else?"

Cathy looked over at Katrina. "You'd better get her a glass of ice water."

After having their Orgasms, Cathy took her turn to order. "Slippery Nipples."

"Sticking with the Bailey's theme, I see," replied the waitress.

"Didn't think about it," replied Cathy. "Just like the drink."

"And love the name!" Stewart added.

As the waitress left, Cathy turned to Katrina and said, "C'mon, Kat, let's hit the dance floor! You too, Iris. Any of you boys man enough to join us?" She paused to see their eyes scatter in all directions. "I didn't think so. Keep an eye on our purses."

The band was a two-piece outfit, guitarist and keyboard player, both of whom sang alternating songs. The range of music jumped all over the map, from country to disco to old and new rock. Cathy didn't really care, as long as it was loud and they could dance to it. The dance floor wasn't crowded, but had enough people bopping around to make it fun. Nothing better than dancing to sweat out the alcohol, she thought. Well, almost nothing better, she corrected herself, thinking of Stewart.

After a half-dozen tunes, Cathy proclaimed she had to use the john, a term she often used on purpose just to see Katrina blush. Iris and Katrina declined, saying they would meet her back at the table after the next song. The women's bathroom was tucked down a short hall, right beside an exit to the back of the building. Cathy wished a few restaurants had this setup when she was going through her blind date phase, providing a really convenient route to skip out on some of her more forgettable dates. Taking her purse to the bathroom never raised suspicion, and she'd be in a cab before the creep, mama's boy, egomaniac, psycho, or loser knew what hit him.

Cathy didn't have the bathroom hang-ups or phobias ingrained in some of her friends, including Katrina at times. Pretty well any port, or porthole, would do in a storm. Even a well clustered bush had served the purpose on the occasional emergency. Cathy actually found it more acceptable to use a dirty public washroom than a dirty bathroom in someone's home. She thought it spoke volumes of the person, but a bar shouldn't be held to such a high standard as it couldn't control what its patrons did in the can. She'd tried explaining her rationale to Stewart, also one to require a clean loo, as he would say, but he didn't get it. To him dirty was dirty, no matter whose toilet or sink it happened to be. So before she opened the door to any public washroom, she imagined the worst in her mind, just in case. In this case, it was unnecessary as the taps sparkled, the floor was clean, and the toilet sanitary in appearance.

Finishing her 'business', as her family called it, she washed up and left the place as clean as she found it. Opening the door, and not seeing anyone waiting, she reached back and flicked off the light. Turning back to the hallway, she took a single step before she felt an arm reach around her waist and a gloved hand come around to cover her mouth, muffling a reactive scream. The little wisp that escaped her vocal chords wouldn't be heard five feet away with a lunch crowd, let alone over the loud Saturday night crowd and music. She kicked her feet, but the attacker was quick and dragged her backwards out the rear door in a matter of seconds. As he swung her around the corner of the building to escape the light over the back door, one of her kicks landed on a trash can sending it rolling across the ground, spewing its contents as it went. Unfortunately for Cathy, it was a plastic can and didn't make much noise, just a mess. The man, as she had suspected by the strength of the assailant, pinned her against the wall, one hand still covering her mouth and the other against her abdomen. A ski mask covered his face.

"I've got a knife against your gut, so don't scream when I uncover your mouth or it will be the last thing you say. Got it?"

Cathy nodded agreement.

"I'm going to ask you a question, then pull my hand away from your mouth so you can answer."

Cathy nodded again.

The man pressed his hand harder into her stomach. "Who is your aunt working with?"

Cathy's eyes must have almost fallen out of her face in surprise. "I don't know what you're talking about."

The man punched her in the gut. "Think harder. Who's Verna Wilkinson working with?"

"Really, I don't know what you mean."

The man punched her a second time, this time harder than the first. He held the knife blade up in front of her face, and it glistened in the little light emitted from a small canister light over the door. Cathy didn't know if she was going to piss her pants out of fear or puke from the gut shots. She puked.

The man caught most of it on his pants. He stepped back in disgust, before his anger flared and the knife made another appearance dangerously close to her pale face. Cathy feared the worst and closed her eyes, waiting for her life to flash by. The creak of the back door opening startled her attacker, and his terrifying grip released Cathy. Still too frightened to open her eyes, she heard the sound of her attacker fleeing.

Katrina had her Slippery Nipple upon return to the table. Or at least that was what she made everyone at the table think. The dancing had helped her avoid drinking anymore, as she'd reached her limit before dinner, well before appetizers had even finished. A guy a few tables over leaned too far back on his chair and went crashing to the deck. In the commotion, Katrina dumped her drink into the short shrubs surrounding the deck. Thinking about the man making a scene, she realized Cathy hadn't returned from the washroom. Standing, she announced to Jake she was going to check on Cathy.

"You've only been back a couple of minutes. There's probably just a line."

He was likely right, but she'd learned from Jake to trust her gut, and her gut was screaming to her. Of course her gut might just be voicing its displeasure with all the shots inflicted upon it.

Knocking on the washroom door, she got no response. Gently turning the handle and slowly opening the door, just in case there was an occupant that didn't hear her knock, she called Cathy's name as she entered. Empty. She turned and went back to look over the dance floor. No sign of her. There was no way she missed her on the way from the table. Cathy would have had to have gone way around the other side of the patio not to be seen, and Cathy was a straight line kind of person, when drinks were involved. Turning back to the washroom area, Katrina's eye caught something out of place through the glass back door. A garbage can lay toppled on its side on the sidewalk. Suspicious, she thought, but why would Cathy go out the back door? Oddly, the thought popped in her mind how it would be convenient to have an escape route near the washroom if you were on a bad date. Thinking back to Cathy, Katrina pushed open the door, surprised by the rusty creaking sound. She saw a man running across the field and wondered why on a hot night like tonight anyone would go jogging wearing pants, gloves, and a hoodie. Not watching her step, she slipped on some of the spilled trash. Grabbing for anything to retain her balance, she caught the corner of the building with her hand, but only by enough to redirect her wipeout. Careening in a new direction, she hit a new patch of something wet and her feet shot up in the air. She landed splat on a puddle of something, before her eyes refocused to see Cathy doubled over in front of her.

"What happened?" Katrina asked her friend.

"Mugged," Cathy panted, still trying to find her wind. "Get Jake!"

"Sure," Katrina agreed and she put her hand down to lift herself up. "God, what am I sitting in?" and she put her hand up to smell it.

"I wouldn't …" Cathy began, but it was too late.

"I'm going to be sick …" Katrina held her arm fully outstretched in a failed attempt to move the smell as far away as possible. "Jake. I'll go get Jake."

Cutting through the restaurant, Katrina herself must have looked like the victim of a mugging. Frazzled hair from her wipeout, garbage- stained top, and of course she smelled like vomit. Good thing she wasn't on a first date or the guy would have snuck out the back door on her.

Jake ran to the back as soon as Katrina could spit out that Cathy was hurt. Amazingly, Stewart kept up with him. Katrina had never seen Stewart move so fast, except for his mouth.

"He's long gone by now," Cathy informed Jake.

Stewart sidestepped the pool of puke and leaned down to console Cathy. "Good job, darling. I see you fought him off and kept him from getting your handbag."

"He wasn't after my bag. He wanted to know about Aunt Verna," she said, attempting to stand and accomplishing it with Stewart's support.

"What did he want to know about Verna?" asked Jake, pausing from scanning the scene for clues.

"He kept asking me who she's working with. It didn't make sense. She works at Tim Horton's."

"Interesting," said Jake and Katrina together.

"What do you think it means?" Katrina asked Jake.

"Haven't a clue. But if they kidnapped her to get that information from her, she obviously hasn't given it up."

Katrina looked to ensure Cathy was a few paces away before whispering to Jake, "Unless she's dead and can't tell them."

28   *Hangover*

Cathy awoke to a painful reminder of the night before. She'd found
some Tylenol 3's in Aunt Verna's medicine cabinet and one did the
trick, at least for a few hours. It hurt to roll over, which she did
constantly in her sleep. Frankly, she didn't know how Stewart put up
with it sometimes, but then again, he slept like a log. Another Tylenol 3
sounded good to her, but trying to sit up in bed sent a gut-wrenching
pain through her body. So much for doing any crunches today, she
laughed to herself. As if. She thought that the puking would have
prevented a hangover this morning, and it likely would have if she
didn't have four or five more drinks at the bar while recovering and
waiting for the police. Jake insisted on filing a report that night, while
the incident was still fresh in everybody's mind. She didn't know why,
but Jake looked pissed at Katrina. All the poor girl did was save her
life. If Katrina hadn't opened the door when she did, who knows what
the guy would have done. Then again, she did remember Katrina saying
Jake fretted over her getting into dangerous situations. Like she could
help it this time? Go figure. All that macho crap of guys having to

protect their women. Sure it was nice to have someone want to feel that way, but don't get carried away. What did he want Katrina to do – sit at home and knit all friggin' night?

After what dragged on like four hours to Cathy, but was actually twenty minutes and forty groans of pain, Stewart woke up from his dead sleep.

"Morning, love," Stewart said, Cathy's back to him. He snuggled up and put his arm around her waist.

"Owwww," Cathy moaned.

"Sorry, love. Forgot about your incident last night. Sore, I assume by all the grunting?"

"Sore ain't the half of it. Hungover to boot. Can you get me another one of those Tylenol 3's please?"

"Are you sure you want another one? I doubt you'll be able to function if you have another one."

"And I know I won't be able to function if I don't have another one."

"Right. Be right back with your meds and a glass of water. We'll just pretend we're practising for when we're old and grey. Minus the messy diaper stuff and you trying to stab me with a kitchen knife because you don't recognize me."

"You're just too good to me," she laughed, but only for a second as it hurt like hell. "And maybe you can throw a few ice cubes in a washcloth too. For the bruising."

Returning from his errands, Stewart pulled a phone out of his front pocket.

"Thank God that's a phone. I was afraid your Union Jack was running up the pole."

Stewart chuckled. "I don't think I'll be waving my flag for a few days by the looks of it." He propped up the pillows against the headboard and helped her, amidst the groans, to sit upright. She took her pill and washed it down, before she gingerly laid the ice cube wrap on her abdomen.

Handing her the phone, Stewart said, "I thought you might want to call your mother."

A soft tapping on the door signalled Katrina coming to check on Cathy. Nobody else would knock like they were afraid of hurting the door. Trying to hide her discomfort, Cathy covered her stomach and ice with a blanket. Bravely, she called out, "Come in, Katrina!" She winced to speak so loudly, but didn't want Katrina to smother her with pity.

"I was just wondering how you're feeling. You had a rough day yesterday." Katrina sat down gently on the edge of the bed and held Cathy's hand.

"Thanks, Kat. I'm doing just fine," and she patted Katrina's hand. "How are you? You took quite a tumble last night."

"I'm going to have a nice bruise on my left cheek in a day or two, if you know what I mean."

Cathy laughed, forgetting it would hurt. She winced slightly.

"Are you sure you're okay?"

"Just a flesh wound," she replied. Stewart let out a belly laugh at the reference to one of his favourite Monty Python skits where a brave knight loses limb after limb, and utters the words as he still tries to fight.

Katrina gave a blank stare, unaware of the joke. "Say, Jake and I were discussing the case this morning. We were wondering if you could call your mom and ask if she knew where Aunt Verna would go on her vacations. Maybe she has a number we can call to see if your aunt's just gone there."

"Funny you should ask. Stewart just suggested I give her a call to cheer me up. I'll see what she knows."

"Thanks, Cathy. Do you want any breakfast? I think Jake is going to whip up some omelettes."

"Sure, sounds good. Besides, if I turned down food you'd likely think I was dying or something."

Katrina laughed as she stood up. She knelt over and kissed Cathy on the top of the head. "Rest up. I'll bring your omelette in when it's ready."

Cathy found her mother's name in her contact list and called her. They hadn't talked in a few weeks. They weren't ones to call every day like some mothers and daughters. She didn't need the comfort of her mother's voice every day.

"Hi, Mom. How's everything?"

"You know. Same old same old. I haven't bludgeoned your father yet, although he continues to give me good reasons," the voice laughed the laugh she'd handed down to her daughter -- full and sincere. "How are you doing, baby girl?"

"I've had better vacations. I got mugged last night, but I'm okay. Just a sore stomach, nothing to worry about."

"That's terrible, dear! I'm glad Aunt Verna's there to take care of you."

"Well, that's another thing."

"What do you mean? Is she okay?"

"She disappeared a few days ago."

"Really? I didn't think it was time."

"Okay, now what do you mean?"

"I never told you because I had no reason to tell you, that's all. Don't take it like I was hiding anything from you. Verna takes off every eight months or so to visit a high school friend. It varies when she goes, because she doesn't want to be down south anytime around Christmas."

"Where's her friend live?"

"Arizona. It's the new Florida, you know. Much drier. Better for arthritis."

"I didn't realize she had a best friend. She never mentioned anything."

"There's good reason for that. It's a sad story. When your aunt was eighteen – the drinking age was eighteen back then – Verna and her friend Mary were out partying one night. We all did stupid things back then. It's amazing any of us lived past twenty-five, to tell you the truth. Anywho, they were driving home late from Harrow, I think. She lived in Windsor back then. Mary was driving and Verna had begun to doze off in the passenger seat. Verna woke to squealing tires. Some critter had made its way up onto the road from the ditch, and Mary braked and swerved to avoid it. Unfortunately, she drove off the culvert into the creek, just east of Amherstburg. Why she was going that way, Lord knows. Maybe she was trying to avoid the cops. Maybe she missed Howard Avenue. Don't know. Anyway, the car goes plummeting into the creek and lands upside down. Mary's legs were broken in God knows how many places. How she did what she did is a testament to that girl's inner strength."

"What happened?"

"So here's Mary with scrambled legs, upside down in a car, submerged in water. She gets out and surfaces but can't see Verna. She goes under the water but doesn't see Verna in the car. Back to the surface again, where she sees Verna flailing around like a fly in a toilet bowl. You may not know this, but your Aunt Verna couldn't swim back then. You wouldn't know it by watching her do laps at the Sherk Centre now. So Mary swims over, broken legs and all, grabs a hold of Verna, wings flapping to beat sixty, and drags her to safety on the shore."

"That's amazing!"

"It was. It truly was. Verna would be dead if not for Mary. And Mary's reward? Can never walk again. Stuck in a wheelchair since age eighteen. Sometimes makes you wonder what the good Lord is thinking."

"Do you have a number for Mary? I'd like to call and see if Verna's down there."

"And what if she's not? You'll get Mary all worked up. Let me call her. I'll call to say I lost her address and need it for mailing my Christmas cards. She won't think anything of it. If Verna's there, I'm sure she'll mention it."

"You're right, Mom. Call me back after you get in touch with her. Love you."

"Love you too. Make that big hunk of a man earn his keep and take care of you. Put him to work. It'll do him good!"

Stewart opened the bedroom door carrying a tray with an omelette, toast, and orange juice. He placed it on the bed next to Cathy and dragged a chair beside the bed. "So, how's Momsie doing?"

"She's fine," Cathy replied as she reached for a slice of toast. Her phone rang before she could take a bite. "Yes, Mom. Any luck? No, not there, eh? Don't worry. I'm sure she's okay. I'll call you tomorrow with an update. Bye."

After a brief recap of the earlier call, Stewart sighed.

"Well, I guess we can cross the annual disappearance off the list. I'll go tell Jake."

"And Katrina," added Cathy.

"And Katrina."

Dale J. Moore

29 *Getting to the Point*

Katrina wasn't sure the knowledge of the reason for Aunt Verna's annual disappearance was a good thing. Sure, it took one possibility off the list, but it was one of the scant good outcomes she had imagined. Jake had his spaghetti-looking 'mind map' diagram that he used to try and keep all the clues straight. In the map, or perhaps the maze, inside Katrina's mind, four scenarios remained. The only favourable one in the bunch had Aunt Verna hitting her head, suffering from amnesia, and wandering around Essex County not knowing who she was or where she lived. Certainly someone would have come across her by now and brought her to the police, or a hospital.

The three negative outcomes boiled down to kidnapped, drowned, or killed. If killed, why did her sweater wash up on shore? Wouldn't she have been murdered in the sweater and buried in it to hide any evidence? That bought her to drowning. If she'd drowned, why did only her sweater drift to shore? Did she take it off to try and swim more easily, but succumbed regardless? If so, where was the body? Then again, Lake Erie was a big lake with strong currents around Point Pelee.

So strong, in fact, that Cathy had told them there were serious warnings about swimming in the Park.

And then there was kidnapped. But she'd never heard of a kidnapping where the family wasn't contacted for money. Either with one of those funky notes made from letters clipped out of a magazine, or with the computer-distorted voices that resembled Darth Vader on drugs. Then again, Verna Wilkinson didn't really have any family – no husband or kids. What if they tried to call and nobody was there? Aunt Verna didn't have an answering machine – her rationale was something like, 'if I'm not here, I don't need to talk to them.' Or what if the kidnappers had contacted somebody, but that somebody hadn't told them? Like Don and Faith. She bounced her idea off Jake, who pried himself away from his 'mind map' to listen.

"So what if the kidnappers contacted Don and Faith about Aunt Verna?"

"Why would they do that?" Jake asked.

"What if she's not being held for money, but as leverage to get them to sell their property?"

"It's an interesting idea, but I just don't see it. For starters, if the kidnappers were after the deed to the property, they'd have to register the name change with the province. As soon as they do, busted."

"Hadn't thought of that," Katrina said, disappointed at how easily her idea got shot down. "What if the kidnapper isn't the one that registers the property, but a third person who sells it to Canawine?"

"Same outcome, I think. Canawine would likely be considered an accessory or something. I doubt they would buy it off a kidnapper, knowing the rightful owner of the property."

Katrina wanted to make the kidnapping angle work, because it at least gave hope to Aunt Verna coming out of it alive. "So why kidnap someone and not ask for a ransom?"

"It's rare, that's for sure," Jake sighed, knowing where Katrina was headed. "I only remember one case. A few years back I heard about some rich guy getting kidnapped before a big stakeholder meeting. There was a key vote on the direction of the company, and without this rich guy present to cast his block of votes, his brother was able to take control. The police eventually proved the brother was behind the kidnapping. Come to think of it though, even then there was a ransom note, and it was one of the key clues."

"Did they find fingerprints or some other evidence with the note?"

"No, actually they were tipped off by the kidnappers only asking for $100,000. The guy was worth hundreds of millions of dollars. Certainly if you kidnap a tycoon you're going to ask for a few million bucks for your trouble. The police determined by the note that there was another motive, and it pointed right at the brother."

"I doubt that's the case here. I don't think Verna's secretly a key stakeholder in Tim Horton's, or anywhere else."

"Don't be fooled by these little old ladies that live by modest means. Sometimes they're very wealthy, as they've never wasted their money on frivolous possessions. Just what they need to get by. They often sock away a lot of dough."

"Still don't see it as a kidnapping," Katrina said, sitting as she sighed.

"Me neither," Jake replied. "Since we've got time before we head back to the festival this afternoon, do you want to head into Point Pelee for a few hours? I'd hate to come all this way and not see it."

"Sure. Let me tell Cathy and Stewart where we're headed."

"Great. I'll go outside and tell Iris... I mean Iris and Tate."

The drive to the Point Pelee gate took under five minutes, even cruising at a not so meteoric pace of thirty-five kilometres per hour. They could have walked if the gate was their final destination. While paying their day use fees, Jake picked up a map, which he spread out on a nearby picnic table. They had a four kilometre drive to get into the actual park and probably another nine or ten to the tip.

"How about we start with renting a canoe for an hour?"

"Is it safe to go onto the lake near here in a canoe? Don't they have bad currents?"

"It would be unsafe for us. I'm sure there are lots of experienced canoeists that can handle it. They'd know where to avoid the currents. We're going to take a nice leisurely paddle through the marsh, along the boardwalk, not in the lake."

"Sounds romantic," Katrina said, snuggling up to his muscular arm.

"Then I want to drive down to the Point to check it out. If we have time, we can take a stroll on the boardwalk."

"Sounds good. Do you want me to use the map while you drive?"

"You can, but I think it will be pretty hard to get lost."

Katrina looked again at the map. "I see what you mean. There's only one road."

Within minutes they'd found the canoe rental place, done the paperwork, and were doing up their life vests. Jake took the back of the canoe, after helping Katrina get settled up front. Back home in Pipton, she'd ventured out in a homemade canoe that one of her cousins had built in shop class. She wasn't a pro by any stretch, but knew the basics and got out a few times each summer. Of course, a few years had passed.

"Just paddle on the right side. That'll likely be easiest for you since you're right-handed," Jake shouted up to her.

"I'm only a few feet away, you don't have to yell."

"Sorry, just using my outside voice."

Jake guided them through the marsh, following alongside the boardwalk. Katrina admired the cool view looking up at the wooden structure. A couple her parent's age waved down to them as they glided along the water. Her canoeing skills were coming back, even if they were limited. At least Jake hadn't yelled at her or even corrected her. Looking away from the elevated walkway, she spotted a couple of small colourful birds darting amongst the reeds protruding from the water.

"Look at the birds, Jake!" and Katrina spun around to point, continuing her stroke through and out of the water. Her paddle carried a load of water backward, landing squarely on Jake's lap.

"Hey! Watch what you're doing."

"Oops! Sorry, didn't mean to. Are you okay?"

"Just a little damp," Jake said.

Katrina appreciated that the remainder of the canoe trip was peaceful, and without further incident. The air out on the marsh felt cool and refreshing. Different types of birds flitted around and flew overhead. No wonder so many birders came here. She'd heard the number of birds and variety of species was amazing in the fall, with the Point a regular stopping spot on the migration south. Made sense as the southern-most point of the northern shore of the lake. The colours would likely be awesome too.

"Hey, Katrina," Jake said to get her attention.

"What is it, Jake?" she said turning to see him.

"Did you ever see the movie 'Paddle to the Sea' when you were younger?"

"Paddle what?"

"It's called 'Paddle to the Sea.' My mom borrowed it from the library one day when she was on a nostalgia trip. I think the movie came up at her class reunion or something. Anyway, she popped it in the VCR one day when I was in my early teens and we watched it together."

"What's it about?"

"This kid in northern Ontario, near Sault St. Marie, I think, makes a little wooden canoe with an Indian in it."

"You mean a native Canadian," Katrina corrected him.

"Yes, you know what I mean. Anyway, in the winter this kid carves this canoe and little Indian, I mean native Canadian, dude. The kid carves a trench on the bottom and fills it with lead for buoyancy."

"With lead? Really? They'd never be able to show that now with all the lead toy scares coming from China."

"This movie was from 1960 or something like that. I don't think they even thought cigarette smoking was bad back then. Can I just finish the story?"

"I don't know what's taking you so long in the first place."

Jake took a deep breath. "So this kid carves on the bottom of it, 'my name is paddle to the sea – if you find me put me back in the water."

"He carved all of that on a little wooden canoe?

"Yes, so if anyone found it, they'd know to put it back in the water instead of keeping it. When spring came, the canoe started its adventure from Lake Superior out to the Atlantic Ocean. The little canoe runs into all kinds of peril, but eventually makes it to the sea, where a lighthouse operator in Newfoundland re-paints it."

"Newfoundland and Labrador."

"Back then it was just Newfoundland."

"Did the canoe get returned to the little boy?"

"No, the lighthouse operator set it free, to travel to Scandinavia or Africa, or wherever the currents might take it."

"I bet the boy would have liked to have known that the canoe made it to the ocean."

"Probably, but it's not like he put his home address on it."

"Maybe he should have carved his address on it instead of all that other stuff."

"Maybe," Jake said, shaking his head, wondering why he'd bothered to tell the story. They'd turned around and were almost back to where they started. Jake quietly guided their craft back to the landing. The rental operators were assisting another couple get into a canoe.

"Just stay sitting. I'll help you out," Jake told her. Tucking his paddle into the canoe, he moved toward the middle of the canoe before standing with one foot on the dock to keep the canoe from drifting. "Okay, I'm right behind you. I'll keep us balanced as you get up."

Katrina pushed up slowly off her seat, and felt one of Jake's hands loosely support her back. Standing completely upright, she turned her body to step out of the canoe. Unfortunately for Jake, she had not let go of her paddle. With her turn, the paddle came across Jake's body and knocked the unsuspecting detective off his feet, over the canoe, and into the shallow water. Katrina had somehow managed to leap free of the tipping canoe, landing safe on the shore, paddle still in hand.

Katrina blushed. The two rental operators laughed out loud. Jake looked angry as he stood in the waist deep water, but seeing the people on shore laughing, he smiled and broke out in laughter as well.

Katrina felt relieved. She already was concerned that she and Jake were on delicate ground. At least he couldn't accuse her of putting herself in a dangerous situation this time.

Jake lifted himself onto the dock, dislodging his fee from the mucky marsh bottom. Discarding his life jacket as he stood, he looked half human and half swamp creature with his seaweed-covered legs. His t-shirt clung to his chest, showing off the muscular torso beneath. Taking off his shirt and wringing it out, Katrina couldn't help but admire his frame. She noticed the female rental operator, and part-time guide, also soaking up the view.

"I'm just going to leave it off for now," Jake said, looking at the wrung-out ball in his hand. "It's not like I need a shirt today. But I would like to rinse this green ooze from my legs and sandals."

"There's a hose at the side of the building," the female guide said.

Both women watched as Jake hosed down his lower torso.

"You're a lucky woman," the guide quietly said to Katrina.

Jake turned off the hose and hung it back on the hook secured to the wall. Walking toward the girls, his body glistened from the sun.

"You're a *really* lucky woman," the guide mumbled.

"No argument from me," Katrina smiled. She locked her arm in Jake's. "Where to?"

"To the Point."

"To the Point it is."

Katrina wished they had a jeep on a day like today, instead of a family loser cruiser, as one of her more snobby customers called minivans. A jeep would go much better with sun, sand, and surf – and with Jake's bare-chested look. Regardless, the short four kilometre jaunt to the Visitor's Centre was enjoyable. Katrina watched the scenery glide by, disappointed that the trees were much thicker than she expected and offered only infrequent glimpses of the waves through its denseness.

The Visitor's Centre reminded Katrina of the Pipton library. One side covered in windows, the other side completely brick. Jake talked to a pleasant young guide stationed at the circular information counter in the centre of the building, and relayed to Katrina that the shuttle had just left to the tip, but ran every twenty minutes. Jake buttoned up a shirt of Stewart's that he found in the van. Jake didn't have many button-up shirts other than his uniforms, and this one, while a little generous in the middle and generating a snicker from his girlfriend, nonetheless made Jake more comfortable about going inside a public building. The cooler indoor temperature reinforced his decision.

The little exhibits and artifacts were fascinating to Katrina. She always liked that kind of stuff, whether it was Point Pelee, Fort Henry, or Upper Canada Village. Her interest peaked reading a story describing a lifesaving station established in 1901 on the Point due to all the shipwrecks caused by the reefs and currents. Another photo showed a Point Pelee covered with cars – six thousand spots in the park at its peak as a beach getaway. Even then, the lots would overflow. In 1963 over 780,000 people visited the Point, making it the most visited National Park, yet the smallest. The traffic was ruining the park until harsh measures were taken to restore the Point to the more natural state it's in today. Katrina thought that a visitor's guide for sale summed up their location perfectly: 'Where Canada Begins.'

"Look, Jake! They have a theatre. I love it when they show a movie about the place."

"Why do we need a movie? We're here!"

"They always tell you all kinds of trivia and stories about its history."

"I don't really care for that stuff. Kind of bores me."

"To each their own, as my mother would say."

"The shuttle will be here any minute. Let's head out," Jake said, glad to escape movie time.

"Maybe on the way back," Katrina said optimistically.

"Maybe. I doubt we'll have time, but we'll see," he replied, but not really intending to make time.

The train, as the park called it, was really a truck with a couple of tram cars in tow. It reminded Katrina of a stretch golf cart, with rows of fibreglass benches. Like the kind of cart that toured people around the Hollywood movie sets, hoping they'd get a peek of Julia Roberts. As Katrina jumped in, she failed to notice the small television screen hanging down in the middle of the centre row she'd picked. Jake could hear her head smack it.

"Are you okay?"

"Yeah," she replied, gently touching the top of her head. She looked up at the monitor. "Who put that there?"

"Maybe," Jake joked, "you should have worn your helmet."

"I've got something better." Katrina drew a little nylon scarf from her purse and pulled it over her head, tying it below her chin to keep her hair from flying everywhere.

"Sexy look," Jake said.

"You think so?" Katrina asked.

"Maybe to my Grandpa," Jake laughed.

"I've seen Julia Roberts wear one just like this in a movie and she looked awesome," she said in support of her fashion choice.

"She likely did," he replied. "But did she have the price tag hanging from it like you do?"

Katrina felt around her head and embarrassedly found the paper sign bouncing up against her neck. Blushing, she tried to nonchalantly pull the tag off. Unfortunately, one of those unbreakable plastic do-hickies secured it. She managed to tear half the paper off, making it look worse in the process.

"Allow me," Jake said. He leaned in close, Katrina's skin tingling to his warm breath on her neck, initiating wildly sprouting goose bumps. With his teeth he bit off the one end of the plastic tie, freeing the tag from her scarf.

"Thanks," Katrina sighed. "You can do that anytime you like!"

Jake smiled and leaned in to plant a kiss softly on her neck.

"Newlyweds?" An elderly man asked from behind, him and his wife grinning from ear to ear at Katrina and Jake.

"No, sorry," Jake replied.

"Well, maybe you should be," his wife replied.

"Thanks." Katrina had resumed blushing. "First time at Point Pelee?"

"No, but first time in the summer. We usually come in the fall for the birding. Best place in Canada."

"I've heard," replied Jake as the shuttle turned into the circular drop-off area. As it came to a stop, Jake got out of the tram and extended his hand to Katrina.

"Watch your head."

"Thanks. I almost forgot."

Jake couldn't help but notice the elderly man likewise help his bride from the train. Jake smiled at the gentleman. "Enjoy your day."

"Thank you, young man. Have a good day too."

Walking away from the shuttle, Katrina beamed. "Aren't they just the cutest couple you've ever seen?"

"Aside from that honeymoon crack, yeah."

"Well, how was he to know?"

"Just don't be getting ideas," Jake said.

Katrina didn't fixate on marriage like some girls she knew. She hadn't even thought of Jake in that way. Still too early in their relationship to have those kinds of feelings. Regardless, those words hurt. *Don't get any ideas.* Did he mean he wasn't serious at all? Not that she was, but she went into every relationship thinking, or at least maybe hoping, that this was the one. After all, what would be the point otherwise? Well, sex maybe. This relationship consisted of more than that. *Didn't it?*

Lost in thought, she hadn't realized the sand, and the land, gradually disappeared on both sides of them. It truly was a point. In spite of all the pictures she'd just seen, it still surprised her. A sand bar, littered with rocks, jutted out into Lake Erie. By the time the trail ended, there remained perhaps forty metres to the end of the sand spit. Jake had gone ahead of her by a few metres. She recalled seeing the 'No Swimming. Dangerous Currents' sign, and could see why. It looked like currents from each side of the Point converged at the tip, likely the source of all the undertow warnings. She'd seen a lot of lakes in the Muskokas and Algonquin area, and Lake Erie from this vantage point looked as massive as an ocean.

Katrina snapped a lot of pictures with her little camera. She loved the quality of the pictures and didn't see much difference in what Stewart took with his big expensive one. Besides, she didn't have to change lenses or spend time focusing, and she could stash it in her purse or a pocket. Jake had wandered pretty far onto the little strip of sand that meandered into the lake. Katrina was less adventurous and stayed well back of the surrounding water, imagining a wave leaping up and pulling her helpless body under. She watched as Jake entered the water past the tip. She nervously took a quick picture of him, then began frantically waving at him to get out of the water.

Jake came jogging back after a couple of minutes.

"Isn't this just amazing!" He grabbed each of her hands and looked in her eyes. She saw the excitement raging in his. "Farthest south you can get, on the mainland anyway. Looking back at the park, when you're out there, it's kind of freaky. It's like you're standing on the lake." He looked like a little boy who'd just opened a new toy on his birthday.

Jake walked backwards with Katrina along the beach toward the shuttle pickup, avoiding the beaten path taken on the way there. He couldn't take his eyes off the point, even as it got more distant, and waited until the last possible moment to rejoin the trail. He finally snapped out of it on the shuttle.

"That was cool. I could have stayed there for hours, if we didn't have other things to do," and he glanced at his watch. "Looks like we've got a choice to make – boardwalk or theatre. You choose."

Katrina didn't like to have to choose. She wanted to do both, but realized they didn't have time. She could very easily take advantage of Jake's delirious state and make him sit through the movie, but deciding she could likely find the movie on the internet when she got home, she announced the boardwalk as their destination. Back at the Visitor's Centre, Katrina took a minute to run in and buy the 'Where Canada Begins' book. Clutching her purchase as she walked back to Jake, she finally noticed the beautiful picture of the Point on the cover – she was so enamoured by the title she hadn't noticed the picture.

Buckled up in the van, Jake steered the vehicle out of the parking lot. Katrina flipped off her footwear and placed her bare feet on the dash. She flipped on her camera and began browsing her photos. She'd taken more than she'd realized. She looked up at a moan by Jake.

"What's the matter?" Katrina asked.

"I just realized that all the pictures of me at the Point have me wearing Stewart's shirt. I look goofy."

"You look fine. Stop obsessing. You sound like a girl."

"Well, I'm going to stop and take it off as soon as there is someplace to turn into."

Katrina spotted the sign for the group campground. "Just pull in here. I can use the washroom. I forgot back at the Visitor's Centre." Jake turned into a short road with a handful of parking spaces on either side of the barricaded entrance to the campground. Two vehicles were parked.

"A black pickup truck!" Katrina shouted. "Do you think our guy's been hiding out here? Nobody would look out here for him!"

"Don't get your hopes up, but let's see if we can find the owner."

"I've really got to go pee first," Katrina stated, a little jump in her step. "Don't go spying around without me." A short trail through the trees led to the washrooms and the rest of the campground.

With Katrina gone, Jake found a pen and paper in the van and jotted down the licence plate. There was a good chance the owner had taken off to explore the park. Jake could give the plate to the local police to look into. He followed the trail into the common area where Katrina had headed. Jake's eyes panned his surroundings, getting a layout of his vicinity. A quaint campground, that's for sure. Maybe enough room for four or five tents in each area: Little Raccoon South and Little Raccoon North. Kids would love those names. He looked at his watch. It wasn't unusual for Katrina to take her time in a washroom. Whatever women did in there for so long, he had no idea. When it came to public places though, Katrina didn't usually dawdle. In and out, normally, with the out consisting of a grimace on her face, her arms bent at the elbows and tight to her sides, palms facing Jake as they waved quickly back and forth. The look of disgust preceded a description of the foul insides, be it the toilet, the sink, the floor, or all of the above. Complain as she would, Jake could not remember a time when she didn't take care of business. His friend's wife would make the poor sap drive her around until she found a place suitable for her waste – Jake always laughed to himself at the thought. So why was she taking so long? She was so anxious to get to sleuthing, as she called it. He didn't have to wait any longer for an answer.

Katrina poked her head around the brick wall obscuring the entrance to the women's bathroom. She waved frantically at him, mouthing something he couldn't make out. Walking toward her, he could read her lips saying 'Come here, come here.' Like he couldn't tell from her gesturing. "What's up?" he said with a barely raised voice.

"SHHHH," Katrina said back, putting her index finger up to her mouth.

Jake mimicked her quiet sign with his finger. As he got within reach, she grabbed his arm and pulled Jake behind the wall.

"What's up?" He adjusted his eyes as he moved into the shadows.

"Aunt Verna. She's here!"

"You saw her?" Jake turned back to look at the parking lot. "Where is she?"

"Here. I mean here, in the restroom. She won't come out to talk to you."

"So I'm supposed to go into the women's restroom to talk to her?"

"Yes. Do you mind?"

"No, it doesn't bother me. I've had to do it before."

"You have?" Katrina looked bothered by this revelation.

"Sure, it happens on the job. After you," and Jake neatly bowed. Inside the door, Jake picked up the yellow 'Closed for Cleaning' sign, placed it outside the door, and turned the deadbolt.

"Hello, Jake. How are you?" said the missing aunt.

Jake looked at the woman before him and barely recognized her. No Christmas sweater for starters. A floppy hat protecting her face and dressed in dreary grey to boot. He barely knew her up close and would never have picked her out at a distance. They could have walked right by her in the campground and not recognized her. Of course, that was the point.

"More importantly, Verna, how are you? Cathy's been worried."

"Drinking herself into a coma to cope, I hope," she laughed.

They're definitely related, Jake thought. "The point is everyone's been looking for you. A lot of people think you're dead. They found your sweater floating in the lake."

"Oh dear! I didn't mean that to happen. I folded it neatly and stashed it next to the building on the pier."

"Even without the sweater, don't you think people would worry when you disappeared?" Jake asked her.

"I just thought they'd assume I'd taken off without notice again." She looked at Katrina and smiled. "I'm told I'm a little eccentric at times. Figured everyone would shrug their shoulders and go on with their lives."

"Maybe that would be the case if you didn't have out of town visitors," Jake replied.

"And with a detective amongst those visitors, didn't you think he'd investigate?" Katrina asked.

"I suppose. Didn't think that much about it."

"So what *are* you doing out here? Who are you hiding from?" Jake leaned forward as he would to question a suspect. Katrina put a hand on his shoulder to remind him he wasn't on duty and that Aunt Verna wasn't guilty of anything, except maybe bad judgment.

"I am hiding, that's for sure. I've been working with an investigator on a case."

"What kind of case?" Jake asked.

"I can't tell you. He made me promise. Said it would put other people in danger if I said anything to anybody. That's why I'm in hiding. He thought they were closing in on me and that I was in – what did he call it?" She paused briefly and closed her eyes to remember. "Imminent danger, that's it," and her eyes popped open. "Imminent danger. I was in imminent danger."

"From who?" Jake asked.

"From whom," Aunt Verna corrected him.

Jake rolled his eyes. "Okay, from whom?" taking care to emphasize the letter *m*.

"The bad guys, of course."

"Yes, but who are the bad guys?"

"I can't tell you that either. He says it will jeopardize his investigation."

"Got it. So who's this investigator?"

"I can't tell you his name. It would …"

"Yes, I know. Jeopardize the investigation," Jake finished for her. "Can you at least confirm it's the guy in the black pickup truck? It's the only lead we've had. One of your employees told us about a customer at the drive-thru in the same kind of truck."

Verna looked down at her feet.

Jake took that as a yes. He realized his questions were getting him nowhere, so he was glad when Katrina stepped forward. Maybe Verna would open up to another woman.

Katrina bent down slightly to get Aunt Verna to look back. "Can you at least give us a hint about the investigation?"

Verna again looked down at her feet. "Wineries."

"What about the wineries?" Katrina asked.

"I've said too much already. I hope I haven't hurt his investigation."

Jake knew the conversation had ended. Just as well too, as someone pounded on the door.

"I need to get in there!" yelled a woman from outside.

"Just a minute," Jake hollered back, hoping the sound of a man's voice would deter the woman at the door.

"I'm not shy," she answered. "And I have to go really bad!"

"I think we're done in here anyway," Jake replied. "We'll let Cathy and the authorities know you're okay."

"No," and Verna grabbed Jake's hand. "He just needs twenty-four more hours. That's all. If you say anything, word might get out."

"I doubt the police will say anything," Jake said.

"It's a small town, Jake. Everything gets out. You just can't take the chance." Verna's furrowed brows expressed visibly her concern with the idea that the investigation would get tipped off.

"Okay. Twenty-four hours. But you know I'm breaking rules by not saying anything about an active investigation."

"I understand, and I'm very thankful."

"You said just a minute!" screamed the woman from outside.

Jake released the deadbolt and opened the door. The red-faced woman almost knocked him over in her haste to use the nearest stall. Aunt Verna hugged Katrina goodbye, and thanked Jake for his confidence.

Walking back to the van, they saw the parking lot no longer had a black pickup occupying a spot. Jake put the keys in the ignition, but stopped short of starting the vehicle.

"What are you thinking?" Katrina asked him.

"I'm thinking, how is it you are always right about these things?"

"I didn't know she was hiding. I was hoping she'd been kidnapped, remember? Well, not hoping she was kidnapped, but you know what I mean. That was the best chance I thought that she'd still be alive."

"No, I mean about the wineries connection to her disappearance."

"Oh, that. Just a feeling."

"I need to start listening to your feelings more."

"You think?"

30 *Wine Contest*

Returning to Aunt Verna's home, Katrina was, in a way, happy that Cathy was laid up. Katrina knew she had a bad poker face, and she would certainly give away the secret of their Aunt Verna sighting. How could she keep this from her best friend? Certainly it was wrong. But what if saying something would actually put Aunt Verna's life in danger? That would certainly be wrong too. Two wrongs don't make a right – but what the heck did that mean in this situation?

Stewart came outside to where Katrina and Jake sat, Jake straining over his now mangled mind map diagram.

"She's sleeping now," Stewart said with a tone of relief. He looked at his watch. "She'll likely be out until about four. Are we heading down to the wine contest?"

Katrina looked at him, appalled. "You're going to leave her? After what she's been through?"

"Yes, she encouraged it. Besides, she hates pampering when she's sick."

"She's not sick. She was mugged."

"I stand corrected. She hates pampering after she's mugged." Jake laughed.

"It's not funny," Katrina protested. "She's hurt in there," she said, glaring at Jake and pointing toward the house.

"Yes, I'm aware of that," Stewart replied in defence of Jake. "And the best thing for her is sleep. She just took another Tylenol 3 and is in dreamland. She's got her cell phone at her side and we can be back in ten minutes if she needs anything, which I doubt."

"Unless you want to stay with her," Jake offered to Katrina. He knew she didn't. She was as anxious as Jake to get down to the wine judging contest and sniff out more leads, or see if the mystery investigator made an appearance. She would love to talk to him, if given the chance.

"No, Stewart's right," she conceded.

"I am? Yes, I am," Stewart proclaimed, sticking out his chest as only men do upon the sudden revelation that they are right about something. "And I've hidden the Tylenol 3 so she doesn't take anymore until we get back."

Jake folded up his paper and looked at his watch. "Ten minutes good for you?"

"I'm ready now," Stewart responded. "Where are Tate and Virus?"

"Virus?" Jake asked.

"Sorry, Cathy's nickname for her this weekend. Something about the way she's acting. I try to block out all that girl talk."

Katrina smirked.

"Whatever," Jake replied. "Are they coming with?"

"I'll ask. I see Tate in the kitchen now. Meet you out front in ten, unless she needs a few more minutes to get ready. I know Tate doesn't waste any time prepping."

Jake laughed. "I don't know many pot-heads that are meticulous groomers."

Twelve minutes later, the five of them were buckled up in the van as it backed out of Aunt Verna's driveway. Stewart held up his cell phone to Katrina to show that he was ready in case Cathy called.

Looking around the festival grounds, you couldn't tell it held yesterday's tomato stomp or fight. The area reminded her of the park in Pipton after the circus had rolled through town. A large patch of flattened grass lingered as the only evidence something had occurred. The septic truck and its crew had suctioned up the entire tomato mess with the proficiency of a flock of Molly Maids.

The cordoned-off area for serving alcoholic beverages greatly expanded at the back of the bar, on the hill overlooking the beach. On previously vacant park space stood new booths, each hosting a local winery. They extended from where the two sponsor wineries had been set up all weekend. Jake told Katrina that he expected all the winery owners to be at the event, due to the judging and the chance to snag an award. It would be the perfect place for Aunt Verna's investigator to close his case. She tingled with excitement, though secretly hoping she and Jake could figure it out first or provide the investigator with a key piece of evidence to solve the case. One slight problem though – they didn't know the specifics of the case that the investigator laboured over, except that it involved wineries. She bet that Evan and Canawine were at the centre of it though.

Iris and Stewart wasted no time finding the ticket booth and purchasing a strip each. The sign above the ticket booths said each ticket could be exchanged for a two ounce sample. Katrina looked at the sign again. Why was it, she wondered, that bars still spoke in terms of ounces when everything else used metric? She never heard of a bar asking you if you wanted the five hundred millilitre draught or the seven hundred and fifty millilitre draught. And a shot was an ounce, not thirty or forty millilitres, or whatever it equalled. Yet all the beer and wine bottles, and boxes in Canawine's case, had millilitres on the labels. Were they hanging on for the sake of the older generation, or was it for the American tourists – like changing the name of Brewer's Retail to The Beer Store. And why didn't the LCBO follow suit and change their name to The Liquor Store or The Booze Box?

Katrina listened as Stewart informed the group of his plan to sample as many wines as possible. She remembered the winery tour and how he would go through his routine with each taste. He even requested a separate glass to discard the sample after he ran it over his palate. Katrina figured it was a way to avoid getting drunk. Since Stewart's tasting usually consisted of just a taste, Cathy happily obliged by finishing the remainder of the sample. Katrina guessed he'd just be pitching the leftovers today. She wondered if Wally the Wino would drink Stewart's jettisoned mouthfuls, given the chance. It would be truly gross, but if an alcoholic like Wally was desperate for a buzz, how far would he go?

Contrary to Stewart, Iris usually drank each glass down. And based on the roll of tickets, Iris planned on getting hammered. Katrina knew this would be a turn-off for Jake, so she hoped Iris got wasted. *Was that being too mean?* Katrina was certainly surprised, however, when Iris handed Jake, Tate, and Katrina a couple of tickets each. "My treat" was all Iris said. Katrina kicked herself for thinking spiteful thoughts. Her mother always told her to 'think the best of people until they proved otherwise to you personally.' Which usually led to 'form your own opinion and don't take the word of others.' Good advice, Katrina thought, but sometimes hard to follow.

"All right, then," Stewart said. "Do we start at the right or the left?"

"Left," said Jake. "Don and Faith are set up at the far right. We can save them for last. You've had a taste of most of their wines already."

"Excellent reasoning, Jake," Stewart replied. "Port side it is. I wonder if any of these wineries make a nice bold Port."

Walking over to one of the host wineries at the far left, one they hadn't tried yet (or even heard of), Jake held Katrina back as they got halfway there. Quietly, he told her his plan.

"I need you to drink part of your samples and then switch glasses with me. I want it to look like I'm just one of the crowd, having a good time tasting like everyone else."

"Okay, but won't I get wasted that way?"

"You can take a few sips, switch glasses, and then dump the full one when no one is looking."

"Why can't you do that?"

"Because I'm going to be asking a lot of questions, so the winery owners will be watching me. I'll look suspicious if I'm not drinking."

"Can't you just say you're the designated driver?"

"People are friendlier if you buy their product and say nice things about it. I can't do that if they know I'm not drinking."

Katrina didn't buy his logic, but agreed to go along with his idea. She dreaded it would be her that ended up hammered and disgusting Jake. If only she had Cathy's tolerance for booze.

Jake let Stewart do most of the talking at the first booth, but did ask a few polite questions about where they were located and how many bottles a year they produced. The wine glass switcheroo with Katrina worked perfectly, at least for Jake. Katrina already had a mild buzz and they stood in front of the first tent.

The second booth belonged to Migration Route, the winery owned by Pierre Antonio. Katrina and Jake had never met him and talked to him. Katrina's only encounter had occurred at the store when she witnessed Pierre and Don getting into it about the sale of the wineries.

"Pierre Antonio, it is a pleasure to meet you," Jake said as one of the booth workers took his ticket and poured him a glass of Cabernet. Katrina looked at Jake, remembering mixing beer and liquor was not good, but unsure if the same held true with mixing red and white wine.

It likely didn't matter. With about ten more tents to go, the quantity alone would leave her wrecked tomorrow.

"And you are one of Verna's guests from out of town, are you not? The detective, I believe," Pierre responded to Jake. Katrina saw Jake's look of surprise at the recognition. So much for Jake's plan of blending in with the crowd. Verna certainly nailed it about a small town knowing everyone's business. Or perhaps Pierre had something to hide and wasn't above snooping around?

"That's correct. I'm Jake," and he shook hands with Pierre. "And this is Katrina."

"Nice to meet you," Pierre replied with a broad smile. Katrina looked closely at the man standing behind the display of Migration Route's products. He didn't look anything like the man she saw the other day, when he had a little dark storm cloud hanging over his head like you see in cartoons. He'd definitely turned his frown upside down, as her grade four teacher used to instruct their class from time to time.

Pierre added, "Do you have any update on Verna's whereabouts? Is she okay?"

Katrina thought he looked sincere, but it was hard for her to tell sometimes when she first met someone. She didn't have Jake's detective instinct, or the natural instinct that many dogs have about judging people.

Jake replied, "No update. Still missing. We've got our fingers crossed she's okay."

"As we all do. She's a wonderful person." Pierre looked at Jake's still-full glass. "Aren't you going to try my wine? I think the

Cabernet is one of my best ever. I really think it has a shot at an award this year."

Jake looked at his glass and then Katrina. He'd talked so much that he hadn't paused to switch glasses with Katrina, who'd done her part and drank half her glass.

"Oh, yes. Too busy chatting." Jake took a small sip and swished it around his mouth, mimicking Stewart.

"Are you a connoisseur, monsieur?" Pierre asked.

"No, just something I picked up watching my friend Stewart here. He's the one with the picky palate."

"And Stewart, what do you think of my Cabernet?"

"Smooth. Oaky with a taste of berry, but I'm not exactly sure which berry. Blueberries, perhaps?"

"Very good. It's a seventy-thirty mix of blueberry and raspberry, so I suppose the blueberry is more prevalent to most taste buds. I'm glad you enjoyed it."

"Will this be your last vintage, if I may be so bold?" Jake asked.

The bluntness of the question startled Pierre. Katrina could see the man carefully considering his response.

"One never knows in this business. The economy is tough and the wine business tougher. It's all about name recognition in the wine business. Winning even a small contest like this one can make all the difference to a small winery like mine."

Katrina thought it interesting how Pierre answered from a perspective of losing the winery, versus selling it to Canawine. She waited for Jake to ask about the mega winery, but no question came as he pretended to take another drink of his wine. Normally too shy to ask forward questions, she stepped out of personality and blurted out her inquiry.

"And what about your sale to Canawine?"

"What about it?" Pierre asked nonchalantly.

Katrina expected an answer, not another question. And she absolutely expected a startled look, but none appeared. Caught off guard, she didn't know what to ask. Fortunately, Jake did.

"You threatened Don if he didn't sell. What if he won't?"

Pierre stood up straight and took a deep breath, trying to manage his emotions. "Look, I apologized to Don just this morning. I've got a bit of a temper that sometimes gets the best of me. He accepted and we're moving on."

"And that's it?" Katrina asked.

"That's it. Have a good day." With that, Pierre turned and walked away, pretending to be busy by moving some cases around at the back of the tent.

"I can take a hint," Jake said to Katrina, pitching his plastic glass and the remaining contents into a nearby garbage can.

"Recycle, Jake. There's a blue bin right beside it." In the midst of the discussion, Katrina had finished her sample without realizing it. She placed her plastic glass into the round opening of the tall blue recycle can.

Stewart, Iris, and Tate had already finished with the next booth, and were moving toward the next in line. Jake excused himself, spotting one of the local OPP officers across the open area. He told Katrina that he would ask about any updates on Verna, and not reveal what they knew about her or the mysterious investigation in process. Katrina also excused herself to use the ladies room, although she really needed a pretext to avoid drinking more wine. Four ounces and she was already feeling inebriated. *Was she that lame?* It must be due to how much they all drank last night. It must still be in her system and making the new wine react faster. Which reminded her of a theory one of her grade school friends had about using hot water to make ice cubes. The friend's theory was something about the hot water 'picking up speed' in the freezing process as it went, thereby freezing faster than cold water. Didn't make any sense to Katrina, but she wasn't a scientist.

When Katrina returned from the restroom, her companions, minus Jake, were standing in the middle of the area talking. Tate had a Coke and Iris a bottle of water.

"Just thought we'd take a break," Tate explained. "Those glasses are small, but five of those back to back in this heat and I needed a little detoxing."

"You always need a little detoxing," a snarky Iris replied.

"And," Stewart added before Tate could retaliate, "next up is Windmill Farms and we know Jake wants to ask some questions there."

"Right you are," Jake said, returning to the fold. "Did any of you notice who just visited with Marco?"

The whole group turned to look at the Windmill Farms booth.

"He's not there anymore," Jake said. "But could you get any more obvious?" He waited until they turned to face him again. "Evan Batch was lurking in the shadows at the back of the tent."

"I wonder what Evan is up to," Katrina said.

"Don't know, but let's go see what Marco is up to," Jake replied.

One of the girls behind the Windmill Farms counter recognized Katrina as they approached.

"I knew you'd like the Riesling! Back for more, are you?"

Katrina apologetically said, "We haven't had a chance to try it yet."

"Well, here's your chance now. Plus you brought friends too! That's great!"

As she poured the last of their samples, Marco came up from behind her and patted her butt. Katrina noticed the girl didn't flinch. Sadly the girl had likely become used to her boss's unethical behaviour.

"Hey, detective guy and hot girlfriend! How ya doin' today?" Marco stood with his arm around the young lady.

"Not as good as you, by the looks of it," Jake replied.

"What's not to be happy about? The sun is shining, we're at a party, and I'm going to win some awards for my vintages."

"So you're not concerned at all about an investigation?" Jake asked him.

Marco pulled his arm away from his young hostess. "They're all nineteen. I've got copies of their ID. I'd never do them otherwise."

"I'm not talking about your lust for your staff. I mean the other thing."

Marco fidgeted anxiously, shifting the weight awkwardly from his prosthetic leg. Suddenly it had gotten too warm for the owner of Windmill Farms, and little droplets of sweat formed on his brow. "I don't know what you're talking about. I never heard of no investigation. I think you're blowing smoke outta your ass, is what I think."

"Maybe I am, Marco. Maybe I'm not." Jake placed his empty cup on the table in front of him and thanked the young assistant. "I'll see you later, Marco."

Katrina leaned forward and whispered to the girl who had greeted her. "I'd get another job if I were you. Your boss shouldn't be grabbing your butt." Katrina then scurried to catch up to Jake.

"Well Marco seemed awfully nervous when you mentioned the 'other thing,' didn't he? What is the 'other thing,' by the way?"

"Don't know, but he doesn't know that. But now I know he's got a guilty conscience about something."

"Smart, Jake."

"Thanks. Next stop is Nate at Essex County Cellars. Let's see if he's paranoid about anything."

Katrina happily realized that she'd finally run out of tickets. Even the one that Jake had given her when he abandoned the glass switching scheme had been used. Her head was swimming in wine. She'd passed buzzed about two samples ago. There were a few couples waiting to be served as Katrina and company arrived at the station for

Essex County Cellars. She looked around while in line, but couldn't see Nate anywhere. He wasn't easy to miss.

Reaching the front of the line, Stewart handed over two of his tickets.

"What would you like, Katrina? Chardonnay sound good?"

Katrina held up a hand like a stop sign. "Nothing for me, but thanks, Stewart."

"Rubbish. Cathy will tan my hide if I don't buy you at least one drink, no matter how small the glass. Chardonnay it is."

So much for getting out of the deep end of the alcohol swimming pool, Katrina thought. She'd just have to nurse it or simply carry it around with her.

"Hi, Deb. Where's Nate? I wanted to ask him a couple of questions," Jake inquired.

"He's not here. He hates these events. He thinks the judging is only slightly better than figure skating. You know, the winner is decided ahead of time. More a popularity contest for the winery owners, really."

"Does he think other wineries are bribing the judges?" Katrina asked as she received her Chardonnay.

"I doubt that. At least not with money. Favours, maybe," Deb replied. "So, Nate's minding the store at home. What did you want to ask him about?"

"I have just a few more questions about Evan and Canawine."

"Fire away. I should be able to answer your questions."

"Okay. How many times has Evan been in this area in the past three months?"

"Let me think. I'm not positive, but I'd say three. No, make that four. There was one visit we heard about but he didn't stop in to see us. Nate was pissed at first at the slight, but then he found out Evan had just done a day trip, with no stay over."

"Why, does Evan stay with you guys when he comes to town?" Katrina asked nervously, sipping her wine.

"Yes, every time but that one trip. Didn't Nate tell you that?"

"No," both Katrina and Jake replied.

"Evan's been staying with us all weekend, as a matter of fact." Deb surprised Katrina and Jake with this revelation. Jake tried to downplay his surprise.

"Who'd Evan visit on that day trip, do you know?"

"I think Evan told Nate he was just down looking into permits and zoning stuff. Evan apparently didn't visit any of the wineries."

"Thanks again." Jake started to walk away, but stopped and asked another question. "Has Evan made any more progress with his deal?"

"He hasn't said as much, but he's been scurrying around here all day as excited as a squirrel with a fresh acorn."

Jake guided Katrina away from the booths. Stewart, Iris, and Tate remained sampling and chatting it up with Deb.

"Stay right where you are," Jake told Katrina. "I'm watching Evan over your shoulder. He's over skulking around Pierre's booth."

Katrina instinctively turned to look, but stopped with Jake's heeding of "Don't look!"

"What do you think Evan's up to?" Katrina asked, fighting the urge to peek.

"I'm not sure. I'm guessing he's trying to seal his deal. I haven't seen him at Don and Faith's booth yet, but I wasn't looking for him earlier. If he made a deal with them, Evan may just be spreading the good news to the others. It could explain why both Marco and Pierre seemed so happy. They're about to come into a bunch of money."

"I just don't believe Don would sell," Katrina protested.

"Maybe he didn't have a choice."

"But we know Evan didn't have Aunt Verna kidnapped."

"But Don and Faith don't know that. I know I said before that a kidnapper wouldn't do that because they'd trace the land sale back to them. But what if Evan said he would harm Verna if Don didn't sign the deal? Nothing could be traced back to Evan because he didn't actually kidnap Verna. He's just leveraging that Don *thinks* he did. Extortion wouldn't stick as it would be word against word."

"That would be very clever. Evan can't be convicted because he committed no crime. What about bugging Don to catch Evan making the threat?"

"Too late. If that's Evan's plan and the deal is done, the threat's been made."

"So what can we do?"

"Well," Jake paused, "first we need to talk to Don and Faith. We've just done a whole lot of speculating without any proof."

Katrina noticed her empty wine glass. She'd drunk it all without realizing during the excitement. She looked around for a recycle bin. Jake noticed her and suggested she toss it when they got to County Estate Vineyard's tent. Midway across the trampled grassy area, a voice rang out through some speakers by the judging table.

"Ladies and gentleman, the judging is complete! We will compile the results, and announce the winners in all categories in about ten minutes. Please grab your favourite sample, or samples if you wish, and gather around the stage area. I'm sure you'll want to toast the winners! We also ask that the representatives from each winery come up now and be seated in the section cordoned off in front of the stage. Thank you everyone, and good luck!"

"Shit," Jake mumbled, as he looked at the County Estates Vineyard booth. "We won't get to talk to them now until afterward."

"Maybe we will," Katrina said. "Faith's giving Don a kiss for luck."

"And?"

"And it means he's going up and she's staying behind. We can at least talk to Faith."

Nearing their destination booth, they were taken aback by the sudden crowd in front of them.

"I guess everyone's trying to get their samples for toasting," Katrina said.

"A lot of good it does us. We'll never get to talk to Faith, and I don't want to ask her my questions in front of her customers. Do you want a glass of wine for the awards ceremony?"

"Please, no!" Katrina exclaimed. "How about you take me over to the concession stand and get me a soft drink or water?"

"Sure, I could use a little sugar too," Jake replied.

"I can take care of that," Katrina said, stopping her boyfriend and planting a kiss on him.

Jake blushed with embarrassment. The flow of people to the stage went by them as they kissed. Katrina avoided displaying affection in public, but the wine had taken its toll on her inhibitions, at least partially.

"What's the matter, big fella," Katrina teased Jake. Half singing, she added, "won't you lay me down in the tall grass and let me do my stuff?" She giggled as she finished, never having seen Jake blush this way. "Relax, there's no tall grass here. It's flatter than a pancake."

"We'd better get those drinks," Jake said, his face returning to its natural colour.

Everyone crowded the winery stands, which meant short concession lines. Seeing the food at the concession, Katrina suddenly had the munchies. Imploring Jake to get some chips, she almost ripped open the bag to get at the contents.

"Parched and famished, I see," said Jake as he witnessed Katrina scarfing and guzzling. Her usual lady-like manners were out the window, at least for a few minutes.

"What?" Katrina muffled with a semi-full mouth.

"Nothing. Just wish I had Stewart's camera, that's all."

"Want some?" Katrina offered the near empty bag of chips to Jake. A few chips the size of fingernails remained.

"No, you can finish them," Jake laughed.

Katrina tipped the bag up in the air to get every last crumb, holding it upright for a few seconds and shaking it in the hope that one last chip clung onto the bottom. Giving up, she tossed the empty package in the garbage. Tilting her plastic pop cup, she waited for the final few drops to descend to her mouth, before pitching the cup in the adjacent recycle bin. Turning back to Jake, something in the background caught her eye.

"Look! It's Don, speaking with Evan."

Jake looked and motioned for Katrina to walk closer with him. They were still far away when they saw Don smiling and shaking hands with Evan, who likely couldn't grin any wider without his face exploding. Katrina couldn't believe her eyes.

"I never thought Don would sell! He loves that place so much," she said.

"Me neither. I'm stunned. The way Don talked about it being their dream and wanting to leave the winery to their daughter. I would have never guessed."

"Another wrinkle to your mind map, eh?" Katrina joked.

"Wrinkle? Might as well scribble over the whole damn thing with black crayon. There are always paths that you take to be certain truths, and your theories take tangents from there. But when the original path is wrong, those tangents all become meaningless."

"It doesn't mean Don is involved in the winery investigation," Katrina tried to assure him his thought process was not a complete waste.

"I don't know," Jake said, rubbing his hand on his hair. "I suppose. After all, Don could be getting involved without knowing that Evan's a crook."

"," she cautioned.

"Who else could it be? He's the one with the most to gain," Jake replied.

"I think all the wineries have a lot to gain too – money, at least. And the town would likely gain as well, with another large employer."

"I agree the bought out winery owners will each make their fortune," Jake said.

Before they could continue, a tapping noise and a blowing sound came over the microphone, followed by the announcer's voice.

"All right! We have numerous awards to give out, so let's get to it, shall we? Mayor, if you wouldn't mind saying a few words."

Katrina whispered in Jake's ear. "The Mayor would have something to gain if Canawine located here. If Evan is bribing people, the Mayor would likely be near the top of the list. You know, get those permits through quickly and all that kind of stuff."

"Maybe," was all Jake said.

"Thanks everyone for coming to this year's festival. It's been a hugely successful weekend and we've been blessed with fantastic weather every day. I hope to see every one of you back next year!"

Some polite applause came from the gathered, and liquored, crowd. The mayor gave the microphone back to the host.

"Our first award is for After Dinner, Fortified, Late Harvest, or Fruit wines, namely the local Ice Wines. I'll announce the top three and you can all come up together for your awards."

"Too sweet for me," Jake said. "Like drinking syrup or something."

"A lot of people like it," Katrina replied.

"Third place for their Reserve Port is Evergreen Mills, second place is Birchtree Woods for their Muscat, and the winner is Pelee Vines Winery for their Vines Ice Wine!"

"All our suspects were shut out of that one," Katrina stated.

"I don't know if any of them even make Ice Wine, do you?" Jake asked.

Katrina shook her head. She watched the handshakes and medals exchange hands.

"Our next couple of awards will be presented by one of our sponsors. I personally want to thank him for his support of this event, Mr. Evan Batch."

Evan confidently shook the Mayor's hand on his way to the microphone, grinning ear to ear.

"Thank you. The first award that I am presenting is for Red Blends, red wines consisting of two or more grapes. There was a lot of good competition in this group. In third place, for their Cabernet Merlot, Essex County Cellars. In second place, for their Malbec Shiraz,

Migration Route Winery, and the winner, for their Meritage, County Estates Vineyard. Let's have a hand for our winners!"

As the three owners got up to receive their rewards, Katrina aired her suspicion with Jake.

"Coincidence? All three are wineries that Evan's looking to buy and he presents the award."

"Maybe that's why we saw him shaking Don's hand. Evan was just giving Don the news in advance."

"Perhaps," Katrina said, unconvinced. "But I bet there's more to it than that."

"Even Don and Pierre are hugging up there, like nothing ever happened. I just don't get it."

"Maybe they made up. Don't guys fight and then make up?"

"I don't think ' make up' is the right term. Guys fight then tolerate each other."

"Well, maybe they're tolerating each other because they're in a public place," Katrina offered.

"Likely what it is," Jake replied. "Or they struck a deal with Evan and they're all buddy-buddy now."

"Do you think Evan bought the results? You, know, bribed the judges?" Katrina asked.

"I thought of that, but wondered what there was to gain. If he buys them out, their name brands will most likely die out as they just produce wine for Canawine's brands. Seems like a waste of money to promote their brands by buying off judges."

"Yeah, I guess so," Katrina said dejectedly.

Evan picked up the microphone and began to announce the next awards. These medals were to be handed out for Blended Whites, the last award prior to the Wine of the Year award. "And our winners for Blended Whites are…" and he paused for a second. "I hope some of you gentleman didn't get too comfortable in your seats. Third place for their Sauvignon Blanc is Windmill Farms. Second goes to County Estate Vineyards for their County Estate White. And the winner of the Blended Whites, for their Sauvignon Blanc is Migration Route!"

"This is looking mighty fishy," Jake agreed with Katrina's earlier assessment.

"They do make good wines," Katrina stated.

"You should know. I think you tried most of them today."

Katrina looked at Jake and put her hands on her hips. "That's not fair. You asked me to drink them so you wouldn't have to. I can't help it if I can't hold my liquor."

"Relax, I didn't mean anything by it. I just meant we visited a lot of tents."

"Okay."

"I just can't figure out what Evan is up to. Is he part of some fraud, and that's what's the investigation's about? I doubt the Ontario Ministry of Agriculture would go to this much trouble over fixing a wine contest. Especially this contest – it can mean that much of a difference to the sales of a small winery. So I don't think Evan could be getting a kick-back from the winery owners for them winning."

"You are just rambling all over the place, Jake." Katrina looked at him. "Give me your mind map."

"Why?"

"Just give me your mind map."

Jake pulled the mangled piece of paper from his back pocket. "I told you this is full of bad assumptions that make it invalid."

"I know that." Katrina unfolded the doodle fest and held it up. "See this mess? This is what your brain is like right now. Your thoughts are running all over the place, with no order at all." She put her hands on Jake's shoulders. "You need to stop just blurting out every opinion or possibility. That's what I do." This evoked a smile from her young detective. "You, on the other hand, use reason and logic to figure things out. Slow that express train in your brain down for a few minutes and think before blurting out any more wild ideas. Got it?"

"Got it.

The host had picked up the microphone, and looking to see that all the vintners had returned to their seats, began his next announcement.

"Well deserved to all winners. Now the moment you've waited for! We had a superb field of entries for our Wine of the Year category. Personally, I've had a bottle or two of all of the wines submitted for this prestigious award. With the quality of wines that our local wineries are producing, I may end up becoming a drunk!"

A heckler from the crowd yelled out, "What do you mean *may end up a drunk*, John? You're already there!"

The announcer laughed. "My brother Tom, everyone. All I can say is it takes one to know one."

The crowd enjoyed the good humoured jousting.

"Now if I can get back to business without further interruption from my little brother, I'm pleased to announce the entries. If you could each stand when I call your name, and show off a bottle of your prized wine. From Windmill Farms, Marco Genoso, and his Windmill Farms Riesling."

Applause greeted Marco as he stood, raising a bottle of his finest high above his head. He let out a couple of woo-hoo's and fist pumps as he did. Katrina thought how this type of behaviour would be thought as very boorish by Stewart and his fellow wine snobs.

"From Migration Route, Pierre Antonio and his Migration Merlot."

Katrina was pleased to see Pierre cleaned up and sober looking. He held up his wine in front of his face, obviously proud of his product but not putting on a frat house display.

"From Pelee Vines Vineyard, Tomas Svengard, and with a wine that has already won an award today, his Vines Ice Wine."

Katrina and Jake had edged up to the front of the crowd. She looked around the spectators, many of whom cheered. Some of the crowd sat their glasses down to applaud. A guy a few feet away tried to hold his plastic wine glass in his teeth so he could applaud, and ended up with most of the grape beverage on his chest.

"From Essex County Cellars, Nate South and his Cellar Chardonnay."

Katrina realized they hadn't bought any of Nate's and Deb's wine to take home. She'd tried a glass of the Chardonnay earlier in the day, but by then she'd had so much wine that the glass could have contained vinegar and she wouldn't have noticed. She'd have to pick up a bottle of their Chardonnay before leaving so she could try it at home.

"And last, but not least, from County Estates Vineyards, Don and Faith, and their CEV Meritage, also a winner already today."

Katrina hadn't noticed Deb slip into the seating area to join Don. They both beamed from ear to ear. They were definitely living the dream and Katrina felt happy for them, so much so that she felt a tear escape. She really was a mush puppy at times. She could understand why they wouldn't want to sell. So why the change of heart?

"Let's give them all a round of applause." The announcer set down the microphone and clapped along with the crowd. "All right," and the man took three envelopes from an assistant. "The bronze medal winner for Wine of the Year … Windmill Farms Riesling, Marco Genoso, Windmill Farms!"

Katrina clapped politely, while Marco's display didn't resemble anything polite or humble. He jumped up and down like he'd won the lottery, more 'woo-hoos', fist pumping, and yelling 'effin right!.' Katrina assumed he had to be intoxicated. She also marvelled at how well a guy with one artificial limb could jump. She could tell the announcer at the front was embarrassed by Marco's display, but he still shook hands and presented the medal to the third place winner.

"Well, someone is certainly happy," the host joked. "Just think if he'd won the gold medal."

Katrina laughed along with the others watching.

"Now, the sliver medal winner." The announcer blushed. "I mean *silver* medal winner," and he tore open the envelope. "Migration Merlot! Pierre Antonio and Migration Route Winery."

Quite contrary to Marco, Pierre's expression showed complete surprise. He stayed seated, like the announcer had called someone else's name. Katrina wondered if maybe he was drunk after all.

"Pierre, come get your silver medal!" the announcer called out.

Pierre stood up, and even from five metres away where Katrina stood, she could see his hands shaking. The bottle of Merlot in his right hand moved quickly from side to side, like a wine pendulum. As the announcer reached out his right hand to shake, Pierre extended his hand, bottle of Merlot still firmly in grasp.

"A little nervous, Pierre?" the announcer joked.

"Sorry," Pierre replied, shifting the bottle to his left hand and shaking hands. The announcer draped the medal around Pierre's neck. Pierre touched the hanging trophy and stared at it.

The announcer whispered, "Take your seat, Pierre. I have to announce the gold medal." Pierre looked up, embarrassed, then turned and took his place.

"I'd like to thank all of our sponsors, and forgive me if I forget a few, Shoppers, Tim's, Zehr's, Canadian Tire, and Heinz. And of course our winery sponsors, Canawine and Pelee Vines Vineyards. The gold medal, and Wine of the Year goes to..." and he paused to extract the winner's name from the last envelope, "CEV Meritage, County Estates Vineyard! Don and Faith!"

Don and Faith stood, pausing to hug before claiming their prize. Both grinned as they came forward, hand in hand. The announcer shook Don's hand before hugging Faith.

"Would you like to say a few words?" the announcer asked, holding the microphone out for Don to speak into.

"Oh, sure," Don said, rubbing his chin as he thought about what to say. "First, I'd like to thank my lovely wife, Faith. My best friend, my soul mate, and my lover."

Katrina smiled at the reference to a song by a local musician friend of Don's that he had played for them on Friday night. She listened as Don continued.

"It's been a remarkable few years. I want to thank the entire community for your support, and look forward to what lies ahead. Thanks!" Don stepped away from the microphone and hugged Faith again.

Katrina didn't notice Evan re-approach the front, but he yanked the microphone out of the announcer's hand and began to talk.

"As a sponsor of today's wine judging, Canawine is thrilled with the community participation in this event. Give yourselves a round of applause."

There were a few random claps. Evan continued undaunted.

"We are especially thrilled with the quality of the wines that we've seen here today. We are even more thrilled with all three winners of the Wine of the Year contest."

Katrina knew the bomb was going to drop.

"Canawine," Evan went on, "is extremely pleased to announce the pending acquisition of Windmill Farms, Migration Route, and Essex County Cellars, as well as a partnership with County Estates Vineyards."

A rumble of murmurs bounced around the crowd. The timing of the announcement astonished Katrina. Talk about stealing the spotlight and grabbing glory from the winners. She looked at the owners of the mentioned wineries and they all looked stunned by the timing.

Jake stood very quiet during the whole awards ceremony. Katrina wondered if he'd taken her little speech too far about not blurting out every little thought that came to his head.

"So they're all involved," Jake said. "I have to admit I'm surprised. But then again, I likely should have seen it coming. Everyone has their number, someone once said. I guess Evan finally found Don's."

Evan stood his ground, clenching the microphone.

"Canawine, and myself personally, look forward to building a strong relationship with Leamington and the surrounding communities. We look forward to bringing new jobs to the area."

He'd finally hit on something that the crowd thought worth applauding. The economic downturn in the area still affected some area residents, and they welcomed any news of jobs.

"Like that will ever happen," Jake doubted. "They'll consolidate and jobs will be lost. Companies like Canawine care more about profit than the community. It's all smoke and mirrors right now."

"Look!" Katrina exclaimed. She pointed, although her mother always told her that pointing was rude, to someone entering the cordoned- off winery area. It was Wally the Wino.

"This should be interesting," Jake laughed.

Wally's beggar slouch had vanished and he looked broader and taller than the previous times they'd met him. With the element of surprise on his side, he easily jerked the microphone out of Evan's hand and pushed him aside.

"I hate to interrupt the celebration," the wino started, "but I have some news."

A heckler in the crowd yelled out, "What, did you piss yourself again?"

"Funny. I suppose I deserve that," Wally responded.

Evan tried to regain control of the microphone, but Wally shrugged him aside. Evan hollered out, "Get this wino out of here!"

Katrina saw a couple of the local police approaching the area. Wally didn't see them off to his side.

"I have some news of my own," he began to say when a firm hand landed on his shoulder from one of the officers.

"Come with us, Wally. We'll let you sleep if off in one of our nice cells."

"Just a minute," Wally countered, and he reached inside his baggy pockets.

Not taking any chances, the officer grabbed Wally's arms and pushed him to the ground, face down. The officer began to cuff Wally.

During the scuffle, something fell out of Wally's pocket, and it wasn't a weapon as the officer had feared.

The other officer held up a badge and read it.

"Ministry of Agriculture, Investigative Unit."

"Will you let me up?" Wally asked.

"Sorry," the first officer replied, uncuffing his suspect and helping him off the ground.

"No problem. Would have done the same, I suppose," the investigator replied. "As I was about to say, I hate to throw a damp cloth on your party, but I'm here to make an arrest."

Evan backed slowly away from the group.

"Relax, Batch. It's not you. Not this time, anyway. As the officer here said, I'm an investigator from the Ministry of Agriculture." He put his hand over the mic and said something to the officers, who retreated and took position at the exits to the area. "During a regular inspection of water quality in the area, some irregularities were detected. Upon further investigation, we found someone tainted the water for personal gain. This tainting cost one man his job, almost twice, as the water filtered into grapes harvested by two local wineries, producing foul batches of wine. The latest incident occurred just this weekend and sealed the investigation."

Katrina wondered how Wally knew about Don's bad batch of Meritage. She then recalled how they'd spotted him in the ditch alongside the wineries. He looked to be drinking the water, but he had to be collecting samples. It wouldn't have taken much for Wally to sneak up to the barn at County Estates Vineyards and overhear Don and Romeo arguing about the foul tank full of wine.

"Officer," Wally added, "if you could be so kind to arrest Pierre Antonio for public endangerment. He knew the source of watering for both incidents, and seeded them with a high enough concentration of a home-made chemical to sour the fruit without affecting their growth. His background in science tipped me off, but the proof is always harder to obtain."

The officer secured Pierre with handcuffs, and stood holding the dejected winery owner.

"And, by accident I came across a case of fraud," the former wino continued. "During my investigation I came across someone using imported bottles and affixing labels of an expensive wine to them. Instead of selling his wine to the LCBO for a few dollars a bottle, he sold the same wine as Chateau Sur La Mer to the black market for over a hundred dollars a bottle. Arrest Marco Genoso, please."

Katrina and Jake looked at each other and laughed, thinking Stewart must be embarrassed beyond belief that his favourite wine was nothing more than a re-labeled local brand. It explained the inconsistency Don had mentioned. Before Katrina could finish laughing, Marco had bolted in their direction trying to flee the officer. Betrayed by his artificial limb and sensing escape as futile, he grabbed Katrina and pulled her over the short ring of yellow tape surrounding the winery owner's section. Marco had Katrina in a headlock, dragging her backwards through the shocked and parting crowd. He firmly struck the bottle of his Riesling against the asphalt parking lot, smashing the neck off the barrel. Marco then held the shard of glass near Katrina's neck.

"Don't move or I'll cut her!" He raised the neck of the bottle to the sky to show everyone the danger to Katrina.

"Just relax," Jake said, hands extended, palms down, trying to calm the attacker.

"You relax," Marco shot back. "You need to help me get out of here."

Jake looked around to see what the other officer was doing. Marco must have followed Jake's eyes, and swung around, tugging Katrina with him. The knife of glass came uncomfortably close to her face.

"Don't try anything funny!" Marco yelled at the officer. The crazed winery owner backed up to position himself with a view of both Jake and the officer. Anxiously, Marco oscillated to keep an eye on both men.

"Where are you going to go, Marco?" asked Jake.

"That's for me to know and you to find out," the assailant responded.

"Think about it," and Jake moved closer to the officer as he spoke, making it easier for Marco to see both of them. Hopefully this would lessen the chance of Katrina getting cut as Marco nervously jerked about. "You're not going to escape. You don't exactly blend in with your artificial leg and decided limp. Face it - you're going to jail."

"I'm not going to jail. I'll get away, with Katrina here as my hostage."

"You're going to jail. Do you want to go to minimum security for a year or two for fraud, or go to a high security joint for kidnapping? They'll beat the crap out of a guy like you in the joint." Jake could read Marco's face to see he'd made points with the winery owner. He also could see it was about to go down any second, and it did.

From behind Marco, Wally grabbed hold of the wrist holding the shard of glass. Simultaneously, he slew-footed the attacker and pulled him away from Katrina. She went sprawling, but away from harm. Wally forced Marco's face hard into the trampled ground just beyond the parking lot. The officer had moved at the sign of the rescue and quickly cuffed the man under siege.

Jake ran over and knelt down by Katrina. Concern reflected on his face. He looked her over for signs she'd been hurt in the scuffle. A beet-red spot on her arm showed where Marco had grasped his hostage so tightly. No sign of lacerations from the bottle on her neck. Jake gently brushed her hair away from the side of her face to reveal a tiny spot of blood on her chin.

"Stay still, you've been cut."

Katrina wiped at her face. Crying, but laughing at the same time, she replied, "I'm okay. I popped a zit, that's all."

31 *Wally*

As the crowd finished their wine and dispersed to other areas of the park or their vehicles, Jake and Katrina approached Wally.

"It's Nick, actually," he stated as he shook hands with the detective. "I'm sorry that I couldn't reveal anything to you sooner than today."

"Understandable," replied Jake. "So you're the one who put Verna Wilkinson into hiding."

"For her own safety, really. Evan was my immediate suspect, and when he tossed that brick through Verna's window, I was afraid he'd taken a turn for the dangerous. Like his old man."

"Sure," said Katrina. "Our friend Stewart told us all about Evan."

"Yes, I know. Stewart Windle and I share some connections, apparently. My guy told me that Stewart started asking around about Evan."

"So what broke the case for you? How did you know it was Pierre and not Evan? My money was on Evan."

"The day you saw me collecting bottles."

"By the ditch! You saw us?"

"Yes, I just didn't let on. I wanted to make you think I was just trying to make some money off empties."

"Had us fooled," Katrina admitted.

"Hey, I made twelve dollars and twenty cents that day," he smiled. "More than enough for a box of Canawine and a package of pepperoni sticks. What more does a wino need?"

"Katrina said she saw you drink the water from the ditch," Jake said.

"Yeah. Was I convincing? I was actually just smelling it, but thought I'd make her think I was drinking it to gross her out."

"It worked," Katrina grimaced, reflecting.

Nick crossed his arms. "Sorry about that. Oh, I forgot to tell you. Verna's safely at home. I figured she was safe, as I knew all my suspects would be here. Egos too big to miss something like this by sending an assistant."

"Cathy will be happy," Jake said, standing with his arm around Katrina. "If her meds have worn off yet, that is."

"I'm sure she is. I just feel bad about not saying anything to her earlier," Katrina frowned.

"You did the right thing," Nick assured her.

"So, Jake," Katrina began, "your suspicion about the Chateau Sur La Mer was correct."

"You figured that one out. I'm impressed," Nick said, wiping off some of his wino makeup.

"Katrina exaggerates a bit. I knew something was up. Why would he have that much expensive wine when he doesn't drink the stuff?"

"That was my tip too. And he was a creep. Creeps are usually up to something."

Jake laughed and pulled Katrina closer. "You sound like Katrina."

"Well he is a creep!" Katrina exclaimed.

"Speaking of creeps," Nick said as Evan approached.

"Just wanted to say thanks, Wally," Evan said.

Nick looked puzzled. "What for?"

"You probably saved me thousands of dollars. I had a morality clause in the deals they signed."

"You. A morality clause. That's precious!" Nick scoffed at him.

"Laugh if you want, but I'm the one laughing now. They'll be desperate to sell now, and I can low-ball them. I'm going to look great back at head office."

"Maybe," Jake said.

"What do you mean maybe?"

"There is a chance that the legal system will tie this up for months, maybe years before the properties can actually be sold," Jake added.

Evan's grin disappeared. "I doubt that," he said. His tone likely didn't even convince himself. Jake could hear Evan quietly cursing as he strode off.

Wally shook hands with Jake. "We made a good pair back there. It was a pleasure working with you, even if it was only for five minutes."

"You too. We'll have to do it again sometime," Jake agreed.

"Good luck with your anger management course," Nick added, catching Jake off guard. "I'm thorough."

The reminder was the first since they'd pulled into Leamington. Back to reality.

32   The End

Dinner back at Aunt Verna's proved a raucous event. Don and Faith had returned with the gang to welcome their missing friend home. Jake and Katrina took turns filling in everyone on the misdoings at the wineries. Don and Faith each wore a medal around their neck, one for each victory at the wine judging contest. Stewart took repeated jabs for his love of Chateau Sur La Mer, or the fake version that Marco Genoso had sold.

"It sure is good to be back home," Aunt Verna said, sporting a sweater vest adorned with dancing elves. "It's so nice to be back in my own clothes. The items that Nick picked out were dreadfully gloomy. I felt the fabric of those ghastly garments sucking the cheer out of my body."

"You look much happier too!" Katrina exclaimed.

"I didn't mind roughing it in a tent for a few days, but I missed my bed and the spirit of my home." Aunt Verna paused to put her hand on Cathy's hand on the picnic table. "And I'm so sorry this had to happen when you were visiting, dear."

"You couldn't help it, Aunt Verna," Cathy replied, placing her other hand on top of her aunt's hand and gently squeezing.

"Katrina," Jake said, "when did you know Wally, I mean Nick, wasn't a wino?"

"Why do you ask?" Katrina responded.

"I was thinking back to the times we crossed paths with him, and you always treated him so nice."

Cathy laughed at Jake's comment. "Honey, you don't know your girlfriend too well! She befriends everyone who crosses her path, no judgment, no questions asked."

Aunt Verna smiled at Katrina. "If only the world had more open hearts like yours, dear."

"So when did you know," Jake persisted.

"I suspected in the store, but I never really knew for sure until he revealed himself at the contest," Katrina replied.

"What tipped you off?" Cathy asked.

"Well, he smelled like booze, but he didn't smell like the other street people I've met," she explained.

Sharing a puzzled look with others around the table, Iris asked, "What do you mean he didn't smell like other street people?"

"I guess," Cathy added, "all that being nice to vagrants paid off, eh, Kat?"

"Street people don't smell so much like booze as they smell like filth. Even the winos. No mistaking the smell of cheap liquor on them, but it's overpowered mostly by the smell of not bathing regularly."

Stewart looked at the sleuthing girl. "Sherlock Holmes would be proud of you, Katrina. Using more than just your sense of sight to solve a crime."

"Well, it was also his eyes. Most winos look like they've been to hell and back with permanently bloodshot eyes. Wally's eyes were so brilliantly blue and clear that they seemed to sparkle."

"Once he got cleaned up a bit," Iris said, "he did look pretty hot."

Katrina blushed. "I just meant he had nice eyes."

"I'll help you out by changing the subject, Katrina," Don said. "For those of you who think Faith and I were selling out to Evan, we weren't."

"But he said …" Katrina started before Don cut her off.

"He said we were forming a partnership. He wasn't buying us out like Marco, Pierre, and Nate."

"What's the difference?" Katrina asked.

"Canawine was going to use our wines to start a new Canawine Prestige line of wines. They're apparently trying to change their image."

Stewart reached for his glass of wine, and sarcastically added, "If someone held up an ink blot of a box of wine, I'd blurt out Canawine as my answer."

"I think most people would," Don agreed. "So our wine would be labeled 'Canawine Prestige presents CEV Meritage,' or some such thing. Our name has to be twice the size of the rest of the wording, per our deal."

Katrina nodded. "So you get more exposure for your wine, and I'd assume more sales means more money."

Stewart expressed concern. "If people get past the image of Canawine, it would mean more sales."

Faith smiled, and rubbed her thumb and fore finger together like a money sign. "Either way, we'll be okay. We got a big chunk of cash up front, retained ownership of the winery, and can get out of the deal if sales don't reach specific levels."

"Sounds like you got a sweet deal," Tate said, finally joining the conversation.

"And it's not tied to the other deals," Don grinned, "so it doesn't matter if Canawine buys Migration, Windmill, or Essex County Cellars. I do feel sorry for Nate and Deb, though. They're the big losers in all of this."

Faith looked in her husband's eyes to reassure him. "They'll be fine, dear. They're holding their own, and they're two of the happiest, most positive people I've ever known." She turned her head, "Well, next to you, Verna."

Verna returned the smile to Faith. "How about you, Don, and I clear the table and let the young 'ens enjoy the sunset.

Katrina's back to the lake, she could have broken her neck by how fast she turned to see the sunset beginning.

"C'mon, Jake. Let's go down to the beach to watch it!" Katrina's enthusiasm was flowing from every bit of her smile.

Finally sitting on the narrow strip of sand to watch the sun go down in a blaze of glory, Jake looked at his girlfriend.

"It's been one hell of a weekend."

"I hope you mean that in a good way."

"Some of it was great. I loved the trip to Point Pelee."

"And Don and Faith were a lot of fun."

Jake nodded. "The tour and tasting at their winery was fun too."

"So what was so bad about the trip?"

"Well, let's see. For starters, Aunt Verna disappeared. You pissed off a London police officer in a parking lot."

"I didn't know the truck belonged to a cop."

"You got in the middle of a brawl in a store, and Cathy got mugged."

"Okay, so there were a few down points."

"And you almost got killed by a lunatic with a broken bottle."

"Oh yeah, that." Katrina looked down, dejected.

"It's not easy having you as a girlfriend sometimes. You seem to be a magnet for trouble."

Katrina tried to put a positive spin on it. "But it makes life more exciting, doesn't it? And we solved another case together. That was cool."

"I think Nick solved the case more than we did."

"We got parts of it, and he himself said that we were invaluable to him closing the investigation."

"Yes, he did, didn't he?" Jake perked up a bit.

"And everybody is safe and sound, right? I'd call it a successful weekend away. I doubt we would have had this much excitement lying on the beach in Mexico."

"I don't know. Like I said, magnet for trouble."

"Maybe. But for now let's just enjoy the sunset. It goes on forever over the lake. It's the most gorgeous sunset I've ever seen."

"I can't argue with that," Jake said, looking into her alluring green eyes just before closing his eyes to kiss her.

Finishing a long kiss, Katrina leaned back on her elbows in the rough sand.

"Let's enjoy the rest of the night. In no time we'll be back to reality."

The End

A Trials of Katrina Novels Series

Novel 1   Novel 2

"I enjoyed Friends of the Deceased by Dale J Moore tremendously, a novel with all the right ingredients to thrill, chill, and keep the pages turning! Witty dialogue, likable--and dislikable!--characters. Katrina keeps moving forward, and I look for more in this line of books."

Heather Graham, New York Times and USA Today Bestselling Author:

Check out the FIRST book in the series,

Life of the Party

Maureen P. Moore

'Outgoing? Gorgeous? Enjoy P/T evening work? Good fun! Good pay! THIS IS PERFECTLY LEGAL!' The ad in the Toronto paper sounds just about perfect for Katrina. Except for the 'outgoing' part. Desperate to escape a creepy roommate and a scary landlord, she must find some way to supplement her meager café salary to flee to a new apartment.

Eye-popping beautiful but woefully shy, when Katrina is hired as a professional guest (aka PEST) for a company called Life of the Party, her nerves get the best of her. Before she can make a total fool of herself and lose her new job, she's saved by a dashing and mysterious stranger who vanishes into the night.

With the help of her newfound friend and fellow PEST Cathy, Katrina tries desperately to find her mystery man. Her search, and her life, gets disrupted by the nefarious affairs of her roommates, landlord, and new boss. Along the way, Katrina learns that she may be shy - but she's certainly no wallflower.

And the Second book in the series,

Friends of the Deceased
Dale J. Moore

How does a small town girl end up investigating crime at a funeral home in Toronto? Drop-dead gorgeous Katrina is trying to run her new salon and take her relationship to a new level. The unexpected death of a client and struggles with her salon lead her to the Shady Rest funeral home.

As she stumbles her way through the personal problems that plague her world, Katrina ends up immersed in the world of preparing people for the next world.

With the help of a ruggedly handsome police detective, some old friends, and a few new ones, will she get to the bottom of what's going on, or end up buried by it? One thing is certain; when Katrina gets involved, chaos and comedy will ensue.

"Friends of the Deceased features Katrina (Kat), a heroine who refuses to be daunted by lies and treachery and finds a silver lining because of her kindness." **Carolyn Hart, Author of the Death on Demand series.**

"Behind-the-scenes hijinks at a funeral home will have you cheering for hairdresser Katrina and her gang when they delve into stolen goods, fraud, and charity scams. Katrina has to unravel the mysteries before the next ultra luxury casket is made for her. **Nancy J. Cohen, Author of the Bad Hair Day mystery series**

Other books by Dale J. Moore

Dale J. Moore

UbiquiMed: We're Everywhere, For You!

The world had changed. A violence Plagued nation, torn apart by a financial crisis, struggled to find its way back. Disease and poverty were rampant. Government assistance led to government intervention. Thus emerged Ubiquitous Medical, a federally funded health organization designed to fill every need of a desperate public.

"UBIQUITOUS MEDICAL is a fast paced ride that will keep you guessing. Twists and turns keep you on the edge of your seat, while the characters grow and deepen with every page. Dale J. Moore's voice shines through in this unique tale of a chilling future." **Gemma Halliday, award winning author of the High Heels Mysteries**

A brilliant researcher isolated in search of a cure.
The star of a media parody broadcast with a favourite target.
A young couple with decisions to make about their children's future.
The corporate executive driven by his vision.
Such is the influence of Ubiquitous Medical.

Made in the USA
Charleston, SC
04 June 2013